Penguin Books
Appleby Talking

Michael Innes is the pseudonym of J. I. M.
Stewart, who has been a Student of Christ
Church, Oxford, since 1949. He was born
in 1906 and was educated at Edinburgh
Academy and Oriel College, Oxford. He
was lecturer in English at the University of
Leeds from 1930 to 1935, and spent the
succeeding ten years as Jury Professor of
English in the University of Adelaide,
South Australia.

He has published several novels and a
volume of short stories under his own name,
as well as many detective stories and
broadcast scripts under the pseudonym of
Michael Innes. His *Eight Modern Writers*
appeared in 1963 as the final volume of
The Oxford History of English Literature.
Michael Innes is married and has five children.

Michael Innes

Appleby Talking

Twenty-three detective stories

Penguin Books

Penguin Books Ltd, Harmondsworth,
Middlesex, England
Penguin Books Australia Ltd, Ringwood,
Victoria, Australia

First published by Victor Gollancz 1954
Published in Penguin Books 1973

Copyright © J. I. M. Stewart, 1954
Made and printed in Great Britain by
Hazell Watson & Viney Ltd,
Aylesbury, Bucks

Set in Intertype Plantin

Contents

Appleby's First Case

'My first case?' Appleby looked at his friends with the appearance of considerable surprise. 'Do you know that nobody has ever asked me about that before? It's always the latest case that people are curious about.'

The Vicar nodded. 'News is more popular than history nowadays. It is only one symptom, I fear, of a deplorable –'

'Precisely, my dear Vicar.' The Doctor's interruption was hasty. 'How right you are. But let Appleby tell us his story. For I can see that there is a story. That manner of squinting into the bowl of his pipe is an infallible sign of it.'

'My first case was quite a small one.' Appleby finished squinting and began to puff. 'I'd say about eighteen inches by ten. And certainly not more than three inches deep.'

The Vicar looked bewildered. 'This case was about a *case*?'

'It was about this rather small case. But then, of course, I was rather small too.

'To be exact in the matter, I was just fourteen – a solemn child with somewhat precocious intellectual tastes and no notion of becoming a policeman. At thirteen I had been a geologist, littering my room with sizable chunks of any hills I could get within hammer's reach of. At fifteen I was going to be a tremendous authority on comparative religion. But at fourteen my line was the fine arts. I spent my holidays in the National Gallery or the Tate, and I particularly liked the delightful business of paying a shilling, and sixpence extra for a catalogue, in order to look at the picture-dealers' shows in the West End.

'This case that I'm telling you about contained a dozen

exquisite pieces of jade, and it was exhibited on a table in the inner room of the Ferrarese Gallery, off Bond Street. The place may be familiar to you. It certainly hasn't changed from that day to this, and it had then, as it has now, a habit of running two exhibitions concurrently. I had gone there to look at Impressionists in the larger rooms. The jade and other Chinese stuff in the room at the back wasn't part of my programme for the occasion. I'm sure I *had* a programme, laid out with admirable neatness, and that it indicated the study of Oriental Art as not due to begin until six weeks later.'

The Doctor chuckled. 'You may have been a little prig, Appleby. But you were a systematic one. And system was to lead you on to sterner things.'

'No doubt. But I remembered that I had paid my shilling for *both* shows, and so I did make a quick survey of the Chinese things. The Impressionists had drawn a big crowd, but there was only a handful of people here at the back. I took a look round, and then stuck my head into the room lying farther back still. It's not much more than a large cupboard, where they sometimes exhibit a single picture or work of statuary under a rather *recherché* lighting. I don't remember what was actually on show there on this occasion, but I do remember the man with the red beard. Indeed, he is one of the three or four human beings I am quite certain I shall never forget.

'He was alone in the little room – an elderly man of shabby but cultivated appearance, muffled in a shapeless old ulster, and carrying under his arm a sheaf of papers and an enormous folio volume in an ancient leather binding. I looked at the folio with great respect – I had a large reverence for learning as well as the arts, and here clearly was a scholar in the grand tradition. I also looked at the red beard. There was something fascinating about it. Indeed, I must positively have stared, because I remember suddenly recollecting my manners, and turning in some confusion to whatever artistic object was on view. When I looked at the scholar again a rather startling thing was happening. He was picking up his beard from the floor and hastily replacing it on a perfectly clean-shaven face.'

Appleby paused, and the Vicar rubbed his hands. 'Capital!' he said. 'Here was swift observation, my dear Appleby, leading to your first triumph. Proceed.'

'I was a bit staggered, and no doubt rather scared. It was with a feeling that there was safety in numbers that I retreated to the crowd milling round the Impressionists. But my mind was moving swiftly. At least that was my own instant conviction in the matter, since I had read time and again how Sexton Blake's mind invariably worked swiftly on similar occasions. It was true that any passion for that eminent detective already lay – or seemed to lie – several years behind me. But of course, as the psychologists assure us, past obsessions rise up again in traumatic situations.

'Conceivably my swift thinking might have led in the fullness of time to the formulating of some line of positive action. As it was, events again took the initiative. I became aware that somebody was shouting, and a second later an attendant or commissionaire rushed out of the inner room. I caught the single word "jade". And at that my tender intellectual faculties really *did* move with tolerable speed. I saw the whole thing in a flash – or *almost* the whole thing. I knew the villain – for are not villains invariably disguised? And I knew just what he had done – for would not the show-case with those priceless little jades fit exactly into that assuredly bogus folio volume? It was a tremendous moment. And yet more tremendous was the moment immediately succeeding it. For there was the red-bearded man not six paces in front of me – and making unobtrusively for the street.'

Appleby again halted in his narrative – this time to tap out his pipe. It might have been the heat of the fire that had brought a slight flush to his features as he sat back again.

'I gave a great yell. At least I thought I did – and was a good deal surprised to hear nothing. It was like the sort of dream in which you cry out and no sound comes. But a second attempt was more successful. Indeed, it commanded the instant attention of every soul in the place. "That's him!" I yelled – and I don't doubt that I was horridly conscious of the bad grammar even amid the very triumph and relief of achieving articulate speech. As I yelled I pointed. And as I pointed I sprang. For there had come to me – with utter inevitability, you will admit – the one unquestionably correct course of action at such a juncture. Attendants were already closing on the red-bearded man. But I got there first, grabbed that beard with both hands, and pulled. The next instant I was aware that he was yelling too. He was yelling with pain. There were tears in his eyes. A single tuft of hair did actually come away. But his beard was as genuine as the childish down on my own lip. And the folio that ought to have been no more than a box concealing that little show-case lay open on the floor – a perfectly ordinary and authentic book.'

'But this is terrible!' The Vicar was dismayed. 'It was a shocking situation for any sensitive boy. Whatever happened next?'

Appleby smiled. 'I certainly experienced all the standard things – like wishing that the floor would open and swallow me up. The establishment, clearly, would have liked to wring my little neck. Only for the first few moments they were too much occupied with apologizing to my outraged victim, asking him if he wanted a doctor, offering to call him a taxi, begging to be allowed to rebind the folio, and a great deal more besides. That allowed me to get a second wind.'

'A second wind!' The Doctor was startled. 'You didn't sail in again?'

'Certainly. It was the only thing to do. I had come quite clear-headed at last, and I knew that this fellow must absolutely be held on to like grim death. I fought so hard, and did a lot of damage, that the police when they arrived felt they must send for an Inspector. He sorted the thing out, and a check-up on the man with the real beard eventually led to the tracking down of the man with the bogus one. That was what, in the end, I *had* seen: that if there were two men like that, they must be in a plot together. They had worked out a clever technique of distraction, particularly suitable for playing off against a boy. As soon as Bogus Beard had contrived to let me see that his *was* a disguise, he simply thrust that disguise away and did the stealing. Whereupon his confederate, Real Beard, planted himself before me in turn, and elicited the response that diverted everybody's attention while Bogus Beard, still beardless, got away with the booty. If I hadn't stuck it out, Real Beard would have got away in his turn, loaded with handsome apologies for my irresponsible imagination and outrageous conduct.' Appleby chuckled. 'And what a bewildered little ass I'd have felt.'

Pokerwork

George Arbuthnot was a novelist by trade – rather sordid social comedy was his line – and he had not been broadcasting for long. But already he was popular on the air, potentially far more popular than he would ever be as a fabricator in finical prose of witty if unedifying drawing-room romances. The microphone had brought to the surface a lot of secondary personality, perhaps more effective than genuine, the chief characteristic of which was an abounding and cheerful moral earnestness. Arbuthnot's confident voice with its buoyant nervous tone momentarily smoothed out life's difficulties for thousands. During a precious fifteen minutes weekly his hearers could believe that all might be well with their particular private world.

But Arbuthnot's own private world was a mess. He had married a beautiful and slightly crazy girl whose completely amoral nature caught his rather cynical professional interest. It had not been a sensible thing to do; craziness and amorality are not likely to go with hard-wearing domestic virtues; and certainly the wise and confident voice on the air would have condemned the alliance out of hand. Arbuthnot was paying for his rashness now.

His wife had taken a lover, a disgusting man called Rupert Slade, whose suave manners and faint contemptuous smile he had come violently to loathe. And unfortunately the situation left Arbuthnot – humiliatingly as if he were a weak-willed wronged husband in one of his own novels – baffled and indecisive. For one thing it was Slade who, being in on broadcasting, had got him this new means of adding substantially to his income. Probably Slade could do him no harm in the matter now. He was too well established as a star performer. Still, the thing added to life's awkwardness.

And so when he came home from delivering his weekly talk Arbuthnot was often irritated and restless. He was restless to-night – more so than he could remember for some time. It was as if he were endeavouring to thrust back into the depths of his mind impulses to which it would be dangerous to give conscious attention. He tried a cigar, he tried the gramophone, he tried a book which had been listed as 'Curious' in his bookseller's catalogue. But nothing served. The book was obscene without being in the least amusing – which might be the plight, Arbuthnot gloomily reflected, in which he would eventually find himself as a novelist when the sands of his talent began to run low. As for music – well, by that he was secretly bored at any time. And the cigar for some reason kept going out.

He got up and prowled the living-room of the apartment. He stood before its handsome but unwelcoming electric radiator and thought that it was like his wife. His brow darkened, and his chin went up; almost one might have thought that he had achieved one of those clear-cut decisions that he so confidently recommended over the air – and that in the novels were so seldom achieved. But the issue of this appeared not so very dramatic after all. He stubbed out the unsatisfactory cigar, switched off the cheerless radiator, moved to a door, opened it and spoke down a passage.

'Roper,' he called, 'I shan't be writing tonight, and I'm going to bed. Don't either of you wait up, for Mrs Arbuthnot will be very late.'

George Arbuthnot flicked off the lights and left the living-room in darkness.

2

'A fellow called Slade,' said the Sergeant. With a sense of sub-dued drama he gestured in the air. 'Just hit hard on the back of the head with a poker. The resourceful old blunt instrument. A very simple and fairly certain manner of killing.' The Sergeant's voice indicated a sort of qualified professional approval. 'And no finger-prints either. Here we are.'

A smoothly accelerating lift whirled them upwards. The door of the Arbuthnot apartment, by which a constable stood guard, was handsome and enamelled in a delicate cream. The sort of place, Detective-Inspector John Appleby reflected, which ate money and bred nervy folk ... They entered the living-room, and he glanced curiously about him. 'Arbuthnot the novelist?' he asked.

The room gave at a first appearance the impression of gracious and civilized standards. The walls were lined with books – for the most part either new or very old – in French and English. A large late Matisse displayed its salmon pinks and acid greens on the wall opposite the window. But the whole place had been efficiently decorated and furnished in terms of some delicately considered scheme, and nothing was visible that did not almost ostentatiously blend with the whole.

'A sterile room, Sergeant, for sterile people living by the laws of cocktail-bars and arty magazines. Have you any kids? Imagine them let loose in a place like this.' Appleby took off his hat. 'And who,' he asked unprofessionally, 'cares which of them killed whom? Still, no doubt we'd better find out.'

Slade's body still lay prone on the carpet, covered with a sheet. Appleby twitched this away and looked down on the sprawled figure in evening-clothes which was revealed to him. It was just possible to distinguish that on the back of the dead man's head there had been a bald patch which would have made a very fair target even in virtual darkness. And the blow had been terrific. Blood, brains, and shivered glass lay around. There was a faint smell of whisky. It looked as if the assailant had struck while Slade was standing beside a small table having a drink. Decanters and syphon were still disposed where they had been set the night before.

'Nasty,' said the Sergeant. 'Doesn't have the appearance of something that happened in the heat of a quarrel. Nothing face to face about it. Matter of stepping up softly from behind while the poor devil was believing himself hospitably entertained. Unmanly, I call it.'

'Unmanly?' Appleby frowned. 'That blow looks like the work of a blacksmith. But perhaps . . . ?'

The Sergeant nodded. 'Just so, sir. It seems there are skulls and skulls. And this was one of the egg-shell kind. So it seems to be quite possible that the lady –'

'I see.' And Appleby once more drew the sheet over Slade's body. 'The lady first.'

And Mrs Arbuthnot was brought in. A striking woman with haunted eyes, she strode forward in uncontrollable nervous agitation. 'My diamonds!' she exclaimed. 'They have been stolen from the wall-safe in my dressing-room. Often I forget to lock it, and now they have simply disappeared.'

Appleby's glanced moved from Mrs Arbuthnot to the sheeted figure on the floor. 'Loss upon loss,' he said drily.

Mrs Arbuthnot flushed. 'But you don't understand. The disappearance of the diamonds explains this horrible thing.'

'I see. In fact, you suppose them to have been stolen by the man who killed your – who killed Mr Slade?'

'But of course! So it is idiotic to think that the murderer could have been George – my husband, that is.'

Appleby received this in silence for a moment. 'But husbands,' he said presently, 'do sometimes kill – well, lovers?'

Mrs Arbuthnot looked him straight in the eyes, and he saw that she was a woman oversexed to the point of nymphomania. 'No doubt they do,' she answered steadily. 'But they don't steal their wives' diamonds.'

Behind Appleby the Sergeant sighed heavily, as one who has heard these childish urgings before. 'That,' he said with irony, 'settles the matter, no doubt.'

But Appleby himself was looking at Mrs Arbuthnot with a good deal of curiosity. 'Perhaps,' he asked mildly, 'you will give me your account of what happened last night?'

With a movement at once sinuous and weary, Mrs Arbuthnot sank into a chair. 'Very well – although your colleagues have heard it all already. Rupert – Mr Slade, that is – brought me home. It was late and both my husband and our two servants – a man and his wife named Roper – had gone to bed. I asked Rupert in. I thought it quite likely, you see, that my husband would be up, for often he writes into the small hours of the morning.'

Appleby nodded. 'Quite so,' he murmured. 'But it just happened that on this occasion you had to continue entertaining Mr Slade alone.

'I gave him a drink. We decided we were hungry, and I went to the kitchen to cut sandwiches. It was while I was away –' Suddenly Mrs Arbuthnot's voice choked on a sob. 'It was while I was away that this horrible thing happened.'

'I see. And while you were in the kitchen making those sandwiches just what, if anything, did you hear?'

Mrs Arbuthnot hesitated, and Appleby had a fleeting impression of fear and intense calculation. 'I did hear voices,' she said. 'Rupert's and – and that of another man: a totally strange voice. Do you understand? A *strange* voice. It was only a few words, short and sharp. And when I came back into this room Rupert was lying on the floor and I saw that he must be dead. I roused my husband. No doubt I ought to have thought of robbery at once. But the shock was too great for coherent thinking, and it was only much later that I found my diamonds had been stolen.' Mrs Arbuthnot paused. 'I blame myself terribly. You see, I left the main door of the flat on the latch behind us. The thief had only to step in.'

'No doubt.' Appleby looked searchingly at Mrs Arbuthnot. 'He was rather lucky to be on the spot, was he not? And you think that he stole your diamonds and then brained Mr Slade just by way of finishing off the evening strongly?'

'I think the thief must have stolen the diamonds and then ventured to explore this room, hoping to find something else that was valuable – perhaps he had heard of the Matisse. When he found Rupert barring his way he killed him and made his escape.'

3

And this was the story to which Mrs Arbuthnot stuck. It was not, Appleby reflected, without some faint colour of possibility. But one major difficulty was evident. Slade had been struck from behind – to all appearance an unsuspecting man. And he was in no sense cutting off the supposed thief's retreat; the whole geography of the apartment negatived this. To say, therefore, that Slade was barring his way to safety was manifestly unsound.

Was Mrs Arbuthnot, then, shielding her husband with this tale of stolen diamonds? Had the two of them concocted the tale together? Suppose Arbuthnot killed his wife's lover. Was it not very likely that, faced by this frightful act, husband and wife had got together to present the most convincing lie that occurred to them?

Arbuthnot himself was brought in. He was a man, it struck Appleby, who either as witness or accused would make a poor impression on a jury. He was obviously clever and almost as obviously sincere – a man wavering, perhaps, between incompatible attitudes to life, indecisive and therefore unreliable and possibly dangerous. And now he was in an awkward situation enough, for his wife's lover had been found murdered beneath his roof. Nevertheless, at first he faced things confidently.

'I went to bed early and read,' he said. 'I never really go to sleep until my wife gets home.'

'And of late that has frequently been in the small hours?'

The man flushed, hesitated, and then ignored the question. 'But I did eventually doze off, and all I can say is that I heard three distinct voices. Not what they said, but just the sound of them.'

'That's it!' Mrs Arbuthnot broke in anxiously. 'My voice, Rupert's voice, and then the voice of the thief and murderer. He must have tried to bluff when he blundered in on Rupert.'

Appleby ignored this. 'You mean,' he asked Arbuthnot, 'that you heard three voices engaged in conversation?'

'I couldn't say that. And I can't be sure that the third voice said very much. But the other two were Slade's and my wife's, all right. So I suppose her explanation fits well enough.'

'Do you indeed?' Appleby spoke drily. 'By the way, was this third voice a cultivated voice?'

Arbuthnot hesitated. 'Well, yes; I'm pretty sure it was. I sleepily felt something rather disconcerting about it, as a matter of fact.'

'A gentleman cracksman. And one, incidentally, who turned with some facility and abruptness to murder.' Appleby paused. 'Mr Arbuthnot,' he continued abruptly, 'you must be very aware of one likely hypothesis in this case. Are you prepared to swear – in a criminal court, if need be – that last night you didn't get out of bed, enter the room while your wife was making sandwiches in the kitchen, and here – well, encounter the dead man?'

Arbuthnot had gone pale. 'I did not,' he said.

'And you are sure that this story of a third voice, and of stolen diamonds, has not been concocted between your wife and yourself?'

'I am certain that it has not.'

Appleby turned to the Sergeant. 'There are two servants – the Ropers. Are they in a position to corroborate this story in any way?'

The Sergeant fumbled with a notebook. And Arbuthnot gloomily cut in. 'Not a chance of it, I'm afraid. I told them to go to bed. And they sleep like logs. It's been a regular joke between my wife and myself.'

Mrs Arbuthnot nodded. 'They wouldn't hear a thing,' she declared confidently.

Appleby moved to the bell. 'We'll have them in,' he said. 'And the whole *dramatis personae* will then be present for the conclusion of the play.'

Arbuthnot started. 'The conclusion, did you say?'

And Appleby nodded. 'Yes, Mr Arbuthnot. Just that.'

The Sergeant buried his nose in his notebook. He was thinking that he had heard his superiors employ that sort of easy bluff before.

4

The Ropers sprang a surprise. They had, after all, been very much awake, for a crash in the kitchen had aroused them. And at this Mrs Arbuthnot's hand flew to her throat and she gave a little choking gasp. 'The breadbin!' she said. 'I knocked it from the shelf.'

'Ah.' Appleby turned to the man Roper, a quiet, wary fellow with the ability to stand absolutely still. 'And, once aroused, will you tell us what you heard, either from this room or from any other room in the apartment?'

'We heard three people talking in here: Mr and Mrs Arbuthnot and the dead man, Mr Slade.'

'It's a lie!' Arbuthnot had sprung to his feet.

And his wife too sprang up, quivering. 'How dare you,' she gasped, facing the servants. 'How dare you tell such a wicked untruth.'

But Roper merely looked very grim. 'There's no lie in it,' he said quietly. 'It's true we both quickly fell asleep again, perhaps before the murder happened. But your three voices we can swear to. So it is Mr Arbuthnot who is lying when he says he never left his bed.'

There was a silence. Appleby turned to Mrs Roper, a pale, nervous woman who was softly wringing her hands. 'You have heard what your husband has just said. Do you corroborate it in every detail?'

Mrs Roper nodded. 'Yes,' she said. 'Yes, it's true – God help them.'

'Do you know anything that you believe it would be useful to add?'

But Mrs Roper shook her head. 'No, sir. There isn't anything more.'

Arbuthnot was now pale to the lips. 'There were three voices,' he said hoarsely. 'But not mine. I didn't stir.'

Suddenly Mrs Arbuthnot gave a shrill, hysterical laugh and turned to her husband. 'George,' she said, 'it's no good. They heard you. My fibs about burglars and diamonds are useless. There's nothing for it but to confess that you came out of the bedroom and – and quarrelled with Rupert as you did.' Again she laughed wildly. 'You had reason enough, God knows. And I will admit it – admit it openly in court. Perhaps that will save you.'

Arbuthnot was staring at his wife with dilated eyes. 'For God's sake –' he began.

But the Sergeant closed upon him. 'George Arbuthnot, I

arrest you on the charge of the wilful murder of Rupert Slade. And it is my duty to warn you –'

Appleby, who had been making a quick tour of the room, intervened. 'No,' he said. 'Mr Arbuthnot is entirely innocent. It was his wife who killed Slade.'

5

'She wanted to get rid of both of them – her husband and Slade,' Appleby explained later. 'Heaven knows why – probably some uncontrolled passion for another man.'

The Sergeant nodded dubiously. 'Well, sir, I must admit she looks a bit that sort.'

'Sex-crazy, no doubt. But she has brains as well. She planned the whole thing. And there was more to it than you might think.'

'There was more to it than I can make head or tail of.' The Sergeant was slightly aggrieved. 'For instance –'

'Take it quite simply, and step by step. Mrs Arbuthnot brought Slade home with her at an hour to suit herself. Her husband never really slept before she returned, and so she knew that he would be awake or dozing and hear the sound of voices. She knew that by knocking down the bread-bin she could arouse the Ropers and ensure that *they* heard the sound of voices too. And in that way she would gain the conflicting – and damning – testimony she desired.'

The Sergeant looked increasingly perplexed. 'But that's just where the puzzle lies! The evidence on the voices *is* conflicting, and you appear to be accepting Arbuthnot's story. But why disbelieve the Ropers? You haven't shaken their evidence in the least. And they both swear that the third voice –'

'Was Arbuthnot's. Well, so it was. But it came from a disc on the gramophone. I found it there before Mrs Arbuthnot had any chance to remove it.'

'Oh, come, sir.' The Sergeant was expostulatory. 'That's an old trick enough. But here it simply doesn't fit the facts. For Arbuthnot himself, whom it appears we are to believe, swears that he stopped in bed, that from there he heard this third voice, *and that it was a strange voice.*'

Appleby nodded. 'Precisely so. But you will find that the trick *does* fit the facts. And that it's not an old trick, but a very new one.

'Consider what Mrs Arbuthnot wanted to contrive: that the Ropers should hear a voice which they knew to be Arbuthnot's, and that Arbuthnot should hear a *strange* voice. Once Arbuthnot had told his story, and it appeared to be disproved on the evidence of the unexpectedly wide-awake servants, and she had turned round upon him with her devil's trick of appearing to see the uselessness of shielding him further and urging him to confess – once she had got him there it would seem there was only the gallows before him. She would be rid of both husband and discarded lover at a stroke. She and the public executioner would have shared the job between them.'

Appleby paused and gazed sombrely round the room. Slade's body had been lugged away; Arbuthnot had made off to some country retreat; beyond the kitchen the Ropers could be heard packing their trunks. In this expensive setting life had dried up and come to a stop.

'On what, then, did Mrs Arbuthnot's plan turn? On a very simple psychological fact, well known to anybody who has recorded for broadcasting and had the result played back at him. Under these circumstances a man is utterly unable to recognize his own voice – although, of course, everybody else does so. People have even been known indignantly to deny that these noises could possibly be theirs! Now, Arbuthnot had recently taken to broadcasting, and his wife got hold of a recorded talk – conceivably through Slade himself, who had some sort of connection with that sort of thing.

'She brought her victim – her first victim – home and gave him a drink. She went to the kitchen and made enough row to waken the Ropers. She knew that her husband, too, would hear any voices in this room. Then she invited Slade to listen to a bit of the record – perhaps as some particularly choice idiocy of her husband's. So the Ropers were sure they heard Arbuthnot in this room, and Arbuthnot was equally sure he heard a stranger. Nothing more was required. The moment had come, and she hit Slade hard on the head.'

Appleby paused. 'How did I tumble to it? Well, Arbuthnot mentioned that the strange voice had some rather disconcerting quality, and I chewed on that. But the first step was earlier. It was when I saw that we had to do with a premeditated crime, and not with the result of some flare-up of passion on the spot. The poker, you know, must have been thoughtfully provided beforehand, since this room has nothing but that electric radiator.'

And Appleby reached for his hat. 'A beastly sterile room, Sergeant, as I said at the start.'

The Spendlove Papers

'Two novels and a detective story.' The Vicar's tone was disconsolate, and he set down with every appearance of distaste the three books he had been carrying. 'I don't know what our local library is coming to. Again and again I have impressed upon the committee that in biographies and memoirs is to be found an inexhaustible store of edification and pleasure.'

'But they keep on ordering fiction, all the same?' Appleby drew a second chair to the fire in the club smoking-room. 'I agree with you on the pleasure to be had from memoirs, but I'm not so sure about the edification. Consider the case of the Spendlove Papers.'

'The Spendlove Papers?' The Vicar shook his head as he sat down. 'The title seems familiar to me. But I doubt whether I ever set eyes on them.'

'You never did. In point of fact, they have remained unpublished. And thereby hangs a tale.'

'Splendid!' A man transformed, the Vicar gave his library books a shove into further darkness, and beamed happily on the steward who advanced to set down a tea-tray in their place. 'Pray let me hear it, my dear fellow.'

'Very well. Lord Claud Spendlove never gained the political eminence customary in his family. In state affairs he was much overshadowed by his elder brother, the Marquis of Scattergood, and he never attained more than minor rank in the Cabinet. When it came to social life, however, it was another matter. For more than fifty years Claud Spendlove went everywhere and knew everybody; his persistence in the field of fashion eventually more than made up for any lack of positive brilliance in it; and he had one marked endowment which was never in dispute. Lord Claud was the most malicious man in England.'

The Vicar looked doubtful. 'It may be so, my dear Appleby – although one day you must let me tell you about Archdeacon Stoat. But proceed.'

'Moreover, Spendlove was known to be a diarist in a big way, and it was confidently expected that eventually he would put all the masters in the kind – Greville, Creevey, and the rest – wholly in the shade. There was a good deal of speculation as to just how scandalous his revelations would be. Some declared that the book would be so shocking that publication would be impossible for at least fifty years after his death. Others maintained that such a concession to decency was alien to the man's whole cast of mind, and that he would see to it that his memoirs were just printable pretty well as soon as he was in his grave. In the end it appeared that his second opinion was the right one. On his seventy-fifth birthday Spendlove announced that his book was ready for the press and would go to his publisher on the day of his funeral. He had decided to call it *A Candid Chronicle of My Life and Times*.'

With a fragment of crumpet poised before him, the Vicar shook his head. 'It must have had for some an ominous sound.'

'Decidedly. And presently Spendlove died. He was staying with his aged brother the Marquis at Benison Court at the time, and there was a quiet country funeral at Benison Parva. I myself knew nothing about all this until, on the following day, an urgent message reached me at New Scotland Yard. Fogg and Gale, the dead man's solicitors, were in a panic. The manuscript of *A Candid Chronicle* had vanished.

'At first, I couldn't see that it was particularly serious. But they explained that through the length and breadth of England there was scarcely a Family – old Gale enunciated the word with a wonderful emphasis on that capital letter – that might not be outraged and humiliated by some revelation in the book. Spendlove had let himself go from the first page to the last, but had agreed to some arrangement for pretty stiff editing of what would, in fact, be offered to the first generation or two of his readers.

'It became clear to me that the solicitors were right, and that we were facing a real crisis. In the first place, the missing manuscript was a blackmailer's dream; anyone well up in that line of business could make a large fortune out of its ownership. In the second place, it contained a mass of stuff that could be fed dispersedly into the sensational Press without any acknowledgement as to its source. And in the third place, a great many threatened parties must have had a strong motive to get hold of the thing and destroy or suppress it. I travelled down to Benison that night.'

'A beautiful place.' The Vicar had shamelessly turned his attention to an éclair. 'One of the most mellow of the great English houses. I hope you saw the orangery and the great fountain.'

'My dear Vicar, I had other things to think about. For instance, finding a room.'

'Finding a room?'

'I preferred not to stop at Benison Court itself. And the local inn was full.'

'Ah – the tourist season.'

'Not a bit of it. This was in mid-November. So I was rather surprised to see old Lord Whimbrel crouching over a smoky fire in the lounge, and Sir Giles Throstle gossiping in the bar with Sharky Lee.'

'Sharky Lee? What an odd name.'

'Sharky is one of the smartest blackmailers in England. There were also the Duke and Duchess of Ringouzel, who had been obliged to put up with an attic; and in a yard at the back there was Lady Agatha Oriole, who had arrived with a caravan. I drove on to Benison Magna and then to Abbot's Benison. It was like a monstrous dream. The entire nobility and gentry of these islands, my dear Vicar, were encamped round Benison Court – and the only escape from this uncanny social elevation was into the society of an answering abundance of notorious criminals. They had begun to arrive in the district before noon on the day on which *The Times* had announced that Lord Claud Spendlove was sinking. Some of the more resolute of them – mostly members of the peerage – had openly imported house-breaking implements and high explosives. With the usual resourcefulness of their class, they had contacted the charitable organizations for assisting reformed cracksmen, and had taken the most skilled professional advice.'

The Vicar looked thoughtful. 'Lord Scattergood,' he ventured presently, 'must have felt some cause for alarm.'

'I don't think he did. The Marquis, as I have mentioned, was a very old man; and when I saw him next morning he seemed to have the unruffled confidence that sometimes goes with old age. He took me to his late brother's sitting-room himself, and showed me what had happened. A window giving on a terrace had been forced open, and so had a handsome bureau in the middle of the room. Splintered wood and disordered papers were all over the place, and one capacious drawer was entirely empty. The Scattergood Papers, roughly ordered into *A Candid Chronicle*, had been in that.

'I asked a number of questions – pretty discreetly, for Lord Scattergood had held, as you know, all but the highest office in the realm, and was a person of decidedly august and intimidating presence. He answered with the unflawed courtesy one would expect, and very coherently in the main. If his years showed at all, it was in the way that a certain malice – what one might call the hitherto suppressed family malice – peeped through the chinks of his great statesman's manner. And he was decidedly frank about his younger brother's proposed book. Claud had never acknowledged the responsibilities proper in a Spendlove; his incursion into the Cabinet had been a fiasco; and while he, the elder brother, had toiled through a long lifetime to sustain the family tradition of public service, Claud had done nothing but amass low scandal in high places, and acquire the ability to adorn and perpetuate it with what was undoubtedly a sufficient literary grace. To this last point Lord Scattergood recurred more than once. But I see, Vicar, that you have guessed the end of my story.'

The Vicar nodded. 'I think I have. None of the folk congregated in those nearby inns had anything to do with the disappearance of *A Candid Chronicle of My Life and Times*. The Marquis of Scattergood had himself staged the burglary, and saved his family's honour by pitching the wretched thing in the fire.'

'You are at least half-way to the truth.' And Appleby smiled a little grimly. 'That night I stopped at Benison Court after all – and did a little burglary of my own. Lord Scattergood, too, had a bureau. I broke it open. The manuscript was there.'

'He had preserved it?'

'He had begun to transcribe it. And with a new title-page. *The Intimate Journals of Eustace Scattergood, Fifth Marquis of Scattergood*. It was as a writer that he would have chosen to be remembered, after all.'

The Furies

'The death of Miss Pinhorn,' said Appleby, 'was decidedly bizarre. But it was some time before we realized that it was sinister too.'

'I remember Miss Pinhorn slightly.' The Vicar set down his tankard. 'My daughter called on her once when collecting for European relief. Miss Pinhorn owned a cottage here, I think. She gave the poor girl sixpence.'

The Doctor chuckled. 'She was quite astonishingly mean.'

'She would have lived, if she could, on free samples of breakfast cereals,' said Appleby. 'But she died, nevertheless, of something odder than starvation. In a sense, she died of drink. But I see I must tell the story.'

'Capital,' said the Doctor. 'And we'll try a second pint ourselves.'

'Amelia Pinhorn was a woman of considerable fortune and marked eccentricity.

'For most of the year she lived in London the normal life of a leisured person of her sort. Then for a couple of months each summer she came down here and led a solitary and miserly existence in a small cottage.

'She had no contacts with anybody – not even the milkman.

'I don't exaggerate. Everything was sent down from town before she arrived. She lived on tins.

'And then one day she was drowned. Or at least, it is supposed that she was drowned.

'For we never, you see, recovered the body. The poor lady went over the cliff just short of the lighthouse. You must know about the current that sweeps in there and then goes out to sea again past the Furies.

'And this was awkward when the rumours began to go round. It might have been particularly awkward for Miss Pinhorn's niece, Jane. Old women over their teacups would have credited the poor girl with the most masterly crime of the age.'

The Vicar looked disturbed. 'This is not *really* a crime story, I hope?'

'It certainly is – but whether masterly or not, you must judge. The initial facts were perfectly simple, and fell within the observation of a number of people who were about here at the time.

'Miss Pinhorn emerged from her cottage, locked the door behind her, and set out on what appeared to be one of her normal solitary rambles. She came in the direction of this pub, and as she neared it she was seen to be hurrying – like a seasoned toper, somebody said, who is afraid of being beaten to it by closing time.

'But she wasn't known to drink, and she had certainly never been in this very comfortable private bar before.

'Well, in she came, talking to herself as usual and looking quite alarmingly wild. She called for two pints of beer in quick succession, floored them, planked down half a crown, and bolted out again. By this time she was singing and throwing her arms about.

'It was only when she had gone some way that she appeared to lose direction and wheel round towards the brow of the cliff.

'By that time she was in a thorough-going state of mania, and she went straight to her death.

'Perhaps, you may say, she had a repressed tendency to suicide, and the need for that took charge when her inhibitions were destroyed by the poison. For this is a story of poisoning – as you, Doctor, have no doubt realized.

'My aunt was the first person to suspect foul play. That needs qualifying, maybe.

'For the notion of poisoning seems to have arisen almost at once at what you might call a folk-level. Everybody was whispering it.

'What my aunt certainly spotted was the significance of the

beer. It indicated, she said, a sudden pathological thirst. Together with the very rapid onset of a violent mania or delirium, it should give us a very good guide to the sort of poison at work.

'When I say "us", I mean, of course, the local police and myself. It's a queer thing that I seldom quit Scotland Yard to spend a week in Sheercliffe with my eminently respectable kinswoman without her involving me in something of a busman's holiday. But I felt bound to peer about.

'For a very little thought suggested to me that my aunt – in this instance at least – was talking sense. Had the body been recoverable. I'd never have bothered my head.

'Miss Pinhorn's cottage was not a difficult place to search thoroughly.

'There was a tremendous store of patent medicines – something quite out of the way even with a maiden lady – all put up in very small packs. But each was more utterly harmless than the last.

'They were, in fact, almost without exception, free samples which had been stored away for a long time.

'A related inquiry to this was that into the dead woman's recent medical history.

'We learned from her maids in town that a few months previously she had been having trouble with her eyes, and that for some unknown reason she had to be hurried off to a nursing home.

'But now I must tell you about the chocolates.

'You see, it really comes down to a sort of sealed-room mystery. Miss Pinhorn is poisoned – and yet *nothing* has gone into her cottage for days.

'Or so we thought until I happened, during the search, to take a second look at this half-pound box of chocolates. It was lying in the sitting-room with the top layer gone.

'It wasn't anything about the chocolates themselves that struck me. It was the lid.

'You know that slightly padded sort of lid that confectioners go in for? It was of that kind. And just visible on it was the impress of three or four parallel wavy lines. That box had been through the post, lightly wrapped, and here was a faint trace of the post-mark.'

'Most astonishing!' The Vicar was enthusiastic. 'My dear Appleby, a fine feat of detection indeed.'

'I don't know that I'd call it that. But at least it sent me to the waste-paper basket. And there, sure enough, with a London postmark and Miss Pinhorn's address, was the scrap of wrapping I expected.

'And there was something more – a slip of notepaper with the words: 'To Aunt Amelia on her birthday, with love from Jane.'

'So I hunted out the postman. Apart from a few letters, he had delivered nothing at Miss Pinhorn's for weeks – until the very morning of the day on which she died. On that day he had delivered a small oblong parcel.

'I looked like being hot on a trail. That evening, while the remaining chocolates were being analysed, with what was to prove an entirely negative result, I went up to town and sought out Jane Pinhorn.

'And I didn't care for what I found. Jane was as nice a girl as you could wish to meet, and she had liked her eccentric aunt. This birthday box of chocolates had been an annual occasion with her. She was a highly intelligent girl, too.

'Miss Pinhorn's symptoms, so far as we knew about them, were consistent with the ingestion of some poison of the atropine group. The sudden thirst, and the delirium resulting from incoordinate stimulation of the higher centres of the cerebrum, were consistent with this.

'Deadly nightshade, as you may know, is not in fact all that deadly. But one could no doubt cram a chocolate with quite enough to cause a great deal of mischief, and Jane Pinhorn had possessed the opportunity to do this.

'Moreover, she had a motive. Along with a male cousin – a ne'er-do-well in Canada – she was the dead woman's only relative and co-heir.

'I saw suspicion inevitably attaching itself to this girl.

'I came back to Sheercliffe that night seriously troubled, and as soon as I arrived I went straight out to the dead woman's cottage.

'The rest of that night I spent prowling from one room to another.

'And then, quite suddenly, I found that I had come to a halt in the little hall and was staring at an envelope lying beside the telephone directory on a small table. It was a plain manila envelope, stamped ready for post, and creased down the middle.

'For a second I didn't see the significance of that crease. What had touched off some spring in my mind was the address – a single-spaced typescript affair of the most commonplace sort. International Vitamin Warehouses Limited, if mildly absurd, was nothing out of the way and wouldn't have troubled me.

'The snag lay in what followed. I know my East London fairly well. And the streets in which this pretentious organization claimed an abode contains nothing but mean private houses and a few shabby little shops.

'And so the truth came to me ... The truth, to begin with, about that crease. This envelope had come to Miss Pinhorn folded inside another one.

'I slit the thing open there and then. "*Send no money. Simply fill up the back of this form ...*" It had been a diabolically clever scheme. And it had, of course, been a completely fatuous one as well.'

Appleby paused. The Vicar was looking largely puzzled. But the Doctor drew a long breath. 'The nephew in Canada?'

'Precisely. He knew about the sealed-room effect. He knew about Jane's annual birthday gift. And he knew about his aunt's idiosyncrasy to belladonna.

'Some months before, its use by her oculist in a normal clinical dose had made her so seriously unwell as to take her into a nursing-home. The nephew believed that he could get on the gum of a reply-paid envelope a quantity which in her special case would be fatal.

'Miss Pinhorn, you remember, could never resist a free sample of anything. So she would fill in the form, lick the envelope – and perish!

'The envelope, if posted, would go to what was in fact a shady accommodation address in London, and our precious nephew would pick it up when he came over to England. He would also pick up the half of his aunt's fortune – or the whole of it if the unfortunate Jane was hanged on the strength of her chocolates.

'But this amateur in poison had confused a lethal with a toxic dose.

'With this particular drug, as it happens, the margin between the two is unusually wide. Having her special susceptibility to it, poor Miss Pinhorn did go horribly delirious, just as she had on a previous occasion.

'But that she chose to hurry on to this pub near the cliff, and thus put herself in the way of tumbling into the sea when the attack was at its worst, was pure chance.'

Appleby paused and stood up. 'It wasn't, as it happened, the last stroke of chance in the Pinhorn case. You may wonder what happened to the nephew.'

The Vicar nodded vigorously. 'Yes, indeed. He was certainly a murderer.'

'He had aimed at being that, and showed a certain efficiency.

'But he hadn't the stuff that an effective killer is made of. No sooner had he set his plot in motion, it seems, than he cracked up badly and went on a drinking-bout. Staggering home one morning in the small hours, and making his way through some public park, he fell into a very small pond and was drowned in six inches of water.

'At just about the same hour that tremendous current must have been drawing Amelia Pinhorn's body to unknown depths beneath the Furies.'

Eye Witness

'It is sometimes alleged,' the Doctor said, 'that the law and medical science don't always see eye to eye. And it may be true in regard to one big problem – that of what constitutes an understanding of the wrongfulness of a course of action.'

The Vicar nodded. 'Pleas of insanity, and that sort of thing?'

'Precisely. But in the main, the law has been very quick to accept and profit by scientific progress in medicine. The light that blood-grouping can sometimes throw on matters of disputed paternity is a good instance.'

'And what a lot of them there are!' Appleby had glanced up from the newspaper he was reading. 'But I suppose the Pelter case was unique – an upside-down business.'

'The Pelter case?' The Doctor shook his head. 'I don't remember it. And what do you mean by calling it upside-down?'

Appleby let his paper drop to the floor. 'In most of these affairs some unfortunate woman is trying to establish that a particular man – also sometimes unfortunate – is the father of her child. In the Pelter case the claimant was a *man* attempting to establish legal paternity. He came forward to declare that Peter Pelter, then a five-year-old boy, was his legitimate child. I'm surprised you don't recall the affair.'

'We neither of us do.' The Vicar produced his pipe. 'Which gives you a chance of telling us about it.'

'Very well – I'll try. And although it may sound a bit complicated at first, it was in its essence a tolerably simple affair.

'Some time in the nineteen-thirties an English girl called Sylvia Vizard, coming of a wealthy family in good society, kicked over the traces in a mild way, and went off in defiance of her parents to become an art-student in Paris. She was dead serious about it, apparently; got herself into a suitable *atelier*; and for the rest lived a lonely sort of existence, working like mad. Then she met a young American, Terry Pelter, who was also an art-student, and who had a similar somewhat unsociable slant on life. And this was important, as you will presently see.

'These two got married – in an unquestionably valid but, again, thoroughly unobtrusive way. Then they departed back into a sort of ·shifting and impermanent studio life that leaves very little trace of itself behind. Later, it was going to prove extraordinarily difficult to find anybody with precise memories of them. Vague impressions abounded – but, so to speak, the crucial eye-witness was missing every time. Nor did the marriage last long. In fact, it broke up within eighteen months.'

The Vicar looked distressed. 'Montmartre, I am afraid, would not be the best place in which to build a stable union.'

'It was certainly far from being that. Mrs Pelter turned up on her parents. She brought an infant son, Peter Pelter, and the news that her husband had cleared out. She rather thought that he had gone off to fight in the Spanish civil war.

'So the Vizards cared for the mother and child, and refrained from asking too many questions. About a year later there was a letter with a foreign stamp waiting for Mrs Pelter at the break-fast-table. She read it; said in a steady voice "Terry's dead"; and then walked across the room and threw both letter and envelope in the fire. She remained calm and dry-eyed all day. The next morning she was found drowned in a small pond where she had sailed boats as a child.

'Nothing could be discovered about the fate of Peter Pelter. I think the grandparents may have made no more effort than was legally discreet, for they were devoted to the child and anxious to enjoy its custody. Nothing happened for some years – nor ever might have, but for an odd circumstance. An eccentric and extremely wealthy sister of Lady Vizard's died. She believed that more vigorous inquiries should have been made, and she bequeathed a large sum of money to Peter Pelter and his father equally.'

'Well I'm blessed!' The Doctor sat forward attentively. 'I call that an uncommonly interfering thing to do. And it produced a claimant?'

'It did indeed.'

Appleby had nodded grimly. 'It produced as Terry Pelter a young American who seemed at first to be not at all a bad fellow. He had a very colourful story – the Spanish civil war came into it – and for a time it looked like being accepted without question. But Sir Charles and Lady Vizard – no doubt because they wanted to keep the child themselves – decided first to dislike him and then to question his identity. They had investigations opened up all over the place – in America, Paris, Spain – and eventually they turned up a fact of prime significance. Terry Pelter had been one of identical twins. And his brother, a dental surgeon somewhere in the Middle East, had disappeared not very long before the man claiming to be Terry turned up in England. Once more there was an explanation, involving, this time, a revolution in some South American republic. The claimant, in fact, had something like proof that his brother the dentist was dead. And he had enough evidence about his own supposed identity to promise a rather ticklish case.'

The Vicar looked up. 'What about blood-groups?'

'As between identical twins, they couldn't possibly help. What did help was the swift intelligence of Geoffrey Bellyse.'

'The Q.C.?'

'Yes. He led for the Vizards, and looked like having a rough time. Young Capcroft was for the claimant – and he was just beginning to build up the big reputation he has today. It was, of course, jury matter; and Capcroft knew from the start where his strength lay. It was in the apparent personality of the claimant – and still more, perhaps, in his mere physical appearance.

'Pelter – there was no disagreement about his surname – was tall and athletic, with regular features, fine brown eyes, a serious expression occasionally lit by a frank and friendly smile, and the best of American good manners. In fact, he was an examining counsel's dream – and correspondingly as hard a nut for cross-examination as Bellyse had ever had to tackle.'

Appleby paused. 'Bellyse would ask himself, you know, "What

is this man's weak point?" And he would answer, "The obverse of his strength. His strength is his good looks. His weakness will be personal vanity. I must try to get him on that."

'So towards the close of a very unspectacular cross-examination Bellyse shifted his ground. The material question was whether the claimant was Peter Pelter's father. What Bellyse worked round to asking was this: *How can you be confident that Peter Pelter is your son?* The judge didn't like it, but he held his peace for a vital couple of minutes. It went rather like this:

' "I believe, Mr Pelter, that you have been allowed to see the boy you claim as your son?"

' "Yes, sir – two or three weeks ago."

' "When had you last seen him before that?"

' "Just before I felt compelled to leave my late wife in order to fight in Spain."

' "The child being then only a few weeks old?"

' "That is correct, Mr Bellyse."

' "When you saw Peter as a five-year-old boy recently, you could yourself have no possible means of identifying him as your son?"

' "No very certain means, I suppose. But the child at least has my eyes."

' "You mean that you have brown eyes and that the child has brown eyes?"

' "Well, yes – and perhaps a little more. They are my sort of brown eyes, I figure."

' "Ah, yes – splendid brown eyes, I suppose you mean. Would it be correct to say, Mr Pelter, that you spend a good deal of time before your mirror?"

' "I have to shave."

' "To be sure. The world would not like to lose a chin such as yours behind a beard. Would you go so far as to say that when you saw Peter a few weeks ago you remembered his eyes?"

' "Certainly I did."

' "They had struck you from the first – perhaps as a comforting assurance of paternity?"

' "I never doubted my wife's honour, if that's what you mean.

But it was kind of good to see my own brown eyes smiling up at me from the bassinet, all the same."

' "I fear I don't quite follow you, Mr Pelter. You found something appealing in the baby's blue eyes?"

' "Blue eyes?"

' "Yes, Mr Pelter. Blue eyes."

Appleby paused. 'It was a wonderful moment. Pelter was still speaking confidently, but he looked scared. And I shall never forget the softly final way in which Bellyse pounced.

' "Would it surprise you, Mr Pelter, to learn that no baby *ever* has brown eyes?" ' '

'Clever!' The Doctor gave a delighted chuckle. 'Little Peter's eyes could certainly not have gained their pigment at the time this fellow claimed to be admiring their beautiful brown. They could only have been blue.'

And Appleby nodded. 'It was a small lie, but it fatally destroyed the impostor's credit. He's in gaol now. And Peter Pelter lives with his adoring grandparents still.'

The Bandertree Case

'The Bandertree case?' Appleby frowned. 'Well, yes – I did have something to do with it. But it wasn't pretty.'

'No more is the name.' The Doctor looked up from the intricacies of mulling a pint of claret. 'But was it *queer*? I'm all for a bizarre story tonight. And Bandertree sounds promising. Who was he?'

'A deeply unfortunate man.' Appleby, staring into the fire, appeared reluctant to proceed.

'How did his case begin?'

'As yours might, or mine, if fate had a whim that way. Bandertree's troubles started with people beginning to talk. Every day, you know, and in every little suburb, people *are* beginning to talk. You can never get at the first whisper – the first starting up of a suspicion in some acute or timid or dirty mind. Hundreds of these notions just die away. But a few become the occasion of persistent, sinister gossip, and may reach the police. If they are not quite clearly mere twaddle, they are investigated. And, every now and again –'

'Quite so.' The Doctor sat back. 'And now we proceed from the general to the particular. Just pass that nutmeg, would you? And then go ahead.'

'Very well. Bandertree was a middle-aged man with a small private income, a small strange talent as a painter, and a large and intermittently explosive temperament. He had been in bad trouble once as a younger man – I believe over some freakish brutality to a friend who had betrayed him in a love-affair – and the rumour of this had followed him to the little village of Chingford, where he lived by himself in a cottage standing by itself on the south bank of the stream. He lived there for years, a great recluse, and it seems that all sorts of odd yarns were told about him. Even when one discounts the greater number, it is evident that he was becoming very eccentric. And then he got married.'

The Doctor nodded. 'With what might be called a composing and normalizing effect? I thought so. It's a not uncommon result – for a time.'

'Bandertree married a war-widow called Agnes Mole. That must have been in 1943; and for a couple of years all went well. They were a devoted pair, despite the lady's being a completely commonplace person, incapable of telling a Picasso from a Modigliani. What you might call a thoroughly successful, thoroughly carnal marriage.'

Cautiously the Doctor tested his claret with a silver spoon. 'And with rocks ahead.'

'It might be better to say a single submerged reef. For what the couple presently ran up against was something thoroughly unexpected and treacherous. Mrs Bandertree proved not to have been a widow after all.'

'This being, in fact, one of those Back-from-the-Dead yarns?'

'Just that. Rupert Mole had been captured, not killed; and for some reason no news of him had ever come through. It was partly, I believe, because he had done one of those brilliant escapes that were apt simply to land a man in hiding with friendly folk in enemy-occupied territory. Anyway, at the end of the war Rupert Mole came home, and presently traced Agnes to Bandertree's cottage.

'Just what happened at first, I never got fully sorted out. Probably – as so often with such predicaments in real life – it was nothing very clear-cut. I suppose a tug of emotions, of appetites, memories, decencies, loyalties now one way and now another – and, as a result, a state of pure muddle and misery for all three of those people, such as would have taken some powerful external authority to straighten out. But in the end the jam did look like having some sort of decisive issue. The woman said she was going to stick to Bandertree; Bandertree agreed to keep her; and both of them told Mole to clear off. Only he didn't. He took a cottage just on the other side of the Ching and began a policy of hanging around. It couldn't be called very wise.'

'Nor very noble.' The Doctor poured out his concoction deftly and sat down again. 'But of course it might produce results.'

'What it produced was an abomination. Bandertree began to go queer again. Agnes alternated between clinging to him passionately and moods of guilt and revulsion. And Mole went about pubs and talked.

'This state of affairs continued for some months, and one consequence was that Bandertree could no longer face the world, and ceased absolutely from ever leaving the cottage. He wouldn't so much as go out into the garden. Only when Agnes did her shopping in the village, he could be seen staring out of the window after her in a sort of bestial fear. Mole, remember, was lurking not much more than a stone's throw away, across the stream.

'Well, Mole might be driving Bandertree crazy, but for a long time he didn't seem to be getting much out of the situation himself. He'd sit sullen and silent in a bar parlour of an evening, and then on a third beer he'd open up and curse his wife for her obstinate faithlessness. He was becoming a recognized bore in this way, when there appeared a sudden change in him. For about a week he became strained and utterly secretive. And then one evening he turned up darkly exultant, but taciturn still. It was on gin – something like a bottle of it – that they got him to talk that night. What he had to say was simple. Agnes had promised to return to him next day, and had agreed to their leaving the country together. And she had told Bandertree that she had made up her mind to this.

'And the next day, sure enough, Mole's cottage was seen to be shut up and deserted – nor did anybody ever set eyes on Agnes again. Bandertree was still to be glimpsed occasionally at a window, but his look was now wandering, and he appeared quite demented. He continued never to leave the house, and lived on supplies which he had persuaded some old woman to leave two or three times a week on his doorstep.

'It was only after about a couple of months that people began the talking – the really sinister talking – that I was speaking of. Eventually it reached the Chief Constable down there – a fellow who is something of a connoisseur in the macabre, and who decided to investigate himself. Bandertree proved to be in sober truth the next thing to crazy. But his story was quite simple. Agnes had simply vanished, and he had no doubt that Mole was responsible.

'So the Chief Constable went after Mole. He was eventually found in Dublin – and alone. His story, too, was simple. Agnes had failed to keep her promise; had simply not turned up. Whereupon he had decided he had had enough, and cleared out.

'There was one plain fact in this tangle: a woman had disappeared, and must be accounted for. The Chief Constable returned to Bandertree's cottage – and as well as an inquiring mind he took with him a sharp eye. In the middle of the sitting-room the floor seemed to have shrunk slightly, as if there had been a subsidence. So he got a search-warrant, had the floor-boards up, and dug. Need I tell you any more?'

The Doctor considered, and then smiled grimly. 'My dear Appleby, if I know anything of you, the answer is decidedly Yes.'

'Very well. They dug, and found the woman's body. The question that arose was whether Bandertree would be considered fit to plead. For he was certainly uncommonly strange, and the discovery, as you may imagine, didn't do him any good.

'It was about getting hold of the right medical line on this that I was consulted, and eventually I reviewed the whole case. There is something to be said for being thorough, even in the dullest and most routine way. I got Bandertree's whole history in all the detail I could. Then I got Mole's, and as soon as I read it I went down to Chingford and found what I expected to find. Four months later Mole was hanged.'

'I don't see it.'

'You would have, if you had learnt from the report on him that as a prisoner of war he had become one of the finest tunnel-diggers on record. He burrowed his way under the Ching and beneath Bandertree's house. Then he killed the woman, got her body where he wanted it, and sealed that end of the tunnel with what must have been astounding technical skill. After that he had only to wait a bit, then from a distance somehow contrive to set rumour going in Chingford. He planned, you see, to be revenged on both his wife and her lover. Didn't I say the story wasn't pretty? Let's forget it in this remarkable brew.'

The Key

'There must be *some* key to the affair.' Inspector Cadover turned from the window and stared at his former colleague. But his eyes retained their distant focus, so that Appleby had the sensation of being some remote and inanimate object, just visible on the horizon commanded from this eyrie in New Scotland Yard. 'There's a key to every murder, after all.'

'Undoubtedly there is.' Appleby's agreement was placid. 'Only sometimes it gets buried with the corpse.'

'Rubbish!' Cadover's nerves were frayed. 'And the corpse isn't buried yet, anyhow. They're still on a rather elaborate P.M.

'You see, this Honoria Clodd had been dead at least three days when they found her, and I'm anxious to narrow down the time all I can.

'Of course, it mayn't be murder at all. Superficially it looked just like another dismal head-in-the-oven affair.

'But if that's so, then Honoria was a much more economically-minded girl than one would take her for, all other facts considered. There she was in the kitchen of this discreet country cottage of hers, and her head was cosily in the oven, sure enough.

'But the gas was turned off – and only her finger-prints were on the tap.'

'I see.' Appleby's interest appeared not very lively. 'Could she have reached that tap from where she lay?'

'Certainly she could. And the thing is just conceivable as suicide. She *may* have turned off the tap herself. Not really out of economy, of course. That's only a joke.'

'Ah,' said Appleby.

'She may have thought better of killing herself at the last moment, as so many of them do. And so she may have reached out desperately at the last moment and managed to turn the tap. Indeed, the position of the arm rather suggested it.'

'And this cottage was where she lived?'

'Not as a regular thing. Although she was pretty well retired from the stage, she had rather a flashy flat here in town. The cottage was there on a lock-up, occasional week-end basis. The sort of cottage where you take down your provisions in tins, do all your own chores, and have absolutely no questions asked.

'A man worked in the garden on Wednesdays. I doubt if he'd have been welcome about the place at other times.'

'The suggestion,' said Appleby, 'appears to be that Miss Clodd —'

'Mrs Jolly. She was married – quite legally – to a nebulous person called Jolly. He was, I think, essential to her way of life.'

'Husbands sometimes are.'

'You misunderstand me.' Cadover's solemn gloom grew. 'The woman had more money than she ought to have had, even if she was quite thrivingly no better than she ought to have been.

'Unless I've got it all wrong, she was not merely immoral, but criminal as well. Jolly turned up at awkward moments —'

'And decidedly belied his name. In fact, a particularly filthy kind of blackmail.' Appleby stood up. 'Well, it's nice to hear that things are still going on as usual. And you've got a murderer to hunt for, all right.

'It's overwhelmingly probable that your Honoria was liquidated by somebody who couldn't afford to lose either his reputation or any more money. Don't forget, in the excitement of hanging the fellow, to get the virtuous Jolly locked up at the same time. And now I must be off.'

'And, mind you, there were signs of a struggle.' Cadover was following Appleby doggedly to the door. 'Bruises in various places, broken finger-nails, rather a nasty —'

'Quite so.' Appleby, with his hand on the doorknob, drew back at the sound of a sharp rap from outside. Hard upon it, a young man burst precipitately into the room.

'I say, sir —' The young man checked himself, recognizing

Appleby, and hurried on. 'They've found something. *A key. And it nearly got buried with the corpse.*'

Inspector Cadover sat down heavily at his desk. John Appleby, looked considerably less retired from the C.I.D. than he had done thirty seconds before, was staring at the contents of a small box which the young man had produced.

'A Yale key,' he said, '– and an odd little bit of twisted wire.'

The young man nodded. 'Just found by the post-mortem wallahs in Honoria's tummy.' With the confidence of one whose cheerful grin operates some inches above a most respectable school tie, the young man glanced from Appleby to his chief.

'A flood of light.' Appleby was immobile and his lips scarcely moved. Only his hand had gone out and, very gently, his fingers were at play upon the little twist of thin, spring-like wire.

'You mean that this – this lunacy positively improves matters?' Cadover had risen, taken three strides to his window, and was contemplating a considerable area of London with every appearance of extreme malevolence.

'There *ought* to be a flood of light in it. Remember Dupin?'

'Dupin?' The young man looked up as one who delights in the fruits of an extensive literary education. 'You mean Poe's Frog?'

'Exactly. Poe's Frog. Poe's immortal and archetypal French detective. Look out, he said, for what has never happened before, and pin your faith on that.

'Well, here it is. Never before, I'll be bound, has Scotland Yard found in the stomach of a presumably murdered woman a Yale key and an inch and a half of twisted wire. It's an uncommonly interesting thing.'

'To be sure it is.' Cadover was suddenly convinced and hearty. 'It's a *most* interesting thing. And just the sort of thing to interest you. Now, my dear Appleby, if you should care to look into it, to poke around –'

Appleby shook his head 'The doctors have done that for us. And if your mystery is ever to be solved' – he tapped the box – 'it will be now, on the strength of what is before our noses.'

A knock at the door interrupted them, and a uniformed sergeant thrust his head into the room. 'Beg pardon, sir – but we have Sir Urien Pendragon below, and wanting to see whoever is concerned with the case of the late Mrs Jolly.'

'Good heavens! Well, show him up.' Cadover was very reasonably staggered at the august scientist's name. 'Appleby, do you think he can have been one of –'

'I haven't a doubt of it.' Appleby returned his hat to the peg from which he had taken it a few minutes before. 'By the way, have you a line on the lately bereaved Jolly?'

'He ought to be presenting himself any minute.'

'Capital. I really think I'll stay. Just for ten minutes or so, until the affair is cleared up.'

Breathing hard, Cadover nodded to the young man. 'Clear out,' he said. 'A person like Sir Urien may take two of us. But he certainly won't take three.'

'Poor Mrs Jolly,' said Sir Urien, 'was a near neighbour of mine in the country. We were quite intimate friends. So naturally I am much distressed.'

'And you feel that you may have valuable information to give?' Cadover's reaction to his visitor's eminence was to turn eminently official and grim.

'Well, yes – although the matter is rather a delicate one.' Sir Urien adjusted his eyeglass and for a moment let his fingers stray over his beautifully trimmed grey beard.

'The fact is that there was – um – almost a sentimental element in the relationship – on poor Mrs Jolly's part, that is to say. I was really afraid that a distorted view of it might affect her relations with her husband, who is a most violent and ungoverned man. They were already on very ill terms, and indeed rarely saw each other.'

'We have some ideas on *that*.' Cadover tapped his writing-pad. 'And you say, Sir Urien, that you have been abroad?'

'I have. It was indeed a sense of this possible awkwardness that made me decide to go abroad some ten days ago. I went to my friends the Mountroyals, at Mentone' – Sir Urien paused as if to let this impressive information sink in – 'and I intended to stay for some three weeks.

'But government business brought me home a couple of days ago, and I heard of the shocking tragedy only this morning.'

Appleby, who had been standing silently by the window during these preliminary exchanges, suddenly spoke. 'May I ask, Sir Urien, if during your holiday you were constantly in the society of your friends?'

'Most certainly.' Sir Urien looked blandly surprised. 'Charles Mountroyal and I are very old friends. Arcades ambo would be a just description of us.'

'Thank you.' Appleby appeared to relapse into abstraction.

'Sir Urien, the facts as we know them are these.' Cadover's tone was quite expressionless. 'The body of Mrs Jolly – or Miss Honoria Clodd – was discovered yesterday morning by a hiker who, having lost his way and got no reply at the door, was sufficiently curious to peer through the kitchen window.

'She had died of coal-gas poisoning at some period which could not have been less than three, or more than six days previously.'

'Dear me, I am more than ever distressed. Had I not been abroad, I might have done something to prevent so rash an act.'

'We think it was murder.'

'You appal me. But I am not wholly surprised. Her husband is unbalanced – is subject, indeed, to overwhelming fits of pathological jealousy. And while one must admire, as in Shakespeare's Othello, the devotion from which such a passion takes its rise ...'

'Sir Urien, I have to tell you that our information in this matter is quite different. As we see it, Mrs Jolly was not a virtuous woman. And she and her husband conspired to exploit the fact in a manner that would have brought them well within the grasp of the criminal law.

'Jolly posed as the outraged husband of his wife's infidelities, and then accepted money as the price of his silence and, I suppose, complaisance.

'Your picture of an outraged husband committing murder in a fit of uncontrolled jealousy is therefore nonsense.'

'You pain me inexpressibly. You horrify me.' Sir Urien, who had certainly gone a little pale, nevertheless again stroked his beard comfortably enough. 'And if I may say so, Inspector, I am much disturbed by the fact of a man in your position displaying so strange an ignorance of human nature.

'Suppose – as I do not for a moment admit – the position to be as you describe. It is tolerably well known that a man who exploits a woman after the fashion you mention is particularly likely to react with an insane fury should that woman import any element of – um – genuine regard into a relationship initially entered into for gain.'

Cadover, thus blandly schooled, breathed harder than ever. And once more Appleby stirred by the window.

'That,' he said, 'is perfectly true. I see, Sir Urien, that you possess some insight into the minds of the criminal classes. You know this fellow Jolly?'

Sir Urien hesitated. 'We have met. He is not a person whom I should wish to admit to my familiar acquaintance.'

'I believe it might be interesting if you met him again.'

And Cadover, taking the hint, leant forward at his desk and pressed a bell.

Jolly was a grey and clammy creature, at once insubstantial and acutely disagreeable.

'We appreciate that you were not often in your wife's society.' Cadover had the air of gazing straight through the human cobweb before him.

'But it will at least not be difficult to prove that she was your only visible means of support. She had money, Mr Jolly, and you knew how she came by it.

'I suggest that you need not look far –' and Cadover glanced quickly at the silent Sir Urien Pendragon – 'in order to recall one quite considerable source of income.'

'I tell you, there was no vice in Honoria.' Jolly licked his lips and looked sidelong at Sir Urien with what appeared to be furtive fear and fury.

'There was no vice in her, at all. I don't say she didn't have some very pleasant gentlemen friends. And I don't say she didn't have presents.'

'Might it have occurred to her to borrow a car?'

It was Appleby who spoke. Quite suddenly, he had taken the middle of the room.

'I don't say it wouldn't, and I don't say it would.' Jolly, thoroughly wary and alarmed, seemed to find reassurance in this formula.

'In fact, was there not a particular car? Rather a grand car –'

'I protest!' Sir Urien had risen to his feet. 'In Mr Jolly's interest I protest against this highly irregular interrogation. I demand that he be permitted to withdraw, and to answer no more questions except upon legal advice.'

'I have no objection in the world.' Appleby gently smiled – and simultaneously made a gesture that sent the spare Cadover with an agile bound to the door. 'But with you yourself, Sir Urien, it is another matter.'

'She told her own story.' Cadover and Appleby were again alone, and it was now the latter who, as he spoke, gazed out far across London.

'As to whether there was vice in Honoria, we have our own opinion. But there was certainly brains. And guts, of a sort. She knew she was being murdered, and she was determined that her murderer should pay.

'As for Pendragon, it was the demand for his car that was at once a last straw and an inspiration. They were near neighbours; she had pestered him to have the use of this grand car; he went abroad – and posted her the key of the particular garage in which it was housed.

'At a guess, I should say it was at a little remove from his house. Or perhaps he had sent away the servants and the place was deserted: that will be something for you to find out.

'He knew the wretched woman's mentality; had good reason to know it. She was selfish in her pleasures, and went off to possess herself of the gorgeous new prize alone.

'She unlocked the garage and entered. She got into the car and slammed the door. In a matter of seconds, I fancy, she knew she was done for – that she had shut herself up in a brilliantly contrived lethal chamber.

'Pendragon was a scientist. It wasn't difficult for him to arrange that when the door of that car shut several other things happened simultaneously. The doors locked themselves.

'I have no doubt that the door of the garage – probably of the roll-up sort – slid down and presented a blank and innocent face to the world. And already coal-gas was pouring into the car.

'Honoria struggled, trying to smash her way out through what would certainly be a virtually unbreakable glass. The signs of that struggle were on her body when it was found.

'Within minutes she was dead. And as the date of her death would later be approximately determined by the state of her body, Pendragon with his Mentone alibi would be safe.

'When he did return to England he had only to drive round to Honoria's deserted cottage and leave her with her head in the oven. He used her fingers to turn on the gas for a bit, and then turned it off again – being afraid that a great stink of gas might attract the notice of a passer-by a little too soon.

'Pendragon was invulnerable, or would have been but for the swift working of Honoria's wits, intent on retribution.

'She swallowed the key, which would have carried us a good long way in the end. And she swallowed something else that ought to have cried *motor-car* the moment we looked at it, even though it is twisted a little out of shape.

'You might find that little twist of wire on the floor, or in the glove box of any car, for it is simply the little clip often used instead of a nut to secure a terminal to its sparking-plug.

'Honoria knew there would be a post-mortem, and she sent us the only message she could. One can't but admire her. Even when dying, it must have taken resolution to swallow those things.'

Cadover nodded. 'I hope a jury will swallow them.'

'There's a good chance that they will. The key is indeed the key to the case, for it will certainly prove to be the key of Pendragon's garage. And it is very unlikely that he has had time to remove all traces of the elaborate set-up he had to contrive.'

'He made a solid bid for freedom.' Cadover had joined Appleby, and now both were staring out over the grey city. 'Shall you be sorry if he hangs?'

Appleby considered. 'I didn't like him, but I like Honoria's kind of game no better. So my answer must be like the abominable Jolly's. I shall and I shan't.'

The Flight of Patroclus

'Anything in the news?' Appleby asked the question idly as he sat down and stretched his legs before the clubhouse fire.

'Singularly little.' The Vicar dropped his evening paper on the floor. 'And certainly no sign that world grows more honest. Numerous petty thefts and robberies – and one big one. A valuable painting – a Titian – has been stolen from Benison Court.'

'The place can very easily spare it.' Appleby spoke with a serenity altogether culpable in an Assistant Commissioner of Police. 'And it will probably give its new owner far more pleasure that it gives the Scattergoods and their guests in that chilly long gallery.'

'My dear Appleby, to apply such a criterion is surely to invite the merest moral chaos. But who will the new owner be?'

'Some mad collector in America, building up a whole secret museum of stolen masterpieces. Think of the thrill of that. It would give Titian himself a tremendous kick. Whereas the long gallery at Benison would leave him cold – in every sense. But that reminds me' – Appleby had begun to fill his pipe – 'did I ever tell you about the Counterpoynt affair?'

The Vicar smiled. 'Go right ahead.'

'Even in his early eighties Lord Counterpoynt was an exceptionally handsome man – not merely in his feature, but in his whole figure. As an undergraduate he had refused to stroke the Oxford boat, saying that it would be a waste of time; and there were several other fields in which he was regarded as being, potentially at least, the leading athlete of his generation. His interests, however, were mainly aesthetic; and he was a great patron of the arts.'

The Vicar looked perplexed. 'But surely he became an extremely well-known –'

'Precisely. But back in the nineties, nobody could have guessed that young Counterpoynt would eventually revert to type – family type, I mean – and become a leading philanthropist and writer on social and moral questions.

'Among the painters he encouraged was Orlando Say, at first a great rebel and Bohemian, but eventually a Royal Academician, celebrated for his mythological subjects, and for ambitious figure compositions in classical settings. Nobody thinks much of Say now. But his canvasses have their virtues. In the age of Burne-Jones, when the nude figure commonly had the air of having been painted in indecent pinko-grey tights, Say carried on from Etty the ability to paint honest nakedness – skin that you could really believe had pores to it, glinting above water or shadowed among leaves.'

The Vicar nodded. 'I am not among those, my dear Appleby, who consider the Nude to be a Pity. But if it is to be done, let it be done well.'

'An excellent sentiment, Vicar. And now to my story. One November morning some years ago, the aged Lord Counterpoynt was shown into my room at New Scotland Yard. He was in great agitation. Somebody, he said, had stolen his best Orlando Say. And he asked me to come to Counterpoynt House at once.'

'It was still standing?'

'Yes – and one of the last surviving town houses of that tremendous sort. A Say was small beer in such a place, and I wondered why the old boy was so upset. I presently found out.

'Counterpoynt took me to the smoking-room – an apartment, it appeared, designed exclusively for male habitation, as the Edwardian habit was. Among a good many paintings there was one empty space, and the proportions of this suggested at once that the stolen picture had been a full-length figure-composition. And this was confirmed when Counterpoynt showed me a photograph of it. It was called *The Flight of Patroclus*, and represented a young Grecian warrior, stark naked, hurtling through the picture-space from left to right. Hector presumably was after him, but Hector wasn't in the picture. And now I come to the crux of the matter. The nude youth was quite clearly the young Counterpoynt. That was why the painting had been kept in the smoking-room. It was an utterly blameless and rather lovely thing. But ladies – at least in Victorian or Edwardian times – might conceivably have been embarrassed if called upon to admire their host represented in just that way. And here too, apparently, was the reason why his lordship was so upset. He didn't fancy the notion of his own unclothed image – even if from sixty years back – being carried off to some thieves' kitchen.'

The Vicar considered. 'But was nothing else stolen?'

'An admirable question. Counterpoynt House had been successfully broken into – and nothing but this curious Orlando Say had vanished. And this very smoking-room held a small Rembrandt landscape and a particularly fine Cuyp. It didn't make sense. Or rather it did. Malice rather than any mercenary motive must have been responsible. The thing was a prank – an ill-natured practical joke.'

'But with so old a man –'

'Exactly. Sixty years earlier one could have supposed that some young rips had hit upon a means of discomfiting another young rip. But who could now want to badger this eminent old person? Conceivably another old person, not risen to any eminence, and enjoying a crazy senile revenge. But the actual robbery was an able-bodied piece of work. If a malignant contemporary of Counterpoynt's had conceived the stroke, he had employed some-one else on the job. And that, somehow, seemed unlikely.

'Well, I understood Counterpoynt's being upset – but not his being quite so upset as he was. There wasn't much to do except put some routine measures in operation and promise that the Yard would do its best. A thorough examination of the scene of the robbery yielded nothing, nor did a close watch in certain likely quarters produce any hint of the stolen picture's going on an illicit market. But about a fortnight later there was a very odd development indeed.

'Only one public gallery in the country has any considerable collection of Orlando Says, and that is the Municipal Museum at Nesfield. One of my first moves had been to get in touch with the Director there, since it had occurred to me that he might have made some study of Say, and so possess a chance piece of information that might throw light on the mysterious theft from Counterpoynt House. That particular cast had drawn blank, but now I had a telephone call from him. An oil painting of Say's had been stolen from his gallery in the course of the previous night, and he would be much obliged if I could come down.

'So down I went, wondering whether Say was presently to be universally acclaimed as a transcendent genius, and whether an enterprising criminal had received some species of precognitive intelligence of this shift in artistic taste.

'But as soon as I entered the gallery, I saw that this fantastic explanation, at least, was ruled out. The place was stuffed with Says. There were Homeric heroes on every wall – for all I knew, half the English peerage had posed for them – and there was an equal muster of nymphs and goddesses, knee-deep in water or gleaming engagingly from behind an exiguous screen of leaves. And it was a nymph that had disappeared. The missing picture was called *The Metamorphosis of Daphne.* The Director showed me a photograph. There she was, beautifully naked, and hurtling across the picture-space from left to right. Apollo wasn't in the painting – but presumably he wasn't far out of it, since one of the nymph's arms was already sprouting into a very pretty little laurel-bough.'

The Vicar chuckled. 'As the poet Marvell puts it:

> Apollo hunted Daphne so,
> Only that she might laurel grow.'

'Quite so. Well, light was dawning on me, and I asked if anything was known about the model who had posed for Orlando Say in this picture. The answer was just right. There was an obscure story that it had been a well-known society beauty of the time – now still alive, but as an extremely old and august lady.

'So there you are. *Apollo Pursuing Daphne* had been a very daring prank indeed. Lord Counterpoynt had wisely had it chopped in two – and the half which had represented him as the pursuing Apollo he had retained as a representation of the fleeing

Patroclus. The other half had gone to the lady, who at some time most rashly parted with it.

'I now knew that I had only to wait. And – sure enough – there was presently an attempt to blackmail poor old Counterpoynt. The thefts had been the work of a fellow who had got the whole story from some stray letter of Say's. He was pretty sure that Lord Counterpoynt would pay a lot rather than have such a ludicrous scandal dragged up in his and the lady's respectable old age. When we pounced on this enterprising scoundrel in the end we found that he had even gone to the trouble of having the two halves of the picture put together again. The background showed it to be incontrovertibly one composition. And it was really rather a pretty thing.'

The Vicar had been listening with grave attention. 'And may I ask,' he said cautiously, 'where this – um – improper picture hangs now?'

'Of course you may.' And Appleby smiled. 'But if I were to give an answer – well, that would be telling.'

The Clock-face Case

'It was the convenient sort of case,' Appleby said, 'in which the bullet stops the clock.'

The Q.C. looked sceptical. 'That's something that *ought* to happen from time to time, I've no doubt. But in twenty years on the criminal side I've never actually come across it.'

The Vicar was mildly considering. 'I *believe*,' he ventured presently, 'that it has been used in a detective-story. In fact, I'm almost sure of it.'

Appleby chuckled. 'I suspect that your reading in the genre is limited. Yarns in which the clock stops the bullet and the bullet retaliates by stopping the clock are as thick in the libraries as autumnal leaves are supposed to be in Vallombrosa. But there was another interesting feature in this case. The evidence of one witness – a crucial witness – was complicated by the fact that he had seen only the *reversed image* of the clock.'

'You mean in a mirror?' The Q.C. groaned. 'It's really too much, my dear fellow. All yarns in which the bullet stops the clock in Chapter One regularly introduce a mirror to our notice round about Chapter Five or Six. And you yourself are being wildly improvident. You should sit on your mirror' – and the Q.C. stretched out his arm for the decanter – 'until the port has gone round a second time.'

'I can imagine nothing more gingerly and uncomfortable. I insist on setting my mirror squarely on the table. And, for that matter, my clock too. It is important that you take a good look at it.' Appleby, somewhat to the Vicar's bewilderment, pointed firmly to a dish of walnuts. 'Notice that it is a thoroughly modern clock. You might almost call it a modish clock. And certainly a reticent clock. It bears no figures, but only a plain dot at each hour.'

The Q.C. nodded. 'I've seen that sort of clock. Uncommonly silly notion, if you ask me. But then' – he smiled happily – 'it's clear that you are determined to tell us an uncommonly silly story. It's an art that I can't myself study too carefully. So pray proceed.'

Appleby nodded. 'Very well. Sir Hannibal Green was a prosperous bachelor living in a flat just off Piccadilly, where he was ministered to by a manservant of the name of Snake.'

'I don't believe a word of it.' The Q.C. was uncompromising. 'Outside Restoration Comedy, such a name simply doesn't exist.'

Appleby grinned. 'Well, I'm *calling* the man Snake. And Snake alone lived with Sir Hannibal in the flat, getting along with the aid of persons who came in to oblige by the day. Sir Hannibal wasn't distinguished for anything very much, with the exception of a very fine collection of miniatures. Some of these hung on the walls of his study; others were disposed in showcases; and the majority – I suppose so that the general effect should not be too overwhelming – lived in a big Flemish cabinet which had been steel-lined and fire-proofed for the purpose.

'As you may have guessed, my story concerns an attempt to steal these treasures. It was a successful attempt and a ruthless one – involving nothing less than Sir Hannibal's murder. And it occurred on the day that Sir Hannibal, together with Snake, returned from his annual visit to Italy.'

'Italy?' The Vicar cracked a nut with the air of bringing off an epigram. 'Then Hannibal must have crossed the Alps.'

'Certainly he did.' Appleby smiled tolerantly. 'He did so by rail and through the Mont Cenis – which got him and his manservant back to Victoria round about seven p.m. They drove straight home in a taxi. Sir Hannibal, after satisfying himself that his collection was safe and sound, went to his bedroom to change. And Snake employed himself in preparing a light supper. So much is certain.

'At ten o'clock that night a married sister of Sir Hannibal's named Mrs Gracie called to welcome home her brother on his return from abroad. Having got no answer to her ring on the door-bell, she let herself in with a latchkey – something she commonly had when her brother was away, so that she could drop in from time to time and keep an eye on things. She found the flat in disorder, the greater part of the collection gone, and her brother shot dead in his dining-room.'

The Q.C. set down his glass. 'You suspected Snake?'

'We came to suspect him strongly, although at first he told a story that seemed innocent enough. On his serving the meal he had prepared, his employer asked him if he wanted to go out. He replied that he would like to. He, too, had a sister, to whom he was anxious to give an account of his holiday. And on the chance that he might be free, he had suggested to her by letter that she come round at nine o'clock and wait for him in some caretaker's room downstairs. This apparently was a common rendezvous for people working in this block of flats. Sir Hannibal at once agreed, adding that he would breakfast in his bedroom, and that the present meal could be cleared up by a woman who came in during the morning.

'And now I come to the clock. Snake withdrew, and Sir Hannibal told him to leave the dining-room door open. He had a notion that he might not be able to hear the door-bell, if Mrs Gracie did call.

'Ten minutes later Snake – if his story was to be believed – left the flat. He didn't glance into the dining-room, since it would have been impolite, apparently, to meet his employer's eye. But he *did* glance at a large mirror in the hall. It showed him Sir Hannibal sitting over his wine just as we are doing now. *And* it showed him the clock. Wondering whether his sister would yet be waiting downstairs, he took the trouble to *read* the clock. He could see that it was going, for it had one of those second-hands that sweep across the whole dial. And it said precisely nine o'clock. Snake seemed quite clear-headed about this. It had the *appearance* of reading three o'clock, because – as I have said – he was, of course, seeing its image in reverse.

'Well, out Snake went – and within a couple of minutes was conversing with his sister, a caretaker, and another private servant. He had left his employer alive and well. Or so he said.'

The Q.C. picked up the decanter again in great absence of mind. 'Snake,' he said, 'was in an unpleasant position.'

'It was to become much more unpleasant quite soon. At first, there seemed to be various possibilities. Sir Hannibal's body was found by the open door of his dining-room. It seemed plausible that somebody might have rung the door-bell, been admitted, and then been led into or towards the dining-room to be interviewed. The direction of the shots – there had been three of them – were consistent with this. One had buried itself in the mantelpiece; another had hit the clock, which was standing on the mantelpiece; and the third had shot Sir Hannibal through the forehead. It looked as if a thoroughly nervous criminal had taken two rapid shots at him ineffectively from behind, and had then got him squarely above the eyes as he swung round.'

The Vicar sighed. 'And all to clear the way to a collection of miniatures. What an incredibly brutal crime!'

'Quite so. There was, of course, the question of the criminal's knowing his way about, getting the Flemish cabinet open, and so on. There was nothing here that positively pointed to Snake. But the business of the waiting sister had a suspicious air. It is just the sort of thing that is brought into prominence when a man has been cooking up an alibi.

'Only if that *had* been Snake's game, he had bungled things badly. You will recall that he claimed to have left Sir Hannibal alive and well just on nine o'clock. And you know that one of the bullets stopped the clock.'

The Q.C. considered. '*Before* nine?'

'Precisely. At half-past eight.'

'Admirable!' The Vicar nodded with every appearance of massive intellectual delectation. 'So Snake's game was up.'

Appleby shook his head – and once more pointed impressively at the walnuts. 'A modern clock. Indeed – as you can now see – an *electric* clock. And you know how the simple type of electric clock is set going? You switch on the current, and then simply spin a little knob at the back. The electricity had, of course, been switched off while Sir Hannibal was away on holiday. Presumably just before his man went out he had set the clock by his watch, switched on, and spun. *But he had spun in the wrong direction.*

'That – as you will know if you have ever possessed such a clock – is a very easy thing to do. And it simply sets the clock going *backwards*. Half an hour *after* Snake last saw Sir Hannibal, the clock would be saying not half-past nine but half-past eight. Sir Hannibal had been murdered by someone gaining admission to the flat half an hour after Snake left.'

The Q.C. drew a long breath. 'How did you tumble to this?'

'Snake remembered that he had seen the second-hand definitely revolving in a clockwise direction. It had obscurely disturbed him at the time – as well it might, in view of the fact that he was seeing the thing in a mirror. I was convinced of the truth of his statement as soon as he recalled this odd fact; and it admits of no other explanation than the one I have given you. So I pegged away at the case until I ran the real criminal to earth. One usually does, in the end.'

Miss Geach

'The newspapers nowadays,' Appleby said, 'are full of resourceful persons remembering to dial 999. And a very good thing too. But Miss Geach disliked the telephone, and so she came all the way to New Scotland Yard instead.'

The Q.C. shook his head. 'An imprecise statement, this. Was her journey from John o' Groats or Highgate?'

'It was from Kensington, where Miss Geach had a small flat in a superior sort of warren called, if I remember correctly, Dreadnaught Mansions. Miss Geach herself, however, was somewhat timorous. Or so one had to suppose.'

'Because she disliked the telephone?'

'Because of that – and because she swooned away in my arms as I was going out to lunch. A sergeant on duty in the lobby was so outraged that he did his best to arrest her on the spot. When I got her revived and calmed down a bit she told me rather an odd tale.

'It seemed that behind the marble hall of Dreadnaught Mansions, with its proliferation of palms and resplendent commissionaire, there harboured a shameful secret, which was causing the tenants much discomfort and annoyance. There was something wrong with the drains.'

The Q.C. looked puzzled. 'But would one want to dial 999 about that?'

'You mistake me. The drains were only a remote cause of Miss Geach's agitation. The attempt to patch them up had resulted in a serious breach in her insulation.'

'Miss Geach was insulated?'

'Yes – I believe with seaweed. In other words, noise from the flat below should have been cut out by some stuff or other packed under her floors. But the bother over the drains had in some way put this out of action, and left Miss Geach for the time being abnormally vulnerable to disturbance. The position was worst in her bedroom. There she was obliged actually to overhear a good deal of any conversation going on beneath her. And this distressed Miss Geach very much. I got the impression that, even during the day, she was in her bedroom quite a lot.'

'And Miss Geach came along to you about this?'

'She came along because – if she was at all to be credited – she had overheard a violent quarrel, followed by what she was convinced had been murder. As you know, mild-mannered elderly ladies are constantly enjoying hallucinations of that sort, and it seemed to me that the best thing to do would be to get her straight home again. If there *was* anything in her story, I could investigate it on the spot. So I drove her back.

'She gave me more details on the way. Just who lived immediately beneath her she didn't know. But she had lately come to the conclusion that it must be a bachelor of unsuitable temperament, since what she heard for the most part was simply the voice of a youngish man talking to himself, or even shouting. At this point I was inclined to feel that poor Miss Geach's fantasy might become merely embarrassing, and concern a sort of dream lover. But as she went on I began to take another view. I thought there might be something in it.'

The Q.C. grinned. 'My dear fellow, it's only if there was something in it that I'm prepared to go on listening to you.'

'Very well. The first thing of which Miss Geach was aware on the relevant occasion was the owner of this attractive young male voice calling somebody a dirty hound. Then he talked with great volubility and passion about his family honour, foul slander, and the reputation of a woman who was inexpressibly dear to him.'

The Q.C. shook his head. 'One can picture – can one not? – the reluctance of your Miss Geach to listen in to such stuff. But proceed.'

'Presently the temperature appeared to be rising yet higher, and the young man's voice was saying something about contemptible curs and blackmail. It was at this point that a second voice joined in. Miss Geach described it as a soft sinister foreign voice. And it was demanding some large sum of money. The young man replied angrily that he wouldn't pay, and added that the whole thing was a filthy racket, and too unspeakably low. The foreign voice replied that it didn't care a damn how low it was, the money must be paid. The young voice said something about not putting up with vulgar gangster stuff, and the foreign voice said inflexibly "One thousand pounds". The young voice then rose in real out-and-out rage, and the language, Miss Geach said, was such as she could not repeat, even to an officer of police. But the owner of the foreign voice appeared to bide his time, and when the other had blown off steam came back again with something inaudible but decisive. The young voice suddenly shouted, "Very well, I'll pay – and then you can take yourself out of this and never let me see you again." The foreign voice made what sounded like a speech of ironical thanks, and then there was a silence of some minutes duration, before hell broke loose.'

The Q.C. raised his eyebrows. 'Hell broke loose? That was Miss Geach's expression?'

'It was. Furniture appeared to be hurtling all over the place, and its crashing or bumping was punctuated by what she described as howls of rage. And it was this that broke the poor lady's nerve. She bolted downstairs and into the street, intending to find a constable. But there wasn't one in sight, and she had the odd inspiration of jumping into a taxi and driving to the Yard. When we drew up upon returning to Dreadnaught Mansions I had to take her encouragingly by the arm before she found resolution to enter again.

'I judged it in her best interest not to start inquiring about a rumpus that might never really have happened, and so I walked straight upstairs with her until we reached the flat beneath her own. Its outer door was closed, and there was a porter standing near by, eyeing it doubtfully. I questioned him and gathered that there had in fact been some sort of row; other tenants had complained, and he had been sent along to make discreet inquiries. But there had been no reply to his knocking, and he was wondering whether to hang about or return and report to the management. It seemed to me a case for going right in, and after some police stuff I got hold of a master-key and opened up.

'The flat was deserted, and there was nothing out of the way about it except in its principal apartment, a handsomely furnished living-room which had all the appearance of having been struck by a cyclone. Chairs had been pitched about, a large mirror was smashed, and a whole bookcase had come down, scattering its contents across the floor. I walked over to a desk which was still in tolerably good order, and the first thing my eye fell on was an open cheque-book. The last counterfoil was exposed, and scrawled on it in bold, angry figures was "£1,000".

'At the sight of all this poor Miss Geach sank with a groan into one of the few chairs remaining in a serviceable position. And at the same moment somebody strode in behind us.

'It was a young man who, I felt at once, was vaguely familiar to me. He was flushed – indeed it came into my head that he was blushing – and he looked at us uncertainly, as if wondering whether to feel furious or foolish.

' "I am from Scotland Yard," I said. "Are you, sir, the owner of this flat, and have you been involved in a fight in it?" And quite suddenly as I spoke I was able to put a name to the fellow. He was Merlin Henneker, the rising young actor.

' "A fight? Nonsense! I got worked up and threw things about a bit. So I went out to cool off. And I can't see that it's any business of yours."

' "I think perhaps it may be. Do you deny that you have had an angry interview with a blackmailer; that you were constrained to write him out a cheque for a thousand pounds; and that he has now vanished after what appears to have been a scene of great violence?" '

The Q.C. considered. 'Young Henneker must have been considerably put out.'

'Not a bit of it. Decidedly to my astonishment, he sat down and roared with laughter.

' "Blackmail?" he spluttered.

' "Certainly." I was determined to take a firm line with him.

"The matter concerned your family honour, and the reputation of a lady."

'Henneker stared at me. "My dear sir, I see that somebody has been eavesdropping and has got matters a little mixed. I spent the morning trying to persuade a detestable little impresario that a play in which I had rashly contracted to appear is hopelessly vulgar and *vieux jeu* – a melodrama, stuffed with blackmail and every kind of silliness. But he was unmoved, and insisted that if I backed out I must pay the monetary penalty to which I had bound myself in the event of breaking the contract. So I paid up, and when the little brute had gone I expressed myself – privately, as I supposed – in a somewhat temperamental way about the whole matter."

'And Merlin Henneker glanced from me to poor Miss Geach. "I am afraid," he said, "that your friend is upset. So, unfortunately, are the decanters. So I can't even offer you both a drink." '

Tragedy of a Handkerchief

The curtain rose on the last scene of Shakespeare's *Othello*, the dreadful scene in which Desdemona is smothered, the scene which Dr Johnson declared is not to be endured. But by this audience, it seemed to Appleby, it was going to be endured tolerably well. For one thing, the smothering was apparently to be staged in the reticent way favoured by touring companies that depend on the support of organized parties of schoolchildren. Not that the schoolchildren, probably, would take a thoroughly Elizabethan robustness at all amiss. But headmistresses are different. If their charges must, in the sovereign name of Shakespeare, be taken to see a horrid murder, let it at least be committed in hugger-mugger in a darkened corner of the stage.

But if the audience was not going to be horrified, neither, so far, had it been gripped. Whatever currents of emotion had been liberated behind this proscenium arch – and currents of emotion there certainly were – they were not precisely those intended by the dramatist. Or rather, Appleby thought, it was as if across the main torrent of feeling as Shakespeare had designed it there were drifting eddies of private passion muddying and confusing the whole. Something of the sort one was familiar with in amateur theatricals, in which the jealousies and spites of rival performers excited by an unusual limelight occasionally reveal themselves as absurdly incongruous with the relationships designed by the story. But it is a thing less common on the professional stage, and during the preceding act the audience had been growing increasingly restless and unconvinced. Perhaps only Appleby himself, who had dropped into this dilapidated provincial theatre merely to fill an empty evening in a strange town, was giving a steadily more concentrated attention to the matters transacting themselves on the stage. Around him were the gigglings of bored children and the rustling of stealthily opened paper bags. Appleby, however, studied Desdemona's bedchamber with a contracted brow.

Othello was about to enter with a taper and announce that, *It is the cause, it is the cause, my soul . . .*

But there was a hitch. For one of those half-minute intervals which can seem an eternity in terms of theatrical time Othello failed to appear. The stage stood empty, with the sleeping Desdemona scarcely visible in her curtained and shadowy bed at the back. And this delay was only one of several signs that all was not well behind the scenes.

Most striking had been the blow – that public indignity to which Othello subjects his wife in the fourth act. The crack of an open palm across a face is a thing easily simulated on the stage; the assailant makes his gesture, his victim staggers back, and at the same time someone watching from the wings smartly claps his hands together. But on this occasion there had been the sound of *two* blows: one indeed from the wings and one from the stage itself. And as Desdemona fell back it had been just possible to discern first a cheek unnaturally flushed and then a trickle of blood from a nostril. Almost as if *Othello* were the brutal pothouse tragedy which some unfriendly critics have accused it of being, the hero had given his wife a bloodied nose. . . . And the ensuing twenty lines had been uncommonly ticklish, with Desdemona playing out her shock and horror while covertly dabbing at her face with a handkerchief. No doubt an actor may be carried away. But an Othello who allowed himself this artistic excess would be decidedly dangerous. What if he permitted himself a similar whole-heartedness when the moment for smothering Desdemona came?

Still staring at the empty stage, Appleby shook his head. There had been other hints that private passions were percolating through the familiar dramatic story. *Othello* is a tragedy of suspicion, of suspicion concentrated in Othello himself – the hero who, not easily jealous, is yet brought by the triumphant cunning of the villain Iago to kill his wife because of a baseless belief in her adultery. But among the people on this stage suspicion was not concentrated but diffused. Behind the high dramatic poetry, behind the traditional business of the piece, an obscure and pervasive wariness lurked, as if in every mind were a doubtful speculation as to what other minds knew. Desdemona – Appleby could have sworn – was more frightened than Shakespeare's heroine need be; Iago was indefinably on the defensive, whereas his nature should know nothing but ruthless if oblique attack; Iago's wife Emilia, although she played out the honest impercipient waiting-woman efficiently scene by scene, was perceptibly wishing more than one of her fellow-players to the devil. As for Michael Cassio, he was harassed – which is no doubt what Cassio should chiefly be. But this Cassio was harassed behind the mask as well as across it. Appleby, knowing nothing of these strolling players without name or fame, yet suspected that Cassio was the company's manager, and one despairingly aware that the play was badly misfiring ...

On one side of Appleby a small girl massively exhaled an odour of peppermint drops. On the other side an even smaller boy entertained himself by transforming his programme into paper pellets and flicking them at the audience in the stalls below.

And now here was Othello at last – a really black Othello of the kind fashionable since Paul Robeson triumphed in the part. Only about this fellow there had been a faint flavour of nigger minstrel from the start, and it had long been plain that there was nothing approaching great acting in him. Yet the theatre fell suddenly silent. The man stood there framed in a canvas doorway, the customary lighted taper in his hand. His eyes rolled, fixed themselves, rolled again. His free hand made exaggerated clawing gestures before him. As far as any elevated conception of his role went he was violating almost every possible canon of the actor's art. And yet the effect was queerly impressive – startling, indeed. The child on Appleby's left gulped and regurgitated, as if all but choked by peppermint going down the wrong way. The boy on the right let his ammunition lie idle before him. From somewhere up in the gods another child cried out in fright. Othello stepped forward into a greenish limelight which gave him the appearance of a rather badly decomposed corpse.

Some forty-five seconds behind schedule, the unbearable scene had begun.

> It is the cause, it is the cause, my soul;
> Let me not name it to you, you chaste stars!
> It is the cause . . .

The mysterious words rolled out into the darkness of the auditorium. And – of course – they were indestructible. Not even green limelight, not even an Othello who made damnable faces as he talked, could touch them.

> Yet I'll not shed her blood,
> Nor scar that whiter skin of hers than snow . . .

To the dreadful threat Desdemona awoke. Propped up on the great bed, she edged herself into another limelight which again offended all artistic decorum.

> Will you come to bed, my lord?

With mounting tension the scene moved inexorably forward. Othello – who at least had inches – was towering over the woman on the bed.

> That handkerchief which I so loved and gave thee
> Thou gavest to Cassio . . .

The Tragedy of the Handkerchief, this play had been contemptuously called. And the French translator, Appleby remembered, had preferred the more elevated word *bandeau* . . .

> By heaven, I saw my handkerchief in's hand,
> O perjured woman; thou dost stone my heart,
> And makest me call what I intend to do
> A murder, which I thought a sacrifice;
> I saw the handkerchief . . .

The limelights faded, sparing the susceptibilities of the schoolmistresses. It was just possible to discern Othello as taking up a great pillow in his hands. His last words to Desdemona rang out. There followed only horrible and inarticulate sounds. For, as if to give the now-appalled children their money's worth after all, the players in their almost invisible alcove were rendering these final agonal moments with ghastly verisimilitude: the panting respirations of the man pressing the pillow home; the muffled groans and supplications of the dying woman. And then from a door hard by the bed-head came the cries of Emilia demanding admission. Othello drew the bed hangings to, reeled backwards like a drunken man, plunged into rambling speech as Emilia's clamour grew:

> My wife! my wife! what wife? I have no wife.

From despairing realization his voice swelled in volume, swelled into its vast theatrical rhetoric, and from behind the hangings the dying Desdemona could be heard to moan anew.

> O, insupportable! O heavy hour!
> Methinks it should be now a huge eclipse
> Of sun and moon, and that the affrighted globe
> Should yawn at alteration . . .

Emilia was calling again. Othello drew the hangings closer to, staggered to the door and unlocked it. The woman burst in with her news of disaster, and in rapid colloquy Othello learnt that his plot for the death of Cassio had failed. Again his voice rang out in despair:

> Not Cassio kill'd! then murder's out of tune,
> And sweet revenge grows harsh . . .

And suddenly there was absolute silence on the stage. Othello and Emilia were standing still – and waiting. Again, and with a different note of anxiety, Othello cried out:

> And sweet revenge grows harsh . . .

Appleby shivered. For again there was silence, the reiterated cue producing nothing. It was now that Desdemona should call out, that Emilia should wrench back the hangings upon the heroine's death-agony and her last sublime attempt to free her lord from blame. But only silence held the boards.

With a swift panicky bump the curtain fell, blotting out the stage. On each side of Appleby were frightened children, sound-lessly weeping.

'Their names?' said Appleby. 'We'll stick to Shakespeare for the moment and avoid confusion. And I think Cassio is the man who runs the show?'

The sergeant of police nodded. He was uncertain whether to be relieved or annoyed that a Detective-Inspector from Scotland Yard had emerged helpfully but authoritatively from the audience. 'That's so, sir. And here he is.'

Chill draughts blew across the stage. The great curtain stirred uneasily, and from behind it there could still be heard the tramp and gabble of bewildered children being shepherded out. Here amid the flats and tawdry properties everything showed shadowy and insubstantial. The dead woman lay on what seemed a bed, and beneath its grease-paint her face showed as black as Othello's. The players, still in costumes, wigs, and beards to which theatrical illusion no longer attached, hovered in a half-world between fantasy and fact. And Cassio stood in the midst of them, his hand nervously toying with the hilt of a rapier, his weak and handsome face a study in despair. Appleby nodded to him. 'This is your company?' he asked. 'And Desdemona's death means pretty well the end of it?'

Cassio groaned. 'That is so. And it is an unimaginable disaster, as well as being' – he glanced fearfully towards the bed – 'unspeakably horrible and painful.'

'In fact, if somebody wanted to smash you, here would have been a thoroughly effective way of going about it?'

The actor-manager looked startled. 'It certainly would. The sort of audience we get will never book a seat with my company again. But I don't think –'

'Quite so. It is a possible motive but not a likely one. Now, please tell me of the relationships existing between your different numbers.'

The man hesitated. 'I am myself married to Bianca.'

A fellow, thought Appleby, *almost damned in a fair wife*. Aloud he said: 'And the dead woman was actually married to Othello?'

'Yes. And so too with Iago and Emilia.'

'I see. In fact, your private relations are quite oddly akin to those in the play? And you may be said to be an isolated community, moving from town to town, with the rest of your company not much more than supers?'

Cassio licked his lips. 'That is more or less true. We can't afford much.'

'You certainly can't afford murder.' Appleby's glance swept the players who were now ranged in a semicircle round him. 'I suppose you know that your performance this evening was all at sixes and sevens? Even the children were at a loss.' His finger shot out at Othello. 'Why did you strike your wife?'

'Yes, why did you strike her?' Emilia had stepped forward. Her eyes, though red with weeping, snapped fire. 'And why did you murder her, too?'

'Strike her?' Othello, his face a blotched pallor beneath its paint, had been glaring at Iago; now he swung round upon Iago's wife. 'You foul-mouthed –'

'That will do.' Appleby's voice, although quiet, echoed in this resonant space. 'There were six of you: Othello and Desdemona, Iago and Emilia, Cassio and Bianca. Your emotional relationships were a sordid muddle, and tonight they got out of hand. Well, I'm afraid we must have them into the limelight. And if you won't confess to what was troubling you I expect there are minor members of your company who can be informative enough.'

'But this is outrageous.' It was Bianca who spoke – a beautiful girl with every appearance of self-control. 'You can't bully us like that, no matter what has happened.' She looked defiantly at the still figure on the bed and then turned to her husband. 'Isn't that so?'

But it was Iago and not Cassio who answered. He was a dark man with a constantly shifting eye and a lip which twitched nervously as he spoke. 'Certainly it is so. In interrogating possible witnesses in such an affair the police are bound by the strictest rules. And until a solicitor –'

'Rubbish!' Unexpectedly and with venom Emilia had turned upon her husband. 'Let the man go his own way, and it will be the sooner over.'

'But at least there are the mere physical possibilities to consider first.' Cassio was at once agitated and reasonable. 'Just when did the thing happen? And is it possible therefore to rule anyone out straight away?'

Appleby nodded. 'Very well. Opportunity first and motive second.'

'At line 83 Desdemona was alive.' Appleby glanced up from the text which had been handed to him. 'And at line 117 she was dead. Throughout this interval she was invisible, since at first she was lying within heavy shadow, and subsequently the bed-hangings were drawn to by Othello. It is clear that Othello him-self may simply have smothered her when the action required that he should appear to do so. But there are other possibilities.

'The bed is set in a recess which is accessible not from the main stage alone. Behind the bed-head there is only a light curtain, and it would thus be accessible to anybody behind the scenes who was passing forward towards the wings. Othello ceased to have Desdemona under his observation at about line 85. There are then nearly twenty lines before Emilia enters. These lines are taken up partly by Othello in desperate soliloquy and partly by Emilia calling from "without". When Emilia does enter it is by the door close by the bed-head. And it follows from this that Emilia could have smothered Desdemona during these twenty lines, some five or six of which she had to speak herself. It would be a procedure requiring considerable nerve, but that is no argument against it.

'A third possibility however, remains. After Emilia has entered, and until the moment that Desdemona cries out that she has been murdered, there are some twelve broken lines, with a certain amount of time-consuming mime increasing the suspense. During this period yet another actor, standing near the wings, might have slipped to the bed-head and committed the murder. So the position, so far, is this: Othello and Emilia are definitely sus-pects, so far as opportunity goes. And so is anybody else who could have approached the bed-head unobserved during the twelve lines after Emilia's entry.'

'Which rules me out.' Cassio spoke without any apparent re-lief, and it was clear that with him the disaster which had befallen his company overshadowed everything else. 'I was on the prompt side with the electrician when we heard the cue for Emilia's going on. I just couldn't have made it.'

'But your wife could.' And Emilia, who had broken in, turned with venom on Bianca. 'For I saw you not far behind me when I stepped on stage.'

'No doubt you did. And I saw your husband.' Bianca, still perfectly calm, turned a brief glance of what was surely cold hatred on Iago. 'I saw him standing in the wings there and wondered what he was about.'

Iago's lip twitched more violently than before. Then he laughed harshly. 'This will get the police nowhere. And what about all the other conventional questions, like who last saw the victim alive?'

Suddenly Othello exclaimed. 'My God!' he cried, and whirled upon Emilia. '*You* know whether I smothered her. Every one knows what your habit is.'

'What do you mean?' Emilia's hand had flown to her bosom, and beneath the grease-paint she was very pale.

'When waiting to come on you have always parted the curtain at the bed-head and had a look at her and perhaps whispered a word. I can't tell why, for you weren't all that friendly. But that's what you did, and you must have done it tonight. Well, how was it? Was she alive or dead?'

'She was alive.' It was after a moment's hesitation that Emilia spoke. 'She didn't say anything. And of course it was almost dark. But I could see that she – that she was weeping.'

'As she very well might be, considering that her husband had actually struck her on the open stage.' The police sergeant spoke for the first time. 'Now if you'll –'

But Appleby brusquely interrupted. 'Weeping?' he said. 'Had she a handkerchief?'

Emilia looked at him with dilated eyes. 'But of course.'

Appleby strode to the body on the bed, and in a moment was back holding a small square of cambric, wringing wet. 'Quite true,' he said. 'And it was right under the body. But this can't be her ordinary handkerchief, which was blood-stained as a result of the blow, and will be in her dressing-room now. So perhaps this is –'

Cassio took a stride forward. 'Yes!' he said, 'it's the love-token
– Othello's magic handkerchief which Desdemona loses.'

And Appleby nodded sombrely. *'Sure,'* he said slowly, *'there's
some wonder in this handkerchief.*

Remorselessly the investigation went on. Cassio is the last
person in whose hand the handkerchief is seen – but on going
off-stage Cassio had tossed it on a chair from which anyone
might have taken it up. And it seemed not unlikely that a Desdemona overcome with grief had done so.

Emilia's story, then, was plausible, and if believed it exonerated
both Othello and herself. What followed from this? It appeared
that of the rest of the company only Iago and Bianca had possessed a reasonable opportunity of slipping from the wings to the
bed-head and there smothering Desdemona in that twelve-line
interval between Emilia's going on-stage and the play's coming
to its abrupt and disastrous end. But farther than this it was
hard to press. And Appleby turned back from opportunity to
motive.

Othello and his wife Desdemona, Iago and his wife Emilia,
Cassio and his wife Bianca: these were the people concerned.
Desdemona had been murdered. Cassio was not the murderer.
And upon the stage, just before the fatality, there had been per-
ceptible an obscure interplay of passion and resentment. What
situation did these facts suggest?

Not, Appleby thought, a situation which had been common
property for long. For it was unlikely that the company had been
playing night after night in this fashion; either matters would
have come to a head or private passions would have been brought
under control at least during the three hours' traffic of the
stage. Some more or less abrupt revelation, therefore, must be
the background of what had happened tonight.

Three married couples living in a substantially closed group
and with the standards of theatrical folk of the seedier sort. The
picture was not hard to see. Adultery, or some particularly
exacerbating drift taken by a customary promiscuity, was the
likely background to this Desdemona's death. And Appleby felt
momentarily depressed. About the last thing that a man plan-

ning some petty fornication would think to do would be to witness – or take this proposed mistress to witness – Shakespeare's *Othello*. Before such cataclysmic poetry and passion human amorousness shrivels and dies. And yet these actors . . .

Appleby turned abruptly back to them. Detective investigation requires more than the technique of reading finger-prints and cigarette-ends. It requires the art of reading minds and hearts. How, then, did these people's emotions stand now?

Othello was horrified and broken; with him as with Cassio – but more obscurely – things had come to an end. Well, his wife had been horribly killed, and that shortly after he had struck her brutally in the face. In a sense then, Othello's immediate emotions were accounted for.

What of Iago? Iago was on the defensive still – and defensiveness means a sense of guilt. He was like a man, Appleby thought, before whom there has opened more evil than he intended or knew. And, in whatever desperation he stood, he seemed likely to receive small succour or comfort from his wife. Emilia hated him. Was it a settled hate? Appleby judged that it had not that quality. It was a hatred, then, born of shock. Born of whatever abrupt revelation had preluded the catastrophe.

There remained Bianca, Cassio's wife. She, perhaps, was the enigma in the case, for her emotions ran deep. And her husband was out of it. Cassio was the type of chronically worried man; he expended his anxieties upon the business of keeping his company financially afloat, and emerged from this only to play subsidiary roles. As a husband he would not be very exciting. And Bianca required excitement. That hidden sort did.

The analysis was complete. Appleby thought a little longer, and then spoke. 'I am going to tell you,' he said quietly, 'what happened. But only the principal actors need remain.'

There was a sigh from the people gathered round. Like shadows they melted into the wings – some with the alacrity of relief, others with the shuffle of fatigue. It had grown very cold. The curtain stirred and swayed, like a great shroud waiting to envelop those who remained.

'It began with Desdemona's seduction, or with the revelation of this. Is that not so?' Appleby looked gravely round. There was absolute silence. 'Is that not so?' he repeated gently. But the silence prolonged itself. And Appleby turned to Othello. 'You struck her because of that?'

And abruptly Othello wept. His blotched black face crumpled. 'Yes,' he said, 'I struck her because I had discovered that.'

Appleby turned to Iago. 'You seduced this man's wife. And the result has been wilful murder. But did you know the truth was out? Or was it you yourself who smothered her to prevent confession and disclosure?'

Iago stepped back snarling. 'You've got nothing on me,' he said. 'And I won't say a word.'

From this time forth I never will speak word ... But Appleby was now facing Emilia. 'Your husband had betrayed you. You had discovered he was sleeping with this man's wife. Did you, in the frenzy of your jealousy, smother her?'

Emilia's face had hardened. 'These accusations mean nothing. Nobody knows who smothered her. And you will never find out.'

There was a pause. Appleby turned slowly to Bianca. 'And you?' he asked. 'For how long had you been Iago's mistress? And what did you do when you found that he had cast you off?'

'Nothing! I did nothing. And she's right. Nobody saw. Nobody can tell anything.'

'And so the mystery will be unsolved?' Appleby nodded seriously. 'It is not impossible that you are right. But we shall know in the morning.' He turned to Cassio. 'Did Desdemona have a dressing-room of her own? I'll just look in there before I go.'

'They probably won't hang her,' Appleby said next day to the police sergeant. 'It was a crime of sudden impulse, after all. And of course there was provocation in the adultery she had discovered.' He paused. 'Will it be any consolation to her in prison to know that she has made history in forensic medicine. I suppose not.'

The sergeant sighed. 'It's been neat enough,' he said. '– and something quite beyond our range, I must admit. But how did you first tumble to it's being Emilia?'

'It was because she changed her mind about whom to blame.

At first she had resolved to plant it on Othello simply as the likeliest person. '*And why did you murder her, too?*' she had asked him. But later on she told a story that pointed to either Bianca or her own husband, Iago. Desdemona, she said, had been alive and weeping when she looked through the curtain at the bed-head. And that, of course, let Othello out, as he had no subsequent opportunity for the murder.

'I asked myself what this change of front meant. Was it simply that Emilia had no grudge against Othello, and altered her story in order to implicate her unfaithful husband whom she now hated? Somehow, I didn't think it was that. And then I recalled a gesture she had made. Do you remember? It was when Othello revealed that she was accustomed to draw back the curtain behind the bed and speak to Desdemona before going on-stage.'

The sergeant considered. 'I seem to remember her hand going to her bodice. I thought it a bit theatrical – the conventional gesture of an agitated woman.'

Appleby shook his head. 'It wasn't quite that. What you saw was a hand flying up to where something should be – something that was now lost. And that something was a handkerchief. I saw the truth in a flash. She had lost a handkerchief – tear-soaked handkerchief – while smothering Desdemona. And my guess was confirmed seconds later when she made her change of front and declared that she had seen Desdemona alive and weeping. For of course her story came from a sudden feeling that she must account for the presence of the handkerchief beside the corpse.'

'I see.' The sergeant shook his head. 'It was clever enough. But dangerous, as being an unnecessary lie.'

'It was fatal, as it turned out. But first I saw several things come together. A man may weep, but he won't weep into a small cambric handkerchief. Emilia showed signs of weeping, whereas another suspect, Bianca, was entirely self-controlled. So what had happened was pretty clear. Emilia had discovered her husband's infidelity and had been under strong stress of emotion. She had snatched up the handkerchief – Othello's magic handkerchief – while perhaps running to her dressing-room, and there she had wept into it. When her call came she thrust it into her bodice. Later, when she yielded to an overwhelming impulse and smothered Desdemona, the handkerchief was lost in the struggle, and the body rolled on top of it.

'But how could all this be proved? Perhaps, as those people said, it couldn't be, and we should never get further than suspicion. But there was one chance – one chance of proving that Emilia had lied.

'A substantial proportion of people are what psysiologists call secretors. And this means, among other things, that there is something special about their tears. From their tears, just as well as from their blood, you can determine their blood-group. Well, I had Desdemona's blood on one handkerchief and I had tears on another. I went straight to your local Institute of Medical Research. And they told me what I hoped to learn. *From a person of Desdemona's blood-group those tears could not have come.*'

The sergeant sighed again. 'Yes,' he said, 'it's neat – very neat indeed.'

'And we shall certainly learn, as soon as the law allows us to make a test, that the tears could have been Emilia's. And as Bianca, who has allowed herself to be blood-grouped, is ruled out equally with Desdemona, the case is clear.'

And Appleby rose. 'Incidentally, there is a moral attached to all this.'

'A moral?'

'The moral that one savage critic declared to be all there is to learn from Shakespeare's play. Housewives, he said, should look to their linen. In other words, it's dangerous to drop a magic handkerchief – and particularly in the neighbourhood of a dead body.'

The Cave of Belarius

'This year's fête,' said the Vicar, 'seems to have been even more devastating than usual. There was everything from a grand historical pageant of Sheercliff history down to a jumble sale. This first distracted the schoolchildren from their work for a month, and the second has induced my wife to make the most outrageous raid upon my scanty personal possessions and habiliments. Don't you detest the fête?'

Appleby nodded. 'Certainly, I regard it as being distinctly of the kind that is worse than death.'

The Vicar considered this seriously. 'A pardonable exaggeration,' he presently announced. 'Do you know that the enormously popular roundabout – you can see them dismantling it now – turns out to have been operating for purely private profit? Deplorable – quite deplorable. You agree, Professor?'

The Professor looked around him with caution. 'I have quite clear views upon such occasions, I must confess. But about yesterday's fête my lips are sealed. Your townsfolk did my wife the honour of asking her to open it.'

'And you went along too?'

'I have to admit that I cut it.' The Professor was apologetic. 'The afternoon was lovely, and I simply slipped out of our hotel and went for a tramp. For some time I've wanted to see your celebrated cave on the other side of the hill.'

'The cave of Belarius?' The Vicar was interested. 'You had a look at it?'

'I did.' The Professor hesitated. 'And – do you know? – I had a look at Belarius too.'

'You mean you took a copy of *Cymbeline* along with you and read the later acts on the spot?'

The Professor shook his head. 'No,' he said slowly. 'I don't mean that. I mean that I had an adventure . . . and rather a queer one. Perhaps you would care to hear the story. It illustrates an interesting mechanism of the mind.'

'Appleby and I are all attention.' The Vicar smiled. 'And whether the mind be indeed a mechanism is something we can talk about later.'

'In itself, as you know, the cave isn't terribly exciting,' the Professor began. 'It starts off as a mere cleft in the rock, becomes an arched chamber of no great size, and then narrows again to a cleft which, by dint of stooping, one can follow for another fifty feet. If Shakespeare's banished lord had really brought up two young men in it they would certainly have been a quarrel-some couple through sheer irritation at their cramped quarters.

'Nevertheless, I explored the place faithfully enough. Caves are always fascinating. If you are superstitious, you may believe them to be tenanted by the ghosts of your remote ancestors who once inhabited them. If you are a scientist, you know that these ghosts do, at least, still haunt the inside of your own head; they are slumbering there, and special circumstances may at any time prompt them to wake up and walk about. Enter a cave by your-self, therefore, and you have to be pretty strong-minded to remain entirely convinced you are alone. You agree?'

The Vicar nodded. 'Certainly. And it was so on this occasion?'

'Not at first. As I explored the place my mind behaved in a thoroughly rational fashion. I wondered how the cave came to be associated with *Cymbeline*, and I recalled what I had read about prehistoric remains found in the district — that sort of thing. Then, upon coming out, I sat down on a boulder in the sun. It's a pleasant spot, with the cave giving upon a broad, grassy platform on the side of the hill. I reflected that here, perhaps, was the source of the association with Shakespeare's play, since the effect is very much that of a stage. The sunshine was delightful, and I felt lazy and relaxed. I certainly had no sense of anything unusual or paranormal as being about to happen.'

'Nevertheless it did?' Appleby was looking with some interest at the Professor.

'Decidedly. I was quite alone. For a few seconds I may have closed my eyes. When I opened them, it was to discover that I had a companion. Standing in the mouth of the cave was a Stone Age man.'

'A *Stone Age* man?' The Vicar had sat up abruptly.

'Or, if you prefer it, Shakespeare's Belarius. He is commonly played as a bearded, skin-clad figure, so it comes to much the same thing. He was carrying something on his back – it might have been the buck or hart that is also traditional with Belarius – and after looking around him for a moment he disappeared into the cave. I was extremely interested. It was a striking instance of the mind's power to produce eidetic imagery.'

'To produce *what*?' The Vicar was dismayed. 'Do you mean, my dear fellow, that you had experienced a hallucination? And were you not very alarmed?'

'Alarmed?' The Professor smiled comfortably. 'Dear me, no. Had I seen *myself* I should have had some cause for uneasiness. The *Doppelgänger* type of hallucination is rather a bad symptom. But eidetic imagery of this sort, although intensely interesting, is the most harmless thing in the world.'

Appleby was looking thoughtfully at the ground. 'And that,' he asked prosaically, 'was all that happened?'

'Well, no – as a matter of fact it was not. I sat for some time looking fixedly at the mouth of the cave, determining my pulse-rate, estimating the distance at which the hallucinatory appearance had seemed to stand, and that sort of thing. Reported occurrences of this sort by trained scientific observers, you will realize, are uncommon and can be important. Then it struck me that I had better traverse the cave again, and verify its being, in fact, completely empty. I had just reached its mouth when another figure emerged from it.'

'Bless my soul!' The Vicar appeared yet more disturbed. 'Another hallucination hard upon the first? I wonder whether you ought not really to consult –'

'Nothing of the sort. This second figure was flesh and blood – I happen to know from the very simple fact that he bumped straight into me. And he was, oddly enough, an unmistakable parson in mufti – a rather haggard, clean-shaven fellow in well-worn clerical-grey flannel. He made me a civil apology and then walked straight down the hill. I called after him, but he didn't stop. I was disappointed, because an extraordinarily interesting possibility had struck me.'

'A possibility?' Appleby had suddenly looked up.

'This fellow was certainly agitated. I had remarked that. So what occurred to me was this. Perhaps there had been a small group hallucination – the formation of a joint eidetic image, common to us both, and involving some form of telepathic communication between us.'

'You mean' – the Vicar took this in slowly – 'that the parson too may have fancied he saw Belarius?'

'Precisely so. And being no scientist, he was upset about it.'

'As I should certainly have been.' The Vicar chuckled. 'And did you, in fact, then inspect the cave again?'

'Most certainly. And it was, of course, empty. There are a few cracks in which you could hide a dog or a cat, but there is certainly no lurking-place for a man. That Belarius had no material existence, therefore, we can take to be a matter of certainty. You agree?'

The Vicar looked doubtful, and then appeared to decide that the best reply would be humorous in tone. 'I'll agree,' said, 'if Appleby will agree. Appleby –' He broke off. 'Dear me – where *is* Appleby.'

'Perhaps he has been taken ill. But no – how very odd! I think I can hear him using your telephone.'

'Belarius,' said Appleby five minutes later, 'broke prison across the moor early yesterday morning. At Sheercliff he hung about the fringes of the fête, penetrated into a tent with the costumes for the pageant, and got himself up as an ancient Briton. That gave him a respite, since scores of people were going about in historical costume. He used the opportunity to stalk something which would excite less remark elsewhere, and managed to get away with some of the Vicar's old clothes from the jumble sale. With these in a bundle he made off across the hill, spotted the cave, and slipped into it to change. When he had done so, he thrust the

Stone Age dress into a crack, came out, was startled to meet the Professor, and made off as fast as he could.'

The Vicar shook his head solemnly. 'How very dull the truth can be.'

Appleby, staring across the moor beyond the town, nodded. 'Quite so. It's no fun hunting down a poor devil of an escaped convict. But it would be rather enchanting to capture an eidetic image.'

A Nice Cup of Tea

'A capital game.' The Vicar gave a final brisk rub to his niblick. 'And all the more pleasant, my dear Appleby, for coming after a long day's work. A round of parish visiting makes me feel like Macbeth.'

'Macbeth?' Appleby drew the cover over his own clubs. 'You surprise me.'

'Lady Macbeth described her husband as too full of the milk of human kindness. I finish my duties far too full of its tea. Towards a clergyman, common benevolence expresses itself largely through the medium of a nice strong cup. Sometimes I feel like Mr Tony Weller's acquaintance when similarly regaled – a-swelling wisibly before the eyes. Policemen escape this inconvenience.'

'As it happens, I've known something like it in my time.' Appleby sat down on the bench overlooking the eighteenth green. 'And if it wasn't as a policeman that I started in on it, there was undoubtedly a professional twist to its close. It began, of course, with my aunt.'

'The Yorkshire aunt. A pertinacious and strong-minded woman, to judge from your accounts of her.'

'Quite so, Vicar. And it was her pertinacity and strength of mind that set me off.

'Retired and pensioned retainers are one of Aunt Jane's special lines. I doubt whether either she or her parents ever lived in a particularly large way, but nobody who was once in the family employment is ever dropped off the list. Aunt Jane visits them all about once a month, with a great unloading of admonition, devotional reading, tinned soup, and sacks of firewood. Aunt Jane is honestly domineering and honestly benevolent – a frank anachronism that one can't very decently turn down. So when I've stopped with her from time to time, I've lent a hand with the visiting.'

The Vicar chuckled. 'My dear fellow, this is a new light on your character. One thinks of you as banging on the doors of thieves' kitchens and shouting "Open in the name of the Law". And here you are, tinkling the bells of old women and disgorging tinned soup. The more credit to you. But proceed.'

'Sometimes it was entertaining enough. If I ever heartily regretted being my aunt's emissary, it was the afternoon I visited Nannie Moggs. I believe she had been no more than temporary nurserymaid in some remote branch of the family sixty years before, and she was too peripheral, so to speak, to be among the pensioners in any substantial way. Her circumstances were dismal, and so was she.

'She inhabited what they call a back-to-back house of the most meagre sort – one room up and one room down, with the upper one let off to another penurious old person like herself. The only vestiges of comfort she rejoiced in – or rather was lugubrious over – were an emaciated cat, distinctly disposed to spit, and a minute gas-fire that seemed incapable of as much as singeing the cat's whiskers. It occurred to me that the old woman would do better to scrap the thing and apply to Aunt Jane for a sack of firewood. Meanwhile I planked down those tins of soup and made what conversation I could.

'The wickedness of some local burial society proved to be the main field of Nannie Moggs's interest. Indeed, I could get her to talk of nothing else. For years, it seemed, she had subscribed ninepence a week, and the man who collected the money had assured her at the start that this meant solid brass handles and an inscribed plate. But when one of her neighbours – a ninepenny neighbour – died some months before, Nannie Moggs had contrived herself a personal inspection of the coffin and satisfied herself that no plate was provided, and that the handles would be a disgrace at fourpence.'

The Vicar shook his head. 'Deplorable. There is undoubtedly

much exploitation of the importance which the simpler classes attach to matters of that sort.'

'No doubt. Well, we had this sort of chat for some time, and if the old lady didn't get any less dismal, at least she managed to get more excited. I pointed out that there was a metal shortage, and that perhaps it was unpatriotic to insist on carrying lumps of the stuff into the grave. As old Sir Thomas Browne insisted, the commerce of the living is not to be transferred unto the dead.'

The Vicar shook his head. 'Appropriate,' he said. 'But not perhaps persuasive.'

'Quite so. And of course Nannie Moggs was in the right in the matter. She had paid her ninepences, and was entitled to corresponding riches in the adornment of her ashes. Fortunately all her pennies hadn't gone the one way. She had a secret to reveal, and the nearer she got to it the more excited she became. She banged the floor with a stick, and her voice rose to a screech that might have made the cat bolt from the room. "Three-pun ten under the third stair,' she said. 'And a letter to the Royal Fambly respekfully demanding that justice be done."

'It wasn't clear to me how the letter was to reach its august destination, or even that seventy shillings would pay for the brass handles. But Nannie Moggs's spirits began to rise as she surveyed her posthumous triumph, and I did my best to confirm her in this improved nervous tone. Presently I was congratulating myself on having the makings of a successful district visitor after all. The cat had begun to purr, the gas-fire was burning brighter, the tins of soup took on the appearance of a magnificent benefaction, and the old lady was crowing away merrily over her nest-egg. So it was rather disconcerting that, when she hobbled out of the room to let me have a peep at it, it proved to have disappeared.

'So my visiting, Vicar, had ended much like yours: in what might be called a nice cup of tea. Alternatively, you might say that we were in the soup – the tinned soup – or that the fat was in the fire.'

'Nannie Moggs was upset?'

'It was clear that seventy bob out of my own pocket would get us nowhere. She cried aloud for vengeance. So I had to abandon my charitable character, turn back into a policeman, and investigate.

'When had she seen the money last? Apparently it had been not long before I arrived. Her main occupation was taking furtive peeps at it whenever her upstairs lodger, Mrs Grimble, was out of the way. As you can guess, Mrs Grimble seemed to me the first person due for interview, and I climbed straight to her room. It was pretty well a replica of Nannie Moggs's – the same cat, the same miserable little gas-fire, the same suggestion of horrible poverty.

'Mrs Grimble was out. It was an hour before she came back again. She was precisely the miserable old soul I expected, and most suspiciously communicative about her movements. She had been out of the house all afternoon, she declared, visiting the municipal cemetery with her widowed brother.

'I saw that if this story was true she could have nothing to do with the disappearance of Nannie Moggs's nest-egg. And I guessed that there *was* a widowed brother and that the story Mrs Grimble was telling he, too, would tell. It was a reasonable story, too – even if the weather was uncommonly chilly for a long afternoon among the graves.

'Suddenly the truth came to me. I fished a box of matches from my pocket. There was an experiment I could make. You can guess it, of course.'

'Guess it, my dear Appleby?' The Vicar was bewildered.

'The gas-fires. There had been a point, you remember, at which Nannie Moggs's fire burnt brighter. In a couple of minutes I had satisfied myself that just this happened as soon as Mrs Grimble's fire was turned *off*. It was a wretched old installation, but I've seen the same effect even with tolerably efficient ones.'

'Did Mrs Grimble confess?'

'Yes. I told her precisely what had happened. Lurking out of mere curiosity outside Nannie Moggs's door, she had heard the secret confided to me, stolen the hidden money, and bolted back to her room. Then she had had sufficient cunning to realize that she must get it out of the place and fake a kind of alibi. So off she went to her brother – who was no doubt as dishonest as she. But, being a thrifty soul, she turned off her gas-fire before she left. And she did confess. My apparently supernatural knowledge of her movements was too much for her.'

'And Nannie Moggs continued vindictive? A constable was called in, and the one wretched old woman got the other sent to gaol?'

Appleby shook his head. 'It was my aunt who was called in. I doubt whether Mrs Grimble ever ventured on dishonesty again.'

The Sands of Thyme

The sea sparkled and small waves splashed drowsily on the beach. Donkeys trotted to and fro bearing the children of holiday-makers who themselves slumbered under handkerchiefs and newspapers. On the horizon lay the smoke of a Channel steamer, on a day trip to Boulogne. And at all this the vicar glanced down with contentment from the promenade. 'Fastidious persons,' he said, 'would call it vulgar.'

'I like a deserted beach myself,' said the Doctor.

Appleby looked up from his novel. Do you know Thyme Bay?' he asked. 'No? It's as lonely as you could wish, Doctor.'

The Vicar removed his pipe from his mouth. 'You have a story to tell us,' he said.

Appleby smiled. 'Quite frankly, Vicar, I have!'

I was there (said Appleby) on special duty with the Security people at the experimental air station. It was summer, and when the tide allowed it I used to walk across the bay before breakfast.

Thyme is a tremendous stretch of sand; you may remember that in the old days they held motor races there.

But the great thing is the shells. Thyme is the one place I know of to which you can go and feel that sea-shells are still all that they were in your childhood. Both on the beach itself and among the rocks, you find them in inexhaustible variety.

On the morning of which I'm speaking, I was amusing myself so much with the shells that it was some time before I noticed the footprints.

It was a single line of prints, emerging from the sandhills, and taking rather an uncertain course towards a group of rocks, islanded in sand, near the centre of the bay. They were the prints of a fairly long-limbed man, by no means a light-weight, and more concerned to cover the ground than to admire the view. But I noticed more than that. The tracks were of a man who limped. I tried to work out what sort of limp it would be.

This had the effect, of course, of making me follow the prints. Since the man had not retraced his steps, he had presumably gone on to the rocks, and then found his way back to the coastal road somewhere farther on. So I continued to follow in his tracks.

Presently I was feeling that something was wrong, and instead of going straight up to those rocks I took a circle round them. No footprints led away from them. So I searched. And there the chap was – tall, heavy, and lying on his tummy ... He was dead.

I turned him over – half-expected what, in fact, I found. There was a bullet-hole plumb centre of his forehead. And a revolver was lying beside him.

But that wasn't all. Suicides, you know, are fond of contriving a little décor of pathos.

On a flat ledge of the rock a score or so of shells – the long, whorled kind – had been ranged in straight lines, like toy soldiers drawn up for battle. Beside them lay an open fountain-pen, and a scrap of paper that looked as if it had been torn from the top edge of a notebook. There was just a sentence: '*As a child, I played with these for hours.*'

Of course I did the routine things at once. The dead man was a stranger to me.

He carried loose change, a few keys on a ring, a handkerchief, a gold cigarette-case, and a box of matches – absolutely nothing else. But his clothes were good, and I found his name sewn inside a pocket of the jacket. A. G. Thorman, Esqre. It seemed familiar.

I made one other discovery. The right ankle was badly swollen. I had been right about that limp.

Thorman was in late middle-age, and it turned out that I was remembering his name from the great days of aviation – the era of the first long-distance flights. He had made some of the most famous of these with Sir Charles Tumbril, and he had been staying with Tumbril at the time of his death.

But he had belonged to the district, too, having been born and brought up in a rectory just beyond Thyme Point. So it seemed likely enough that he had chosen to cut short his life in some haunt holding poignant memories of his childhood.

I took Tumbril the news of his guest's death myself. It was still quite early, and he came out from his wife's breakfast-table to hear it. I had a glimpse of both the Tumbrils from the hall, and there was Thorman's place, empty, between them.

Tumbril showed me into his study and closed the door with a jerk of his shoulder. He was a powerful, lumbering, clumsy man.

He stood in front of an empty fireplace, with his hands deep in his trouser pockets. I told him my news, and he didn't say a word. 'It comes completely as a surprise to you, Sir Charles?'

He looked at me as if this was an impertinence. "It's not for us to conjecture,' he said. 'What has prompted Thorman to suicide can be neither your business nor mine.'

'That doesn't quite cover the matter, Sir Charles. Our circumstances are rather exceptional here. You are in control of this experimental station, and I am responsible to the Ministry on the security side. You have three planes here on the secret list, including the P.2204 itself. Any untoward incident simply must be sifted to the bottom.'

Tumbril took it very well, and said something about liking a man who kept his teeth in his job. I repeated my first question.

'A surprise?' Tumbril considered. 'I can't see why it shouldn't be a surprise.'

'But yet it isn't?'

'No, Appleby – it is not. Since Thorman came down to us a few days ago there has been something in the air. We were very old friends, and I couldn't help feeling something wrong.'

'Thorman didn't give any hint of what it might be?'

'None at all. He was always a reticent fellow.'

'He might have had some sort of secret life.'

'I hope he had nothing as shoddy as that sounds, Appleby. And I don't think you'd find any of the very obvious things: money gone wrong, a jam between two women, or anything of that sort. But serious disease is a possibility. He looked healthy enough, but you never know.'

'Were there any relations?'

'A brother. I suppose I ought to contact him now.' Tumbril crossed the room to the old upright telephone he kept on his desk. Then he said: 'I'll do that later.'

I thought this might be a hint for me to clear out. But I asked one more question. 'You had confidence, Sir Charles, in Thorman's probity?'

He looked at me with a startled face. 'Probity?' he repeated. 'Are you suggesting, Appleby, that Thorman may have been a spy – something of that sort?'

'Yes, Sir Charles. That is what I have in mind.'

He looked at me in silence for almost half a minute, and his voice when he spoke was uncomfortably cold. 'I must repeat that Arthur Thorman was one of my oldest friends. Your suggestion is ridiculous. It is also personally offensive to me. Good morning.'

So that was that, and I left the room well and truly snubbed. All the same, I didn't precisely banish the puzzle of Arthur Thorman from my mind.

And there *was* a puzzle; it was a precisely plain puzzle, which appears clearly in the facts as I've already given them.

Tumbril must have felt he'd been a bit stiff with me, and that I'd shown the correct reactions. At least that, I suppose, is why I received a telephone call from Lady Tumbril later in the morning, inviting me in to tea. I went along at the time named.

Thorman's brother had arrived. He must have been much older than the dead man; his only interest in life was the Great Pyramid of Cheops; and he gave no indication of finding a suicide in the family anything out of the way.

Lady Tumbril coped with the situation very well, but it wasn't a cheerful tea. Tumbril himself didn't appear – his wife explained that he was working – and we ate our crumpets in some abstraction, while the older Thorman explained that something in the proportions of his pyramid made it certain that London would be destroyed by an earthquake in 1958.

It was only at the end of the meal that this tedious old person appeared to make any contact with the lesser catastrophe of that morning. And what he was mainly prompted to, it seemed, was a concern over his brother's clothes and baggage, as these must still repose in a bedroom upstairs.

The tea-party ended with the old man's going up to inspect and pack his brother's things, and with myself accompanying him to lend a hand.

I suppose I should be ashamed of the next incident in the story. Waste-paper baskets and fireplaces have a strong professional fascination for me. I searched these in Arthur Thorman's room. It was not quite at random. I had come to have a good idea of what I might find there. Ten minutes later I was once more in Sir Charles Tumbril's study.

'Will you please look at this, sir?'

He was again standing before the fireplace with his hands in his pockets, and he gave that sombre glance at what I was holding out to him. 'Put it on the desk,' he said.

'Sir Charles – is there any point in this concealment? I saw how it was with your arm when you stopped yourself from telephoning this morning.'

'I've certainly had an accident. But I'm not aware that I need exhibit it to you, Appleby.'

'Nor to your doctor?'

He looked at me in silence. 'What do you want?' he asked.

'I should like to know, sir, whether Thorman was writing a book – a book of memoirs, or anything of that sort?'

Tumbril glanced towards the piece of charred paper I had laid on his desk. 'Yes,' he said, 'I believe he was.'

'You must know what I've got here, sir. I had to find it.' I was looking at him steadily. 'You see, the thing didn't make sense as it stood. That last message of Thorman's could be the product only of complete spontaneity – a final spur-of-the-moment touch to his suicide.

'But, although it had the appearance of having been written on the spot, there wasn't another scrap of paper on him. That it should just happen that he had just one fragment from a note-book —'

'I see. And what, in fact, have you got there?'

'The bottom of another leaf of the same paper, Sir Charles. And on it, also in Thorman's writing, just two words: *paper gliders.*'

'I must tell you the truth.' Tumbril had sat down. 'I must tell you the truth, Appleby.

'It so happens that I am a very light sleeper. The fact brought me down here at two o'clock this morning, to find Thorman with the safe open, and the P.2204 file in front of him on the desk. He brought out a revolver and fired at me.

'The bullet went through my arm. I don't doubt now that he meant to kill. And then he grabbed the file and bolted out through the french window. He must have opened it in case of just such a need to cut and run.

'He jumped from the terrace and I heard a yelp of pain. He tried to run on, but could only limp, and I knew that he had sprained an ankle. The result, of course, was that I caught up with him in no time.

'He still had the revolver; we struggled for it; it went off again — and there was Thorman, dead. I carried the body back to the house.

'I went up to his room with the idea of searching it for anything else he might have stolen, and there I saw the manuscript of this book he had begun. My eye fell on the last words he had written. I saw them as pathetic. And suddenly I saw how that pathos might be exploited to shield poor Arthur's name.

'My wife and I between us had the whole plan worked out within half an hour. Shortly before dawn we got out her heli-copter from the private hangar — we fly in and out of here, you know, at all sorts of hours — and hoisted in the body.

'Thorman and I were of the same height and build; I put on his shoes, which I found fitted well enough; and then I set out for the shore. The tide was just right, and I walked out to those rocks — limping, of course, for I remembered Thorman's ankle.

My wife followed in the machine, and lowered the body to me on the winch.

'I restored the shoes and made the various dispositions which you found – and which you were meant to find, Appleby, for I had noticed your regular morning walk.

'Then I went up the rope and we flew home. We thought that we had achieved our aim: to make it appear irrefutable that poor Arthur Thorman had committed suicide – and in circumstances which, although mysterious, were wholly unconnected with any suspicion of treason.'

When Appleby had concluded his narrative neither of his hearers spoke.

'My dear Appleby,' the Vicar said presently, you were in a very difficult position. I shall be most interested to hear what your decision was.'

'I haven't the slightest idea.' And Appleby smiled at the astonishment of his friends. 'Did you ever hear of Arthur Thorman?'

The Doctor considered. 'I can't say that I ever did.'

'Or, for that matter, of the important Sir Charles Tumbril?'

The Vicar shook his head. 'No. When you come to mention it –'

And Appleby picked up his novel again. 'Didn't I say,' he murmured, 'that I was going to tell you a story? And there it is – a simple story about footprints on the sands of Thyme.'

The X-Plan

'A mere impression,' Appleby said, 'was all I had to go on in the affair of the X-Plan. But it turned out to be enough.'

'The X-Plan?' The Doctor was suspicious. 'Are confidential documents really given those fancy names?'

Appleby smiled. 'I'm calling it that. Even in a small circle like this, security must be respected.'

The Vicar tapped out his pipe. 'One hears a great deal about security. And the more one hears of it, the less one feels it. But tell us about the X-Plan.'

'Essentially, it was an explanation.' Appleby paused to let this mild pun take effect. 'A committee of the Cabinet wanted a comprehensive and non-technical account of some very important scientific work, and that was what Tilley had prepared for them. Tilley did it out of his head, while on holiday here by the sea. I used to watch him sitting in this very beach-shelter we're in now, jotting it down on a scribbling-pad.'

'How did you know,' the Doctor demanded, 'that what he was busy with was the X-Plan?'

'My dear chap, it was my job, I was the detective guarding him.

'Our people knew Tilley to be pretty vague,' Appleby continued. 'That was why they insisted on a detective. And I must say I've had easier assignments. The chap liked solitude, and would slip away to take a long ramble along the coast, or just bury himself among the rocks at the foot of the cliff here.

'Whether Tilley was feeling active or inactive, I had an equally anxious time. A holiday place like Sheercliff is always tricky. There's a floating population, and you're constantly wondering about one new face or another.

'Again, there's the fact that trippers have no respect for privacy, and walk in on you after a fashion they'd never dream of at home. I'd hear a thoroughly suspicious scurrying after dark, and it would turn out to be a woman from a caravan, filling a kettle in the kitchen, or placidly borrowing the matches.'

The Vicar had lit his pipe again. 'What kitchen would this be?'

'Tilley lodged with an old friend of his called Stepaside, who had the last cottage on the cliff road. Stepaside was a bachelor, and by occupation a prolific but rather unsuccessful novelist. He was no doubt quite glad of Tilley's money – and of mine that went with it.

'There was nobody else in the cottage. We lived on the can-opener, and an old woman came in and cleared up. She was a queer, gobbling creature called Mrs Hodge, from whom one seldom caught an articulate word.'

'I remember her quite well,' the Doctor remarked. 'An interesting speech dystrophy.'

'No doubt. Well, that was the set-up. Stepaside divided his time between tapping interminable fiction out of an old typewriter and going for long brooding walks to think out his plot.

'He was scarcely an entertaining character. A day for him seemed simply a space of time in which he could fabricate so many thousand words. "I've finished chapter four," he'd say; or "I've got her living with her husband again and now I must think up a new lover, blast it." I came much to prefer the queer noises made by Mrs Hodge.

'As for Tilley, he read novels – including some of Stepaside's, for he was a good-natured soul – and scribbled this minute that I'm calling the X-Plan. For my own part, I kept my eyes and ears open and waited for a rather tiresome fortnight to end.

'Everything looked like being thoroughly uneventful. And then, one day in the High Street, I saw Gruber.'

The Vicar chuckled. 'Enter the villain. The well-known secret agent.'

'This Gruber had done time for an offence under the Official Secrets Act, so you describe him fairly enough. His presence in Sheercliff might be coincidental. But I had an obstinate feeling that he was after Tilley and his stuff. I took to carrying a gun.'

'I didn't know you people ever did that.' The Doctor appeared disturbed. 'They're frightfully dangerous things.'

'Gruber was dangerous, too. I warned both Tilley and Stepaside about him – and I even did my best to warn Mrs Hodge. Mrs Hodge made noises like a hen – I imagine she must have had some horrible Freudian experience in a poultry yard when a child – and Stepaside half emerged from his fictional world and promised to keep a look-out.

'But Tilley himself just laughed at the thing as cheap melodrama, and advised Stepaside to cook it up for a yarn. The next morning Tilley disappeared.'

'Capital.' The Doctor was delighted. 'Appleby has quite the Stepaside professional touch – eh, Vicar?'

Appleby shook his head. 'There was nothing funny about it at the time. Tilley left the breakfast-table to walk down the garden and decide about the weather. And he just didn't come back. By ten o'clock I had been round all his nearer haunts, and by eleven I'd summoned the local police to the hunt. A week earlier, I'd have given Tilley rather more rope, but Gruber had got me on the jump.

'It was close on noon, and I was coming back to the cottage to see if there was any news there, when Mrs Hodge met me. "Glookcoop," she said. "Boo-goo-hoo" – and rather more to the same effect. It came to me like an inspiration that these remarks were topographical, and that she was reminding me of a little coign in the cliff no more than a hundred yards off. I'd missed out on it.'

The Vicar was looking sober. 'Tilley had been killed?'

'So I supposed. And then I saw something that was an immense relief. His blessed scribbling-pad was sticking out of his hip pocket. A moment later I found that he was simply heavily asleep.

'Getting him awake was quite a business. He had climbed down here, he said, to see if the tide was right for bathing in a little cove below. And not having slept very well during the night, he had just dropped off in the warmth of the morning sun.

'By the time I got him back to the cottage Stepaside was laughing at me, too, for at my first alarm he had pooh-poohed the notion of any danger, and I'd simply left him at his interminable tap-tapping.

'But in point of fact he appeared uneasy. "I still think there may be something wrong," he said. "After all, the whole morning's gone past. And I saw Gruber on the cliff."

' "So you went out?" I asked.

'He scowled at the litter of typescript on his table. "I finished that blasted Chapter Six, and then I thought I'd better join in your hunt.

' "After an hour down on the shingle I came up to the cliff. And there was your spy. His idea seemed to be to slip off inland. He had all the appearance of a harmless tourist – rucksack, camera, and a hearty stick." '

Appleby paused in his narrative. 'A nasty moment,' the Doctor said.

'It didn't look too good. "Did you tell the police?" I asked Stepaside.

'He shook his head. "I thought I'd better keep it for you, Inspector Appleby. I wasn't sure what you wanted known. So I came back to the cottage and started on the seduction scene. That's Chapter Seven."

'Stepaside pointed at the papers on his table, and something prompted me to take a good squint at them. The next moment I had that gun out. It was a big thing, and I was taking no chances. "Your trick has failed," I said. "Hand over." And there was no trouble. The fellow crumpled at once.'

The Vicar took his pipe from his mouth. 'You mean that Stepaside –'

'He had drugged Tilley at breakfast, and managed to suggest the direction of his stroll. As soon as the hunt began, he had slipped down, taken the scribbling-pad, returned to the cottage and typed out its contents at high speed. Then he'd returned it. It was, of course, my warning about Gruber that had put the treacherous idea in his head.'

The Vicar nodded. 'It was certainly a nasty piece of perfidy. But I don't yet see how you stumbled to it.'

'Stepaside had put a new ribbon in his machine near the end of what he called "the blasted Chapter Six". That gives at first, as you know, a very black rather broad print, which when the ribbon reverses, begins to fine away to normal. The fading process, of course, goes on all through the life of the ribbon, and an expert can always tell whether one sheet has been typed much before or after another.

'In this case, there was evidence visible to my naked eye. Between the end of Chapter Six and the beginning of Chapter Seven, Stepaside had done quite a lot of typing that he was keeping quiet about. It wasn't difficult to guess what it had been.'

The Vicar – not a mechanically minded man – was working it out slowly. 'The impress of the machine upon its ribbon yields a progressively fainter –'

'Precisely. Didn't I say it was a mere impression that I had to go on?'

Lesson in Anatomy

Already the anatomy theatre was crowded with students: tier upon tier of faces pallid beneath the clear shadowless light cast by the one elaborate lamp, large as a giant cart-wheel, near the ceiling. The place gleamed with an aggressive cleanliness; the smell of formalin pervaded it; its centre was a faintly sinister vacancy – the spot to which would presently be wheeled the focal object of the occasion.

At Nessfield University Professor Finlay's final lecture was one of the events of the year. He was always an excellent teacher. For three terms he discoursed lucidly from his dais or tirelessly prowled his dissecting-rooms, encouraging young men and women who had hitherto dismembered only dogfish and frogs to address themselves with resolution to human legs, arms, and torsos. The Department of Anatomy was large; these objects lay about it in a dispersed profusion; Finlay moved among them now with gravity and now with a whimsical charm which did a good deal to humanize his macabre environment. It was only once a year that he yielded to his taste for the dramatic.

The result was the final lecture. And the final lecture was among the few academic activities of Nessfield sufficiently abounding in human appeal to be regularly featured in the local Press. Perhaps the account had become a little stereotyped with the years, and always there was virtually the same photograph showing the popular professor (as Finlay was dubbed for the occasion) surrounded by wreaths, crosses, and other floral tributes. Innumerable citizens of Nessfield who had never been inside the doors of their local university looked forward to this annual report, and laid it down with the comfortable conviction that all was well with the pursuit of learning in the district. Their professors were still professors – eccentric, erudite, and amiable.

Their students were still, as students should be, giving much of their thought to the perpetration of elaborate, tasteless, and sometimes dangerous practical jokes.

For the lecture was at once a festival, a rag, and a genuine display of virtuosity. It took place in this large anatomy theatre. Instead of disjointed limbs and isolated organs there was a whole new cadaver for the occasion. And upon this privileged corpse Finlay rapidly demonstrated certain historical developments of his science to an audience in part attentive and in part concerned with lowering skeletons from the rafters, releasing various improbable living creatures – lemurs and echidnas and opossums – to roam the benches, or contriving what quainter japes they could think up. On one famous occasion the corpse itself had been got at, and at the first touch of the professor's scalpel had awakened to an inferno of noise presently accounted for by the discovery that its inside consisted chiefly of alarm clocks. Nor were these diversions and surprises all one-sided, since Finlay himself, entering into the spirit of the occasion, had more than once been known to forestall his students with some extravagance of his own. It was true that this had happened more rarely of recent years, and by some it was suspected that this complacent scholar had grown a little out of taste with the role in which he had been cast. But the affair remained entirely good-humoured; tradition restrained the excesses into which it might have fallen; it was, in its own queer way, an approved social occasion. High University authorities sometimes took distinguished visitors along – those, that is to say, who felt they had a stomach for post-mortem curiosity. There was quite a number of strangers on the present occasion.

The popular professor had entered through the glass-panelled double doors which gave directly upon the dissecting-table. Finlay was florid and very fat; his white gown was spotlessly laundered; a high cap of the same material would have given him the appearance of a generously self-dieted chef. He advanced to the low rail that separated him from the first tier of spectators and started to make some preliminary remarks. What these actually were, or how they were designed to conclude, he had probably forgotten years ago, for this was the point at which the first interruption traditionally occurred. And, sure enough, no sooner had Finlay opened his mouth than three young men near the back of the theatre stood up and delivered themselves of a fanfare of trumpets. Finlay appeared altogether surprised – he possessed, as has been stated, a dramatic sense – and this was the signal for the greater part of those present to rise in their seats and sing *For he's a jolly good fellow*. Flowers – single blooms, for the present – began to float through the air and fall about the feet of the professor. The strangers, distinguished and otherwise, smiled at each other benevolently, thereby indicating their pleased acquiescence in these time-honoured academic junketings. A bell began to toll.

'*Never ask for whom the bell tolls,*' said a deep voice from somewhere near the professor's left hand. And the whole student body responded in a deep chant: '*It tolls for THEE.*'

And now there was a more urgent bell – one that clattered up and down some adjacent corridor to the accompaniment of tramping feet and the sound as of a passing tumbrel. '*Bring out your dead,*' cried the deep voice. And the chant was taken up all round the theatre. '*Bring out your dead,*' everybody shouted with gusto. '*Bring out your DEAD!*'

This was the signal for the entrance of Albert, Professor Finlay's dissecting-room attendant. Albert was perhaps the only person in Nessfield who uncompromisingly disapproved of the last lecture and all that went with it – this perhaps because, as an ex-policeman, he felt bound to hold all disorder in discountenance. The severely aloof expression on the face of Albert as he wheeled in the cadaver was one of the highlights of the affair – nor on this occasion did it by any means fail of its effect. Indeed, Albert appeared to be more than commonly upset. A severe frown lay across his ample and unintelligent countenance. He held his six-foot-three sternly erect; behind his vast leather apron his bosom discernibly heaved with manly emotion. Albert wheeled in the body – distinguishable as a wisp of ill-nourished humanity beneath the tarpaulin that covered it – and Finlay raised his right hand as if to bespeak attention. The result was a sudden squawk and flap of heavy wings near the ceiling. Somebody had released a vulture. The ominous bird blundered twice round the theatre, and then settled composedly on a rafter. It craned its scrawny neck and fixed a beady eye on the body.

Professor Finlay benevolently smiled; at the same time he produced a handkerchief and rapidly mopped his forehead. To several people, old stagers, it came that the eminent anatomist was uneasy this year. The vulture was a bit steep, after all.

There was a great deal of noise. One group of students was doggedly and pointlessly singing a sea shanty; others were perpetrating or preparing to perpetrate sundry jokes of a varying degree of effectiveness. Albert, standing immobile beside the cadaver, let his eyes roam resentfully over the scene. Then Finlay raised not one hand but two – only for a moment, but there was instant silence. He took a step backwards amid the flowers which lay around him; carefully removed a couple of forget-me-nots from his hair; gave a quick nod to Albert; and began to explain – in earnest this time – what he was proposing to do.

Albert stepped to the body and pulled back the tarpaulin.

'And ever,' said a voice from the audience, 'at my back I hear the rattle of dry bones and chuckle spread from ear to ear.'

It was an apt enough sally. The cadaver seemed to be mostly bones already – the bones of an elderly, withered man – and its most prominent feature was a ghastly *rictus* or fixed grin which exposed two long rows of gleamingly white and utterly incongruous-seeming teeth. From somewhere high up in the theatre there was a little sigh followed by a slumping sound. A robust and football-playing youth had fainted. Quite a number of people, as if moved by a mysterious or chameleon-like sympathy, were rapidly approximating to the complexion of the grisly object displayed before them. But there was nothing unexpected in all this. Finlay, knowing that custom allowed him perhaps another five minutes of sober attention at this point, continued his remarks. The cadaver before the class was exactly as it would be had it come before a similar class four hundred years ago. The present anatomy lesson was essentially a piece of historical reconstruction. His hearers would recall that on one of Rembrandt's paintings depicting such a subject –

For perhaps a couple of minutes the practised talk flowed on. The audience was quite silent. Finlay for a moment paused to

recall a date. In the resulting complete hush there was a sharp
click, rather like the lifting of a latch. A girl screamed. Every eye
in the theatre was on the cadaver. For its lower jaw had sagged
abruptly open, and the teeth, which were plainly dentures, had
half-extruded themselves from the gaping mouth, rather as if
pushed outwards by some spasm within.

Such things do happen. There is a celebrated story of just such
startling behaviour on the part of the body of the philosopher
Schopenhauer. And Finlay, perceiving that his audience was
markedly upset, perhaps debated endeavouring to rally them
with just this learned and curious anecdote. But even as he
paused, the cadaver acted again. Abruptly the jaws closed like a
powerful vice, the lips and cheeks sagged; it was to be concluded
that this wretched remnant of humanity had swallowed its last
meal.

For a moment something like panic hovered over the anatomy
theatre. Another footballer fainted; a girl laughed hysterically;
two men in the back row, having all the appearance of case-
hardened physicians, looked at each other in consternation and
bolted from the building. Finlay, with a puzzled look on his face,
again glanced backwards at the cadaver. Then he nodded
abruptly to Albert, who replaced the tarpaulin. Presumably, after
this queer upset, he judged it best to interpose a little more composing historical talk before getting down to business.

He was saying something about the anatomical sketches of
Leonardo da Vinci. Again he glanced back at the cadaver. Suddenly the lights went out. The anatomy theatre was in darkness.

For some moments nobody thought of an accident. Finlay
often had recourse to an epidiascope or lantern, and the trend of
his talk now led people to suppose that something of the sort was
in train now. Presently, however, it became plain that there was
a hitch – and at this the audience broke into every kind of
vociferation. Above the uproar the vulture could be heard overhead, vastly agitated. Matches were struck, but cast no certain
illumination. Various objects were being pitched about the
theatre. There was a strong scent of lilies.

Albert's voice made itself heard, cursing medical students,
cursing the University of Nessfield, cursing Professor Finlay's

final lecture. From the progress of this commination it was possible to infer that he was groping his way towards the switches. There was a click, and once more the white shadowless light flooded the theatre.

Everything was as it had been – save in two particulars. Most of the wreaths and crosses which had been designed for the end of the lecture had proved missiles too tempting to ignore in that interval of darkness; they had been lobbed into the centre of the theatre and lay there about the floor, except for two which had actually landed on the shrouded cadaver.

And Finlay had disappeared.

The audience was bewildered and a little apprehensive. Had the failure of the lighting really been an accident? Or was the popular professor obligingly coming forward with one of his increasingly rare and prized pranks? The audience sat tight, awaiting developments. Albert, returning from the switchboard, impatiently kicked a wreath of lilies from his path. The audience, resenting this display of nervous irritation, cat-called and booed. Then a voice from one of the higher benches called out boisterously: 'The corpse has caught the dropsy!'

'It's a-swelling,' cried another voice – that of a devotee of Dickens – 'It's a-swelling wisibly before my eyes.'

And something had certainly happened to the meagre body beneath its covering; it was as if during the darkness it had been inflated by a gigantic pump.

With a final curse Albert sprang forward and pulled back the tarpaulin. What lay beneath was the body of Professor Finlay, quite dead. The original cadaver was gone.

The vulture swooped hopefully from its rafter.

'Publicity?' said Detective-Inspector John Appleby. 'I'm afraid you can scarcely expect anything else. Or perhaps it would be better to say notoriety. Nothing remotely like it has happened in England for years.'

Sir David Evans, Nessfield's very Welsh Vice-Chancellor, passed a hand dejectedly through his flowing white hair and softly groaned. 'A scandal!' he said. 'A scandal – look you, Mr Appleby – that peggars description. There must be infestigations.

There must be arrests. Already there are reporters from the pig papers. This morning I have been photographed.' Sir David paused and glanced across the room at the handsome portrait of himself which hung above the fireplace. 'This morning,' he repeated, momentarily comforted, 'I have been photographed, look you, five or six times.'

Appleby smiled. 'The last case I remember as at all approaching it was the shooting of Viscount Auldearn, the Lord Chancellor, during a private performance of *Hamlet* at the Duke of Horton's seat, Scamnum Court.'

For a second Sir David looked almost cheerful. It was plain that he gained considerable solace from this august comparison. But then he shook his head. 'In the anatomy theatre!' he said. 'And on the one day of the year when there is these unseemly pehaviours. And a pody vanishes. And there is fultures – fultures, Mr Appleby!'

'One vulture.' Dr Holroyd, Nessfield's professor of human physiology, spoke as if this comparative paucity of birds of prey represented one of the bright spots of the affair. 'Only one vulture, and apparently abstracted by a group of students from the Zoo. The Director rang up as soon as he saw the first report. He might be described as an angry man.'

Appleby brought out a notebook. 'What we are looking for,' he said, 'is angry men. Perhaps you know of someone whose feelings of anger towards the late Professor Finlay at times approached the murderous?'

Sir David Evans looked at Dr Holroyd, and Dr Holroyd looked at Sir David Evans. And it appeared to Appleby that the demeanour of each was embarrassed. 'Of course,' he added, 'I don't mean mere passing irritations between colleagues.'

'There is frictions,' said Sir David carefully. 'Always in a university there is frictions. And frictions produce heat. There was pad frictions between Finlay and Dr Holroyd here. There was personalities, I am sorry to say. For years there has been most fexatious personalities.' Sir David, who at all times preserved an appearance of the most massive benevolence, glanced at his colleague with an eye in which there was a nasty glint. 'Dr Holroyd is Dean of the Faculty of Medicine, look you. It is why

I have asked him to meet you now. And last week at a meeting there was a most disgraceful scene. It was a meeting about lavatories. It was a meeting of the Committee for Lavatories.'

'Dear me!' said Appleby. Universities, he was thinking, must have changed considerably since his day.

'Were there to be more lavatories in Physiology Puilding? Finlay said he would rather put in a path.'

'A path?' said Appleby, perplexed.

'A path, with hot and cold laid on, and an efficient shower. Finlay said that in his opinion Dr Holroyd here padly needed a path.'

'And did Dr Holroyd retaliate?'

'I am sorry to say that he did, Mr Appleby. He said that if he had his way in the matter Finlay's own path would be a formalin one. Which is what they keep the cadavers in, Mr Appleby.'

Dr Holroyd shifted uneasily on his chair. 'It was unfortunate,' he admitted. 'I must freely admit that unfortunate nature of the dispute.'

'It was unacademic,' said Sir David severely. 'There is no other word for it, Dr Holroyd.'

'I am afraid it was. And most deplorably public. Whereas your own quarrel with Finlay, Sir David, had been a discreetly unobtrusive matter.' Dr Holroyd smiled with sudden frank malice. 'And over private, not University, affairs. In fact, over a woman. Or was it several women?'

'These,' said Appleby rather hastily, 'are matters which it may be unnecessary to take up.' Detectives are commonly supposed to expend all their energy in dragging information out of people; actually, much of it goes in preventing irrelevant and embarrassing disclosure. 'May I ask, Sir David, your own whereabouts at the time of the fatality?'

'I was in this room, Mr Appleby, reading Plato. Even Vice-Chancellors are entitled to read Plato at times, and I had given orders not to be disturbed.'

'I see. And I take it that nobody interrupted you, and that you might have left the room for a time without being observed?'

Sir David gloomily nodded.

'And you, Dr Holroyd?'

'I went to poor Finlay's final lecture and sat near the back. But the whole stupid affair disgusted me, and I came away – only a few minutes, it seems, before the lights went out. I composed myself by taking a quiet walk along the canal. It was quite deserted.'

'I see. And now about the manner of Finlay's death. I understand that you have inspected the body and realize that he was killed by the thrust of a fine dagger from behind? The deed was accomplished in what must have been almost complete darkness. Would you say that it required – or at least that it suggests – something like the professional knowledge of another anatomist or medical man?'

Holroyd was pale. 'It certainly didn't strike me as the blind thrust of an amateur made in a panic. But perhaps there is a species of particularly desperate criminal who is skilled in such things.'

'Possibly so.' Appleby glanced from Holroyd to Sir David. 'But is either of you aware of Finlay's having any connections or interests which might bring upon him the violence of such people? No? Then I think we must be very sceptical about anything of the sort. To kill a man in extremely risky circumstances simply for the pleasure of laying the body on his own dissecting-table before his own students is something quite outside my experience of professional crime. It is much more like some eccentric act of private vengeance. And one conceived by a theatrical mind.'

Once more Sir David Evans looked at Dr Holroyd, and Dr Holroyd looked at Sir David Evans. 'Finlay himself,' said Sir David, 'had something theatrical about him. Otherwise, look you, he would not have let himself pecome the central figure in this pig yearly joke.' He paused. 'Now, Dr Holroyd here is not theatrical. He is pad-tempered. He is morose. He is under-pred. But theatrical he is not.'

'And no more is Sir David.' Holroyd seemed positively touched by the character sketch of himself just offered. 'He is a bit of a humbug, of course – all philosophers are. And he is not a good man, since it is impossible for a Vice-Chancellor to be that. Perhaps he is even something of a *poseur*. If compelled to characterize him freely' – and Holroyd got comfortably to his feet – 'I should describe him as Goethe described Milton's *Paradise Lost*.' Holroyd moved towards the door, and as he did so paused to view Sir David's portrait. 'Fair outside but rotten inwardly,' he quoted thoughtfully. 'But of positive theatrical instinct I would be inclined to say that Sir David is tolerably free. Good afternoon.'

There was a moment's silence. Sir David Evans's fixed expression of benevolence had never wavered. 'Pad passions,' he said. 'Look you, Mr Appleby, 'there is pad passions in that man.'

Albert was pottering gloomily among his cadaver-racks. His massive frame gave a jump as Appleby entered; it was clear that he was not in full possession of that placid repose which ex-policemen should enjoy.

Appleby looked round with brisk interest. 'Nice place you have here,' he said. 'Everything convenient and nicely thought out.'

The first expression on Albert's face had been strongly disapproving. But at this he perceptibly relaxed. 'Ball-bearing,' he said huskily. 'Handle them like lambs.' He pushed back a steel shutter and proudly drew out a rack and its contents. 'Nicely developed gal,' he said appreciatively. 'Capital pelvis for child-bearing, she was going to have. Now, if you'll just step over here I can show you one or two uncommonly interesting lower limbs.'

'Thank you – another time.' Appleby, though not unaccustomed to such places, had no aspirations towards connoisseurship. 'I want your own story of what happened this morning.'

'Yes, sir.' From old professional habit Albert straightened up and stood at attention. 'As you'll know, there's always been this bad be'aviour at the final lecture, so there was nothing out of the way in that. But then the lights went out, and they started throwing things, and something 'it me 'ard on the shins.'

'Hard?' said Appleby. 'I doubt if that could have been anything thrown from the theatre.'

'No more do I.' Albert was emphatic. 'It was someone came in through the doors the moment the lights went out and got me down with a regular Rugby tackle. Fair winded I was, and lost my bearings as well.'

'So it was some little time before you managed to get to the switch, which is just outside the swing doors. And in that time, Professor Finlay was killed and substituted for the cadaver, and the cadaver was got clean away. Would you say that was a one-man job?'

'No, sir, I would not. Though – mind you – that body 'ad only to be carried across a corridor and out into the courtyard. Anyone can 'ave a car waiting there, so the rest would be easy enough.'

Appleby nodded. 'The killing of Finlay, and the laying him out like that, may have been a sheer piece of macabre drama, possibly conceived and executed by a lunatic – or even by an apparently sane man with some specific obsession regarding corpses. But can you see any reason why such a person should actually carry off the original corpse? It meant saddling himself with an uncommonly awkward piece of evidence.'

'You can't ever tell what madmen will do. And as for corpses, there are more people than you would reckon what 'as uncommon queer interests in them at times.' And Albert shook his head. 'I seen things,' he added.

'No doubt you have. But have you seen anything just lately? Was there anything that might be considered as leading up to this shocking affair?'

Albert hesitated. 'Well, sir, in this line wot I come down to since they retired me it's not always possible to up'old the law. In fact, it's sometimes necessary to circumvent it, like. For, as the late professor was given to remarking, science must be served.' Albert paused and tapped his cadaver-racks. 'Served with these 'ere. And of late we've been uncommon short. And there's no doubt that now and then him and me was stretching a point.'

'Good heavens!' Appleby was genuinely startled. 'This affair is bad enough already. You don't mean to say that it's going to lead to some further scandal about body-snatching?'

'Nothing like that, sir.' But as he said this Albert looked doubtful. 'Nothing *quite* like that. They comes from institutions, you know. And nowadays they 'as to be got to sign papers. It's a matter of tact. Sometimes relatives come along afterwards and says there been too much tact by a long way. It's not always easy to know just how much tact you can turn on. There's no denying but we've 'ad one or two awkwardnesses this year. And it's my belief as 'ow this sad affair is just another awkwardness – but more violent like than the others.'

'It was violent, all right.' Appleby had turned and led the way into the deserted theatre. Flowers still strewed it. There was a mingled smell of lilies and formalin. Overhead, the single great lamp was like a vast all-seeing eye. But that morning the eye had blinked. And what deed of darkness had followed?

'The professor was killed and laid out like that, sir, as an act of revenge by some barmy and outraged relation. And the cadaver was carried off by that same relation as what you might call an act of piety.'

'Well, it's an idea.' Appleby was strolling about, measuring distances with his eye. 'But what about this particular body upon which Finlay was going to demonstrate? *Had* it outraged any pious relations?'

'It only come in yesterday. Quite unprepared it was to be, you see – the same as hanatomists 'ad them in the sixteenth century. Very interesting the late professor was on all that. And why all them young varmints of students should take this particular occasion to fool around –'

'Quite so. It was all in extremely bad taste, I agree. And I don't doubt that the Coroner will say so. And an Assize Judge too, if we have any luck. But you were going to tell me about this particular corpse.'

'I was saying it only come in yesterday. And it was after that that somebody tried to break into the cadaver-racks. Last night, they did – and not a doubt of it. Quite professional, too. If this whole part of the building, sir, weren't well-nigh like a strong-room they'd have done it, without a doubt. And when the late professor 'eard of it 'e was as worried as I was. Awkwardnesses we've 'ad. But body-snatching in reverse, as you might say, was a new one on us both.'

'So you think that the outraged and pious relation had an earlier shot, in the programme for which murder was not included? I think it's about time we hunted him up.'

Albert looked sorely perplexed. 'And so it would be – if we

knew where to find him. But it almost seems as if there never was a cadaver with less in the way of relations than this one wot 'as caused all the trouble. A fair ideal cadaver it seemed to be. You don't think now' – Albert was frankly inconsequent – 'that it might 'ave been an accident? You don't think it might 'ave been one of them young varmint's jokes gone a bit wrong?'

'I do not.'

'But listen, sir.' Albert was suddenly urgent. 'Suppose there was a plan like this. The lights was to be put out and a great horrid dagger thrust into the cadaver. That would be quite like one of their jokes, believe me. For on would go the lights again and folk would get a pretty nasty shock. But now suppose – just suppose, sir – that when the lights were put out for that there purpose there came into the professor's head the notion of a joke of his own. He would change places with the cadaver –'

'But the man wasn't mad!' Appleby was staring at the late Professor Finlay's assistant in astonishment. 'Anything so grotesque –'

'He done queer things before now.' Albert was suddenly stubborn. 'It would come on him sometimes to do something crazier than all them young fools could cudgel their silly brains after. And then the joke would come first and decency second. I seen some queer things at final lectures before this. And that would mean that the varmint thinking to stick the dagger in the cadaver would stick it in the late professor instead.'

'I see.' Appleby was looking at Albert with serious admiration; the fellow didn't look very bright – nevertheless his days in the Force should have been spent in the detective branch. 'It's a better theory than we've had yet, I'm bound to say. But it leaves out two things: the disappearance of the original body, and the fact that Finlay was stabbed from behind. For if he did substitute himself for the body it would have been in the same position – a supine position, and not a prone position. So I don't think your notion will do. And, anyway, we must have all the information about the cadaver that we can get.'

'It isn't much.' Albert bore the discountenance of his hypothesis well. 'We don't know much more about 'im than this – that 'e was a seafaring man.'

The cadaver, it appeared, had at least possessed a name: James Cass. He had also possessed a nationality, for his seaman's papers declared him to be a citizen of the United States, and that his next-of-kin was a certain Martha Cass, with an indecipherable address in Seattle, Washington. For some years he had been sailing pretty constantly in freighters between England and America. Anything less likely to bring down upon the Anatomy Department of Nessfield University the vengeance of outraged and pious relations it would have been difficult to conceive. And the story of Cass's death and relegation to the service of science was an equally bare one. He had come off his ship and was making his way to an unknown lodging when he had been knocked down by a tram and taken to the casualty ward of Nessfield Infirmary. There he had been visited by the watchful Albert, who had surreptitiously presented him with a flask of gin, receiving in exchange Cass's signature to a document bequeathing his remains for the purposes of medical science. Cass had then died, and his body had been delivered to the Anatomy School.

And, after that, somebody had ruthlessly killed Professor Finlay and then carried James Cass's body away again. Stripped of the bewildering nonsense of the final lecture, thought Appleby, the terms of the problem were fairly simple. And yet that nonsense, too, was relevant. For it had surely been counted upon in the plans of the murderer.

For a few minutes Appleby worked with a stop-watch. Then he turned once more to Albert. 'At the moment,' he said, 'Cass himself appears to be something of a dead end. So now, let us take the lecture – or the small part of it that Finlay had got through before the lights went out. You were a witness of it – and a trained police witness, which is an uncommonly fortunate thing. I want you to give me every detail you can – down to the least squawk or flutter by that damned vulture.'

Albert was gratified, and did as he was bid. Appleby listened, absorbed. Only once a flicker passed over his features. But when Albert was finished he had some questions to ask.

'There was an audience,' he said, '– if audience is the right name for it. Apparently all sorts of people were accustomed to turn up?'

'All manner of unlikely and unsuitable folk.' Albert looked disgusted. 'Though most of them would be medical, one way or another. As you can imagine, sir, a demonstration of a sixteenth-century dissecting technique isn't every layman's fancy.'

'It certainly wouldn't be mine.'

'I couldn't put a name to a good many of them. But there was Dr Holroyd, whom you'll have met, sir; he's our professor of Human Physiology. Went away early, he did, and looking mighty disgusted, too. Then there was Dr Wesselmann, the lecturer in Prosthetics – an alien, he is, and not been in Nessfield many years. He brought a friend I never had sight of before. And out they went too.'

'Well, that's very interesting. And can you recall anyone else?'

'I don't know that I can, sir. Except of course our Vice-Chancellor, Sir David Evans.'

Appleby jumped. 'Evans! But he swore to me that –'

Albert smiled indulgently. 'Bless you, that's his regular way. Did you ever know a Welshman who could let a day pass without a bit of 'armless deceit like?'

'There may be something in that.'

''E don't think it dignified, as you might say, to attend the final lecture openly. But more often that not he's up there at the far doorway, peering in at the fun. Well, this time 'e 'ad more than 'e bargained for.'

'No doubt he had. And the same prescription might be good for some of the rest of us.' Appleby paused and glanced quickly round the empty theatre. 'Just step to a telephone, will you, and ask Dr Holroyd to come over here.'

Albert did as he was asked, and presently the physiologist came nervously in. 'Is another interview really necessary?' he demanded. 'I have a most important –'

'We shall hope not to detain you long.' Appleby's voice was dry rather than reassuring. 'It is merely that I want you to assist me in a reconstruction of the crime.'

Holroyd flushed. 'And may I ask by what right you ask me to take part in such a foolery?'

Appleby suddenly smiled. 'None, sir – none at all. I merely wanted a trained mind – and one with a pronounced instinct to get at the ruth of a problem when it arises. I was sure you would be glad to help.'

'Perhaps I am. Anyway, go ahead.'

'Then I should be obliged if you would be the murderer. Perhaps I should say the first murderer, for it seems likely enough that there were at least two – accomplices. You have no objection to so disagreeable a part?'

Holroyd shrugged his shoulders. 'Naturally, I have none whatever. But I fear I must be coached in it and given my cue. For I assure you it is a role entirely foreign to me. And I have no theatrical flair, as Sir David pointed out.'

Once more Appleby brought out his stop-watch. 'Albert,' he said briskly, 'shall be the cadaver, and I shall be Finlay standing in front of it. Your business is to enter by the back, switch off the light, step into the theatre and there affect to stab me. I shall fall to the floor. You must then dislodge Albert, hoist me into his place and cover me with the tarpaulin. Then you must get hold of Albert by the legs or shoulders and haul him from the theatre.'

'And all this in the dark? It seems a bit of a programme.'

Appleby nodded. 'I agree with you. But we shall at least discover if it is at all possible of accomplishment by one man in the time available. So are you ready?'

'One moment, sir.' Albert, about to assume the passive part of the late James Cass, sat up abruptly. 'You seem to have missed me out. Me as I was, that is to say.'

'Quite true.' Appleby looked at him thoughtfully. 'We are short of a stand-in for you as you were this morning. But I shall stop off being Finlay's body and turn on the lights again myself. So go ahead.'

Albert lay down and drew the tarpaulin over his head. Holroyd slipped out. Appleby advanced as if to address an audience. 'Now,' he said.

And Appleby talked. Being thorough, he made such anatomical observations as his ignorance allowed. Once he glanced round at the corpse, and out of the corner of his eye glimpsed Holroyd beyond the glass-panelled door, his hand already going up to flick at the switch. A moment later the theatre was in darkness, and seconds after that Appleby felt a sharp tap beneath the shoulder-blade. He pitched to the floor, pressing his stop-watch as he did so. Various heaving sounds followed as Holroyd got the portly Albert off the table; then Appleby felt himself seized in surprisingly strong arms and hoisted up in Albert's place. Next came a shuffle and a scrape as Holroyd, panting heavily now, dragged the inert Albert from the theatre. Appleby waited for a couple of seconds, threw back the tarpaulin and lowered himself to the floor. Then he groped his way through the door, flicked on the light and looked at his watch. 'And the audience,' he said, 'is now sitting back and waiting – until presently somebody points out that the cadaver is the wrong size. Thank you very much. The reconstruction has been more instructive than I hoped.' He turned to Holroyd. 'I am still inclined to think that it has the appearance of being the work of two men. And yet you managed it pretty well on schedule when single-handed. Never a fumble and just the right lift. You might almost have been practising it.'

Holroyd frowned. 'Yachting,' he said briefly, '–and particularly at night. It makes one handy.'

And Albert looked with sudden suspicion at Nessfield's professor of Human Physiology. 'Yachting?' he asked. 'Now, would that have put you in the way of acquaintance of many seafaring men?'

Of James Cass, that luckless waif who would be a seafarer no longer, Appleby learned little more that afternoon. The cargo-vessel from which he had disembarked was already at sea again, and a couple of days must elapse before any line could be tapped there. But one elderly seaman who had recently made several voyages with him a little research did produce, and from this witness two facts emerged. There was nothing out of the way about Cass – except that he was a man distinctly on the simple side. Cass had been suggestible, Appleby gathered; so much so as to have been slightly a butt among his fellows. And Appleby asked a question: had the dead man appeared to have any regular engagement or preoccupation when he came into port? The answer to this was definitive. Within a couple of hours, Appleby felt, the file dealing with this queer mystery of the anatomy theatre would virtually be closed for good.

Another fifteen minutes found him mounting the staircase of one of Nessfield's most superior blocks of professional chambers. But the building, if imposing, was gloomy as well, and when Appleby was overtaken and jostled by a hurrying form it was a second before he recognized that he was again in the presence of Dr Holroyd.

'Just a moment,' Appleby laid a hand on the other's arm. 'May I ask if this coincidence extends to our both aiming at the third floor.'

Holroyd was startled, but made no reply. They mounted the final flight side by side and in silence. Appleby rang a bell before a door with a handsome brass plate. After a perceptible delay the door was opened by a decidedly flurried nurse, who showed the two men into a sombre waiting-room. 'I don't think,' she said, 'that you have an appointment? As an emergency has just arisen I am afraid there is no chance of seeing Dr –'

She stopped at an exclamation from Appleby. Hunched in a corner of the waiting-room was a figure whose face was almost entirely swathed in a voluminous silk muffler. But there was no mistaking that flowing silver hair. 'Sir David!' exclaimed Appleby. 'This is really a most remarkable rendezvous.'

Sir David Evans groaned. 'My chaw,' he said. 'It is one pig ache, look you.'

Holroyd laughed nervously. 'Shakespeare was demonstrably right. There was never yet philosopher could bear the toothache patiently – nor Vice-Chancellor either.'

But Appleby paid no attention; he was listening keenly to something else. From beyond a door on the right came sound of hurried, heavy movement. Appleby strode across the room and turned the handle. He flung back the door and found himself looking into the dentist's surgery. 'Dr Wesselmann?' he said.

The answer was an angry shout from a bullet-headed man in a white coat. 'How dare you intrude in this way!' he cried.

'My colleague and myself are confronted with a serious emergency. Be so good as to withdraw at once.'

Appleby stood his ground and surveyed the room; Holroyd stepped close behind him. The dentist's chair was empty, but on a surgical couch nearby lay a patient covered with a light rug. Over this figure another white-coated man was bending, and appeared to be holding an oxygen mask over its face.

And Nessfield's lecturer in Prosthetics seemed to find further explanations necessary. 'A patient,' he said rapidly, 'with an unsuspected idiosyncrasy to intravenous barbiturates. Oxygen has to be administered, and the position is critical. So be so good –'

Appleby leaped forward and sent the white-coated holder of the oxygen-mask spinning; he flung back the rug. There could be no doubt that what was revealed was James Cass's body. And since lying on Professor Finlay's dissecting-table it had sustained a great gash in the throat. It had never been very pleasant to look at. It was ghastly enough now.

Wesselmann's hand darted to his pocket; Holroyd leaped on him with his yachtsman's litheness, and the alien dentist went down heavily on the floor. The second man showed no fight as he was handcuffed. Appleby looked curiously at Holroyd. 'So you saw,' he asked, 'how the land lay?'

'In my purely amateur fashion I suppose I did. And I think I finished on schedule once again.'

Appleby laughed. 'Your intervention saved me from something decidedly nasty at the hands of Nessfield's authority on false teeth. By the way, would you look round for the teeth in question. And then we can have in Sir David – seeing he is so conveniently in attendance – and say an explanatory word.'

'I got the hang of it,' said Appleby, 'when we did a very rough-and-ready reconstruction of the crime. For when, while playing Finlay's part, I glanced round at the cadaver, I found myself catching a glimpse of Dr Holroyd here when he was obligingly playing First Murderer and turning off the lights. There was a glass panel in the door, and through this he was perfectly visible. I saw at once why Finlay had been killed. It was merely because he had seen, and *recognized*, somebody who was about to plunge the theatre in darkness for some nefarious, but not necessarily murderous, end. What did this person want? There could be only one answer: the body of James Cass. Already he had tried to get it in the night, but the housebreaking involved had proved too difficult.'

The benevolent features of Sir David Evans were shadowed by perplexity. 'But why, Mr Appleby, should this man want such a pody?'

'I shall come to that in a moment. But first keep simply to this: that the body had to be stolen even at great hazard; that when glimpsed and recognized by Finlay the potential thief was sufficiently ruthless to silence him with a dagger secreted for such an emergency – and was also sufficiently quick-witted to exploit this extemporaneous murder to his own advantage. If he had simply bolted with Cass's body and left that of Finlay the hunt would, of course, have been up the moment somebody turned the lights on. By rapidly substituting one body for the other – Finlay's for that of Cass – on the dissecting table, he contrived the appearance first of some more or less natural momentary absence of Finlay from the theatre, and secondly the suggestion of some possible joke which kept the audience wary and quiet for some seconds longer. All this gave additional time for his getaway. And – yet again – the sheer grotesque consequence of the substitution had great potential value as a disguise. By suggesting some maniacal act of private vengeance it masked the purely practical – and the professionally criminal – nature of the crime.

'And now, what did we know of Cass? We knew that he was a seaman; that he travelled more or less regularly between England and America; that he was knocked down and presently died shortly after landing; and that he was a simple-minded fellow, easily open to persuasion. And we also knew this: that he had a set of rather incongruously magnificent false teeth; that in the anatomy theatre these first protruded themselves and then by some muscular spasm appeared to lodge themselves in the throat, the jaw closing like a vice. And we also knew that, hard upon this, a certain Dr Wesselmann, an alien comparatively little known in Nessfield and actually a specialist in false teeth, hurried from the theatre accompanied by a companion. When I also learned from a seaman who had sailed with Cass that he was often concerned about his teeth and would hurry off to a dentist as soon as he reached shore, I saw that the case was virtually complete.'

'And would be wholly so when you recovered Cass's body and got hold of these.' Holroyd came forward as he spoke, carrying two dental places on an enamel tray. 'Sir David, what would you say about Cass's teeth?'

Nessfield's Vice-Chancellor had removed the muffler from about his jaw; the excitement of the hunt for the moment banished the pain which had driven him to Wesselmann's rooms. He inspected the dentures carefully – and then spoke the inevitable word. 'They are pig,' he said decisively.

'Exactly so. And now, look.' Holroyd gave a deft twist to a molar; the denture which he was holding fell apart; in the hollow of each gleaming tooth there could be discerned a minute oil-silk package.

'What they contain,' said Appleby, 'is probably papers covered with a microscopic writing. I had thought perhaps of uncut diamonds. But now I am pretty sure that what we have run to earth is espionage. What one might call the Unwitting Intermediary represents one of the first principles of that perpetually fantastic game at its higher levels. Have a messenger who has no notion that he *is* a messenger, and you at once supply yourself with the sort of insulating device between cell and cell that gives spies a comforting feeling of security. Cass has been such a device. And it was one perfectly easy to operate. He had merely to be persuaded that his false teeth were always likely to give him trouble, and that he must regularly consult (at an obligingly low fee) this dentist at one end and that dentist at the other – and the thing was practically foolproof. Only Wesselmann and his friends failed to reckon on sudden death, and much less on Cass's signing away his body – dentures and all – to an anatomy school.' Appleby paused. 'And now, gentlemen, that concludes the affair. So what shall we call it?'

Holroyd smiled. 'Call it the Cass Case. You couldn't get anything more compendious than that.'

But Sir David Evans shook his beautiful silver locks. 'No!' he said authoritatively. 'It shall be called *Lesson in Anatomy*. The investigation has been most interesting, Mr Appleby. And now let us go. For the photographers, look you, are waiting.'

Imperious Caesar

'It all began,' Appleby said, 'with a Professor writing a learned article called Shakespeare's *Stage Blood*. He wasn't starting a theory that the Bard came of a long line of actors. He was simply showing from a study of the old texts that the Elizabethan theatre was a thoroughly gory place.'

The Vicar nodded. 'Carnal, bloody, and unnatural acts,' he quoted cheerfully. 'Accidental judgements, casual slaughters, death put on by cunning and forced cause –'

'Quite so. But the relevant point was this: when X drew his dagger or rapier on the stage of the Globe and appeared to stab Y, what in fact he did stab was a concealed bladder, full of some sort of red paint. The stuff spurted out all over the place, and gave an engaging impression of a neatly severed artery.'

'Messy. One hopes it came out in the wash.'

'No doubt it did. But the immediate effect was terrific. All concerned simply wallowed in this bogus blood, and the audience got no end of a thrill. Now, no sooner had the Professor published his discovery than it greatly took the fancy of a chap called Cherry, who was the moving spirit of a group of amateur players at Nessfield. Most of his company belonged to the staff of the University there, and this blood-bath business apparently gave very general pleasure to all. It was felt that something should be done to put this discovery about Shakespeare's stage into practice. So Cherry decided that the next play should be *Julius Caesar*.'

The Vicar chuckled. ' "Stoop, Romans, stoop, and let us bathe our hands in Caesar's blood." '

'Precisely. "Up to the elbows, and besmear our swords." Contemplating that scene, Cherry, you may say, simply saw red. As it happened, I was visiting a friend of some consequence in those parts, and he took me along to the performance. For some reason that I didn't gather, it was quite an occasion, and we sat among a whole gaggle of the local nobs, all doing Cherry and his friends proud.

'They played uncommonly well. The scene in the Senate House built up some first-rate suspense, and when at length the conspirators had edged round Caesar and isolated him beside Pompey's statue, the audience was as keyed up as ever I've seen it at a professional production. Then Casca gave his signal, and that dignified group of noble Romans closed in like a rugger scrum, and had a high old time stabbing and hacking for all they were worth. You wouldn't have believed, Vicar, that most of them were Doctors of Philosophy and Readers in Ancient Hebrew and such like. And the gore! It exceeded all expectations. Every one of the conspirators – Brutus, Cassius, Casca, Decius, Cinna, and the rest –'

'Ligarius, Trebonius, and Metellus.' The Vicar rubbed his hands in mild self-congratulation. 'Once learnt, one doesn't forget these things.'

'They were all dripping some beastly stuff supplied, I imagine, by the Department of Chemistry. And the rest of the scene went with a swing – Mark Antony's "Cry Havoc" speech and all. It was only when Antony and the servant of Octavius started to bear away the body that things went wrong. You see, it *was* a body. Caesar had been stabbed through the heart.'

The Vicar looked serious, but his memory did not fail him. '"Imperious Caesar, dead and turned to clay" – eh? What an uncommonly disconcerting business.'

Appleby nodded. 'It was clearly *my* business, whether disconcerting or not. Scotland Yard was in the stalls, and Scotland Yard had to step into the limelight. So I got my august friend to announce my presence in due form, and there and then I took charge. Within half an hour I felt like concluding myself to be at grips with the perfect murder.

'Caesar – I needn't drag up those people's real names – had been an unpopular figure about the place. He was a mathematician with a boring habit of pestering his colleagues with insoluble problems. He and Cassius had had a tremendous row over something entirely technical; Brutus was believed to be his bitter rival for the next Fellowship of some important scientific society; and Casca was convinced that he had done him out of a job.'

'Ah!' The Vicar was impressed. 'There looks to have been quite a field. But I put my money on Casca. "See what a rent the envious Casca made."'

'These things might be far from very substantial motives for murder. But they hinted an atmosphere which might nurse really bad blood – *real* blood, you may say. And now think of the actual melée. There's nothing like a crowd of amateurs for doing that sort of thing in a really whole-hearted way, and for a conspirator meaning actual homicide this bit of stage assassination was ideal cover.

'And all I had to go on was a bunch of confused statements by these people – that, and eight daggers; seven of them trick daggers of the sort that disappear up the sheath, and one of an authentic and deadly kind. The seven were dripping this beastly red muck; the eighth –'

'A nasty contrast, indeed.' The Vicar was sober. '"And as he plucked his cursed steel away, mark how the blood of Caesar followed it." Would there be fingerprints?'

'I hadn't much hope from them – and so I was the more pleased when I suddenly had an idea. I gathered the cast together; told them I believed I knew who was responsible; and announced that I was going to have them enact the scene over again, with myself as Caesar.'

'My dear fellow, wasn't that rather risky? If the crime had been the work, say, of a homicidal maniac, this second chance –'

'There were to be no daggers this time, and no disgusting red paint. Even so, I got well thumped, for those people's zest for violence wasn't to be exhausted by the mere spectacle of a murdered colleague. They found the re-enacting thoroughly enjoyable. And I don't doubt that, at the end of it, they were extremely disappointed when I simply told them to go home.'

'To go home!'

'Certainly. For all I'd wanted to do, you see, was to *count* – to count the conspirators. And my memory proved right. Eight daggers made one too many.

'It's true that there are eight conspirators, and you completed my own list quite correctly. But Trebonius' job, you may recall, is to get Antony out of the way; and so he isn't concerned in the killing. Caesar, in fact, had killed himself. For distressing reasons into which I needn't enter, his life was no longer of any use to him; and it had pleased him to exploit the occasion of his own suicide to set his colleagues, and the world in general, a final little problem.'

'My dear Appleby, this is a very shocking story. Suppose that one of those unfortunate conspirators had actually been suspected of murder.'

'Nothing would have pleased Caesar more. He was a thoroughly malicious fellow – and, like the real Caesar, a good deal of an exhibitionist. He liked staging that sensation for all the important citizens of Nessfield. And had Casca or Cassius been brought to trial, he would have been delighted. He had even left with a crony a letter addressed to the Home Secretary and telling the whole story. It was to be posted –'

'Only in the event of a criminal trial?'

'Only in the event of somebody having been hanged.'

The Clancarron Ball

'I hadn't been in the police long,' Appleby said, 'when they put me into plain clothes. It meant a much more colourful life.'

'Not, I imagine, in the literal sense.' The Vicar knocked out his pipe in the grate and turned an expanse of shabby clerical flannel comfortably to the blaze. 'Plain clothes are commonly drab.'

Appleby shook his head. 'Think of hunt balls and a dozen other such things. They all allow free play to the thwarted male instinct for bright feathers. And I went to all of them. I was the scarlet-coated but otherwise unobtrusive guest, with his eye on the gold plate, the silver cups, the more portable *objets d'art* in unnoticed corners.'

'You kept an eye on things generally?'

'And on people too. At times it was not at all a nice trade. Even in the most polite society efficient peeping and peering uncovers a good deal that is far from edifying.'

'No doubt.' The Vicar pushed his tobacco-jar companionably across to Appleby. 'But, when the gold plate really disappeared, what sort of person was commonly responsible? Would it be a professional criminal, or just a bad baronet or absent-minded bishop?'

'You never could tell until you'd caught your man. That was part of the difficulty, for instance, in the Clancarron affair.'

'Ah!' The Vicar straddled himself yet more comfortably before the fire. 'Now we come to something. Proceed.'

Appleby leant forward and thrust a spill into the flames. 'A big evening party among people of that sort means hosts of tradesmen, caterers, extra servants, and so forth hard at work from early morning. I liked to keep an eye on the whole thing. So I would arrive with the milk, more or less, and looking as if I were the head man from the florist's or the confectioner's.

'Lady Clancarron counted as an important political hostess in those days. She was determined to get her husband out of county cricket, where he was a notable fast bowler, and into the Cabinet, where it was unlikely he would have got things moving so rapidly. When she gave a really large-scale affair she opened up the whole of Carron House, although during the months the family spent in town they commonly made do with about half of it. When I arrived on the morning of her biggest party it seemed impossible that, in a mere twelve hours, order and every appearance of settled splendour and luxury could be extracted from the chaos of the place. The great ballroom, in particular, was like a museum emerging from cold-storage: dust-covers coming off the chairs and chandeliers, a squad of men working on the floor, another on the lighting, and a third bringing in so much vegetation that they looked like a tropical Birnam Wood arriving on an equatorial Dunsinane. Not that the temperature was at all equatorial. Outside it was quite freezingly cold, and yet another army of men were busy draught-proofing the line of french windows which open on the flat roof of the offices.

'And it was pretty well the same all over the house. In such conditions one can do little more than hope for the best. Anybody can walk in, you see, make a grab at anything, and stump off with it as if under orders. A terrible headache these occasions are, you may believe me, both for the police and the insurance people. Particularly as, among the owners of easily vanishing heirlooms and the like, it is decidedly within wheels, so to speak, that wheels sometimes incline to revolve.'

The Vicar chuckled. 'A dark saying! But proceed to the ball.'

'The ball was a relief when it came. If I'd had eyes in the back of my head, and a large endowment of extra-sensory perception, I might really have felt quite on top of things. But don't let me spin the story out. Just after midnight the whole place was suddenly plunged into darkness. The dancing stopped, the band stopped, there was a hum of people exchanging amused and reassuring remarks. But they didn't reassure me. I wasn't surprised to catch, seconds later, the sound of breaking glass and splintering wood.

'And then the light went on again. Some of the nice young people on the floor clapped their hands, to show what fun it all was, and the assembled elder aristocracy who were scattered around the walls just continued conversing as if nothing had happened at all. But a good many of them were guessing, all the same. Indeed, there was something pretty definite to guess about. Those lights had been out for a matter only of seconds. But in that interval the frame of one of the french windows had been splintered and was hanging open.

'I became aware that Lady Clancarron was approaching me from across the room with an appearance of the very largest leisure. She even stopped for a moment to say something polite to a couple of rather obscure guests. Then she came up to me and tapped my shoulder with her large fan. You would have thought she was talking about the next by-election or the Prime Minister's sore throat. "My diamond necklace," she said, smiling charmingly. "It was snatched from my throat the instant the lights went out." And she turned away for a moment to give a particularly delightful bow to some inconsiderable personage – a cultural attaché, perhaps, from a minor legation. It was the *noblesse oblige* business in action. I admired it very much.'

The Vicar nodded. 'Wonderful! But then the nobility are trained to that sort of thing.'

'Quite so.' Appleby smiled ironically. 'Training is uncommonly useful, there's no doubt. I had some of sorts myself, as it happened, that was quite useful on that difficult occasion. But let me continue. Lord Clancarron, who had been standing beside his wife near one of the ballroom's two big fireplaces, now came across to us rather more quickly, but in the same carefree way. "My God, Kate!" he said as he came up. "Some rascal's got your diamonds and made off by that window. What shall we do? Some people have spotted what's up. Beastly unpleasant for them, eh?" He had ignored me as he spoke to his wife, but now he wheeled round on me with his athlete's speed, so that his coat-tails swung in air behind him. "Have you anyone on guard out there, my man? Or will the fellow have got clean away?"

'I shook my head. "I don't think anybody will have got clean away, my lord. And it's possible that the broken window may be a feint."

' "What the devil do you mean?"

' "The thief may still be in this room. He may have managed that business at the window simply to set us on a false scent."

'Lord Clancarron stared at me. "That's a deuced clever idea." He glanced round the room. "Look here – nobody's gone out. What about a search – of every man-jack and woman-jill of us in the room?"

'I believe he meant it quite seriously – that he had no notion of how monstrous and impracticable such a course would have been. I gave a second to looking him squarely in the eye. "Nothing of the sort is necessary," I said.

'It was Lady Clancarron who spoke this time – and quite clearly in the most sincere bewilderment. "'You mean –"

' "I mean that your ladyship's diamonds are quite safe. There is no reason why the ball should not continue on its normal course." '

Appleby took a last puff at his pipe. 'It was three in the morning, and the ballroom was empty except for the Clancarrons and myself, when I got a step-ladder and fished that diamond-necklace out of the great central chandelier – where it had been no more than a few purer points of fire amid a myriad gleams of crystal. Lord Clancarron was very upset. "I can't understand it," he said. He didn't "my man" me this time.

' "A tiresome practical joke, my lord." And I hope I managed to give him a sufficiently nasty look that his wife didn't see. "Somebody had an opportunity to tinker with some of the temporary wiring earlier in the day, so as to control the entire lighting with a flick of a toe. It's a thing very easy to do. And the same person snatched the necklace from her ladyship in the darkness and tossed it into the chandelier. He must have had plenty of practice and a very good aim. But he did something more. He carried round some suitable object in the pocket of his tails – say a cricket ball. It didn't show – except perhaps to a trained eye wondering why those tails didn't swing evenly in a dance. And with that object our practical joker did a really wonderful job – still in the dark, mind you, just before flicking the lights on again. He contrived the effect of somebody's bursting out through that french window."

' "You amaze me." His lordship was now looking pretty green.

' "No doubt." I waited until Lady Clancarron, simple soul, had wandered over to stare at the broken window. "And now, my lord, I must be off. Like the Australians last season" – and I looked round the vast, empty room – "I shall have good reason to remember the famous Clancarron ball." '

A Dog's Life

'Human action,' remarked the surgeon, 'is often oddly disproportioned to the motive prompting it. Men are driven to suicide by mere boredom and to murder by simple curiosity.'

The philosopher stretched out his hand for the decanter. 'I should have thought,' he said, 'that it was the other way about. Boredom makes us long for some decisive action, and killing a man is surely the most decisive action we can achieve. Correspondingly, curiosity is prompted by nothing more acutely than by the secret of the grave. And our chance of solving *that* lies in ourselves descending into it, and not in giving a shove to some other fellow ... My dear Appleby, a capital port.'

'I've seen a good many cases of homicide.' The Q.C. cracked a walnut and inspected its kernel with care. 'That some had boredom behind them and that some had curiosity, I won't deny. But a good many more had respectability.'

'Respectability?' The surgeon put down his glass. 'My dear sir, you alarm me. My own respectability is most pronounced.'

The Q.C. chuckled. 'Well, have a care. The desire to retain one's respectability is a terrible killer, I assure you. And I think our host would tell you the same thing.'

There was a pause, which grew expectant as Appleby silently watched the decanter returning to him round the little table. 'Yes,' he said presently, 'that's fair enough. I've known a woman who poisoned her husband in a particularly horrible and lingering way rather than sully her fair name with the neighbours by just going off with another man. And then, of course, there was the Lorio case. Interesting? Well, you may judge for yourselves.

'I was a young man at the time, and having my first holiday since being sent into the C.I.D. Not a very exciting holiday, for

I was spending it with my aunt at Sheercliff – a retreat to which she withdrew periodically from the harrassing life of Harrogate. It was she who sent me to make the Lorios' acquaintance. Robert Lorio, it seems, came of a good Yorkshire family, which meant that my aunt had him down in a sort of social card-index of persons not altogether to be lost sight of. Most people, I found, *had* lost sight of Lorio, and of his wife Monica too. They lived quite alone, in a farm-house that no longer had anything to do with a farm, about a couple of miles outside the little town. The tremendous cliff from which the place takes its name was hard-by; and about a mile farther on again it piled itself up in the famous landmark called High Head.

'My aunt had no intention of calling on these people herself. They existed, as it were, in too small a type in her index for *that*. It was simply a matter of sending me out with a stately message of recognition. So off I went one windy morning and presented myself. Lorio proved to be a glum, commonplace-looking chap of middle age, whose only notion of impressing the world seemed to have been to grow a short black beard. The dismal condition known as "reduced circumstances" was written all over him, and all over his house. You could see the unfaded places on the walls from which some picture or cabinet had been wafted away to end finally in the family stew-pot. Yet if one had really thought of the culinary aspect of things *chez* Lorio one's associations would have been rather different. Eye of newt and toe of frog, with plenty of baboon's blood for saucing, would have been the predominant image. Monica Lorio, in fact, was decidedly a witch. Dark like her husband, she was at the same time much younger. She had a fine body, which rippled with a sinister grace beneath a slatternly rag of a dress. It was she who entertained me, after a fashion – for her husband, with one hand deep in the pocket of his shabby lovat tweeds and the other playing with the ears of a large shaggy dog, did little more than stare at me morosely. Mrs Lorio stared at me too, for that matter – and then her eyes would wander to Lorio with a look I didn't like, or out of the window to a tumble-down barn at the bottom of the garden, and thence to the loneliness – for it was that – of the moor and cliff beyond.

'You will have gathered, I think, that I hated the whole thing.

What I find difficult to convey is the inexplicable intensity of my feeling. I sat there talking rubbish about my aunt's health, and the innumerable calls upon her benevolence – and all the time there was growing on me the conviction that I had strayed into the presence of some bold approximation to an absolute evil. When I got back that evening, and my aunt asked me about Monica Lorio, a fair answer would have been: "She is a woman who has sold herself into some depth of degradation I can't at all fathom." But that is not the sort of thing one says to an aunt – or not to my aunt. So I held the peace.

'Will it surprise you to learn that I took to walking that way almost every day? The views were magnificent; nevertheless, I don't doubt that it was my infant detective faculties that were at work. On one occasion they actually took me through the yard at the back of the house, although I'd have hated to be spotted by one of the Lorios and sociably received once more. Well, for a moment I thought I had been spotted by Monica, though not to the kindling of feelings at all sociable. For there she was, peering covertly out from the side of an uncurtained window, and glaring at me with a sort of gloating malignity that made my heart jump. Or rather that, momentarily, was what it looked like, and then I realized that she was really glancing straight past me at something else. I turned my head without seeing anything at first except that great dog, lying in the sun scratching itself. Then – just for a second and turning a corner of the barn – I glimpsed a slouching, listless figure in shabby lovat tweed and a black beard.

'Lorio was not a chap I'd taken to, but in that moment I felt uncommonly sorry for him. He was no good; the whole tumbledown place witnessed to that; and his wife, who clearly had vitality and ambition, hated him as a failure. It was a sombre and sordid picture, and I decided that my curiosity had had about enough. Nevertheless, it got another dose later that day.

'I walked a good many miles along the cliffs, lunched in a pub, and came back by the shore – you can do that until you are within about a mile and a half of High Head; from there onward the cliffs drop sheer to deep water, and you have to climb again and go along the top of them. Well, I was down there by the shore still; it was sunny and warm; I sat down in a little coign to read, and very presently I was asleep. I doubt whether I slept very long, and when I woke it was to the sound of voices coming from not half a dozen yards away – from the next little hollow, in fact, among the sandhills. One of the voices was a woman's, which I recognized instantly as Mrs Lorio's. The other was a man's, and it was certainly not her husband's. I didn't hear what was being said. But it wasn't the sort of talk in which the words hold much significance in themselves; in fact, it was unmistakably the low murmuring of lovers. I was extremely disconcerted. You see, I had set out that morning with a restless curiosity about the Lorios in my head. And now here I was, without the least intending it, skulking like a little private inquiry agent at the door of a hotel bedroom. So I bolted – and without a glance. I hadn't yet learnt that policemen can't afford nice feelings. On this occasion, had I just done a little crawling and peeping – but I see that you are getting impatient. I'll hurry on to the kill.'

Appleby paused, and the Q.C. nodded approvingly. 'We are taking it for granted there is going to be a kill. Is it too much to hazard that our friend Lorio comes to a sudden and sticky end?'

'Sudden – yes. But I don't know that I'd call it sticky.' Appleby paused to draw at his cigar. 'There's no mystification about this, you know. I'm just telling you a straight yarn.'

'A simple bed-time story.' The surgeon pushed an ashtray towards the philosopher and chuckled. 'Or that was the turn it seemed to be taking when you broke off. Proceed, my dear Appleby, proceed.'

'Well then, after that I reckoned never to see a Lorio again. But I was out of luck. For the very next day Robert Lorio called on my aunt. That was only right and proper, no doubt. It surprised me, all the same. The fellow had seemed too sunk in his private miseries – whatever they might be – to care twopence for social forms. However, there he was; and when he took his leave I strolled along the front with him and tried to say a civil word. In this it seemed that I was only too successful. For three or four days later he turned up again and suggested we go for a walk.

'And walk we did – then and on a couple of subsequent occasions. Young and conceited though I was, I don't think it ever occurred to me that the thing was a pleasure to him. He did his best to make himself agreeable; we looked at such antiquities as that countryside boasts of; and he talked about them like a chap who had got them up the night before. He had something on his mind. That fact was plain enough. And at first I supposed that he was anxious to unburden himself, and was grooming me for the role of confidential friend. But then I realized that there was more to it than that; and I remembered with a bit of a shock that I was a police-officer in the C.I.D. Perhaps Lorio was clinging to me in my professional character. I had already done some tagging around as bodyguard to one important person or another. Poor Lorio, it occurred to me, was trying to place himself unofficially in the same category.

'The man was afraid. When I grasped that simple and abject truth about him, and when I pictured him in that lonely house, with his hell-cat of a wife, and that wife's lover lurking perhaps in the next village, I – well, I felt thoroughly sorry for the man. His must have been a dog's life. I think I even felt a bit alarmed – although I didn't, so far as I can remember, at all anticipate what you have called a respectability murder, or anything of the sort. He seemed unable to talk – really to talk, that is – and I believe that at the end of our third walk I'd have questioned him outright. Only that third walk never had an end.

'It differed from the earlier walks in two ways. First, we didn't have Rex, the shaggy dog. And that seemed to make Lorio's nervousness and apprehensiveness worse. For normally the creature would take great sweeps round us and he would follow it affectionately with his eye; then it would dash up and fawn on him, and he would give it a quick thrust away with his arm, and away it would go again. Now, not having the dog to look at, he kept looking at his watch instead – for all the world, I thought, as if he were Dr Faustus waiting for midnight. The other difference was in the weather. There was a gale blowing that made walking thoroughly hard work, and the sea beneath us was tremendous. For we had taken the cliff path past Lorio's own house, and were climbing steadily towards High Head. We had been silent for some time — needing, as we did, all our breath to face that tremendous wind — when he muttered something incoherent about the dog. I gathered presently that it had disappeared that morning and that he was worried about it. I tried to sound sympathetic, but I was more worried about the man himself. His agitation was growing, and it struck me that he must be a bit mad about the brute. Perhaps he gave it the affection that it was no good carrying to his wife.

'As it happened, I ought to have been a bit more worried than I was. For Robert Lorio had then just about thirty minutes to live.

'There is a motor road of sorts leading right to the brow of High Head, and as we approached it I saw three or four parked cars and a little knot of people standing at a discreet distance from the edge. That was to be expected, since when a bit of a gale is blowing the spectacle from up there is justly famous. For a stretch of about fifty yards the top of the cliff breaks down into a system of jagged rocks, crazy ledges, and rudimentary caves, with here and there a thorn or a clump of gorse clinging desperately to terra firma above an utter void. Then there is simply sheer precipice, and the breakers that crash and roar and seethe I don't know how many hundred feet beneath.

'I have a pretty tolerable head for heights, but I can tell you that on that morning I was disposed to keep well away from the edge. With Lorio, however, it was otherwise. He seemed drawn to the verge, and I followed him — or at least I kept sufficiently close to hear his sudden cry before it was caught by the gale and blown to limbo. "Rex," he shouted, "Rex! He's trapped!"

'Sure enough, there was the dog, cowering on a narrow ledge some twenty feet below us. It was a horrid enough sight. Yet my instant calculation was that the animal was *not* trapped; and that with a little encouragement it could be persuaded to come up as it had, presumably, gone down. Of any other trap being in question I hadn't a notion.

'Before I knew what he was about, Lorio had started to scramble. I called to him not to be a fool, but he waved his hand and went on. There seemed, as I've said, to be a practicable path, up which Rex might have been whistled. For a man, the difficulty seemed to be that it was in two places sharply overhung. The second of these places, which was right on the verge, so that its passage admitted of not the slightest slip without disaster, was partly obscured by a great boulder. A couple of the spectators up on the Head, seeing that something was happening, had strolled down to investigate; we waited breathlessly together; it was a moment in which it would have appeared like murder to call out a single word.

'Lorio came to this last and critical place, and I could see him hesitate. Then he bent low to creep past the overhang. He head disappeared; then his shoulders in that shabby tweed; then all we could see was a single foot, edging cautiously out of sight an inch at a time. It seemed an eternity before anything appeared at the other side. At last one of the men standing beside me exclaimed softly, and I saw an arm. It was feeling for a hold – and then it was flailing wildly in air. I recall in that horrible instant a most extraordinary association of ideas. What that arm fantastically suggested to me was the conductor of an orchestra, working up some terrific coda. And at that random thought my ears were opened. I heard – what I had been unconscious of an instant before – the roar and crash of the tremendous seas below; and I heard, too, a single ghastly scream. For a split second the whole man was visible – the gale lifting his jacket, his curved back pillowed on the void, his bearded mouth gaping in that last despairing scream. Then he was gone. Have you noticed that when one pictures such a fall one sees the *progress* of it – the object, whatever it may be, on its *journey* through the air? The reality isn't like that; the speed is so great that it is over as one looks. I think I was aware of that tremendous fall not in terms of distance but of size. At one instant a man had hovered in agony before me; at the next a small black blob hit the sea.

'There was, of course, nothing whatever to do. I knew very well that what I had seen was sudden death. Nevertheless, I raced to the coastguard hut on the other side of High Head. For some reason it was deserted. But I knew it had a telephone. So I broke in through a window and sent a message to the lifeboat station in Sheercliff – which was futile enough, but the best that could be done. All this took about fifteen minutes. When I got back to the scene of the accident there was quite a crowd collected. The people who had come up to the Head by car were pointing, jabbering, and gingerly exploring the edge of the cliff; in fact, they were getting more kick out of their expedition than they had expected, by a long way. One group was in particular agitation. And in a moment I saw why. Rex had apparently managed to rescue himself after all – as I had thought he very well might. They were patting him, shaking their heads over him, shouting at him against the gale, and generally driving the poor brute silly. He gave a howl. And at that moment a hand fell on his collar and quieted him. It was Mrs Lorio's. How she had come upon the scene wasn't clear.

'She was as pale as a ghost, and wildly questioning the folk around her. Somebody, indeed, was in the middle of explaining the accident; it was one of the two men who had stood by me and watched the thing happen. But he was confused and stammering. I had no liking for the job, but I saw that I must step up to her and tell her the horrible truth as I knew it.

Or was it she who knew the truth? If suspicion had been slow to stir in me, it came flooding in now. I hadn't actually seen the dead man *begin* to fall. He had disappeared for a second, and then I had seen him actually off-balance and falling. And the terrain down there was quite problematical. I knew only that before the cliff fell away sheer, there were those dizzy little paths and ledges, with here and there niches and shallow caves fit enough for lurking in. What if Monica Lorio's lover had been lurking there – or even the two of them together? What if the dog had been no more than a decoy?

'These questions answered themselves in about thirty seconds. Or rather Rex answered them. He had become restless again, and was straining against his mistress's hand on his collar. Suddenly his restlessness changed to violent excitement; he broke away; and was off along the top of the cliff like a flash. What he was after became clear in a moment. About a hundred yards away a ragged fellow with a largish bundle on a stick was walking briskly towards Sheercliff. He might have been a tramp who had paused on the outskirts of the little crowd to see what had happened, and who was now going on his way.

'Rex was up with him like lightning. For an instant I thought he was going to fly at the fellow's throat. But all he did was to leap up at him in mere joy and affection. And the fellow pushed him off with a quick thrust . . .

'I'd have recognized that gesture anywhere, and I put on a turn of speed that wouldn't have disgraced Rex himself. As I came up on him the fellow turned and faced me. He was dark and clean-shaven – for a tramp, quite absurdly clean-shaven. Our eyes met, and he knew that I *knew*. Horror and despair flooded his face. Then he took the simplest course open to him. He turned, ran, and jumped. This time I didn't see the body fall. But the result could be in no doubt. Robert Lorio had gone to join his victim. Monica Lorio had not the same courage. She was hanged.'

'I think,' said the philosopher, 'that you said there was no mystification in this story?'

'There wasn't very much. Robert and Monica Lorio were devoted to each other – and in penury. Their only possible resource was a very substantial insurance policy on Robert Lorio's life. That was the position when one day a tramp turned up at Mrs Lorio's back door. He was about her husband's build, dark, and of very low intelligence. He was also, as it turned out, open to suggestion – criminal suggestion.

'Her plan must have come to her instantaneously. She housed him in the barn, pretending to conceal his presence from her husband. She admitted him as a lover. Hence the occasion upon which I awakened that afternoon by the sea. And hence, too, the malignity of her glance at him earlier that day, when I had taken him for her husband. She didn't much like what she had been subdued to.

'By that time he was already groomed for his part – wearing Lorio's beard, wearing Lorio's old clothes. You can see what she had persuaded him would happen. They would lurk together in a little cave below the brow of the cliff when Lorio was taking one of his regular walks; they would use Rex as a decoy to lure him down; they would pitch him over the precipice and that would be an end of him. She was very well able to persuade her miserable accomplice, no doubt, that if the body was ever discovered it would be unrecognizable. And meanwhile there would simply be a new Robert Lorio.

'So from the tramp's point of view, you see, it really was a special sort of respectability murder that was going forward. But in actual fact it was nothing of the sort. It was a mercenary murder. And the wretched man was cast for the role not of accomplice but of victim.

The Lorios' plan was complex – but it was feasible. There was to be an observer; and nothing less than a rising young officer from Scotland Yard! The veritable Robert Lorio was to go to the rescue of his dog, disappear for a moment, and then *seem* to fall to his death. But really it was to be the tramp – whose body would almost certainly be recovered some days afterwards and identified as Lorio's. Meanwhile Lorio in the cave was to shave and change, and he and his wife were severally to slip quietly back to ground level. And while she distracted attention by making a scene, he was simply to clear out. When she had collected the insurance money they would have joined up again in Canada.

'Well, it nearly worked. From the moment that Lorio began looking nervously at his watch the timing of the thing was perfect. So was whatever scheme they had down there for instantaneously turning the tables on their miserable dupe – getting him off-balance and over the edge. One can't be very sorry for *him*. His death was decidedly a case of the would-be biter being bit. But the last bite, so to speak, was Rex's. He betrayed the whole thing when it appeared to be all over except the shouting.'

Appleby paused. 'The memory of those two deaths is horrible to me still. But not, in retrospect, so horrible as waking up that afternoon and hearing the murmuring voices of Monica Lorio and the man she was preparing to murder.'

A Derby Horse

'Such curious names,' Mrs Mutter murmured, and let an eye travel vaguely down her card. 'Gay Time and Postman's Path and Summer Rain. Often *witty*, of course – one sees that when one looks at the names of the dear creatures' fathers and mothers – but inadequately *equine*, if you understand me.'

'Nonsense, m'dear.' Mrs Mutter's husband had tipped back his chair the better to scan through his binoculars the vast carpet of humanity covering the downs. 'You couldn't call a likely colt Dobbin, or a well-bred filly Dapple or Daisy . . . But what a tremendous turn-out there is. Biggest crowd, if you ask me, since 'forty-six – Airborne's race.'

'And the time's creeping on, and the excitement's creeping up.' Lady Appleby had glanced at her watch.

'Anxious about your husband – eh?' Mr Mutter shook his head. 'Exacting, being high up in the police. Hope he hasn't been detained by somebody's pinching the favourite. Or perhaps –'

'Nothing of the sort.' A new voice was heard – that of Sir John Appleby himself as he strolled up to join his party. 'But I did not long ago have to do with a Derby horse that went rather badly missing. Have you ever known, Mutter, a strong colt, closely knit and with the quarters of a sprinter, disappear into thin air? Disconcerting experience.'

'But no doubt instructive.' Mutter dropped his binoculars. 'And you've no doubt just got time to tell us about it.'

Appleby sat down. 'It began with a frantic telephone-call from a certain Major Gunton, who trains near Blandford. Pantomime had vanished.'

Mrs Mutter made one of her well-known charming gestures.

'What did I say? Such *curious* names. Who could take seriously a horse called that?'

'Gunton did, and so did the brute's owner. They had entered Pantomime for this very Derby.'

'Hasn't that to be done very young?' Mrs Mutter was eager for knowledge. 'Like Eton boys, and that sort of thing?'

Mutter groaned. 'As yearlings, m'dear. Appleby, go on.'

'Pantomime was being sent from Blandford to Newbury. The journey, which was to be made by road —'

'It would be in one of those horrid little boxes.' Mrs Mutter was expressive. 'Almost like *coffins*, supposing horses to *have* coffins. The poor things can't so much as turn round.'

'It wouldn't be to their advantage to do so.' Appleby took the point seriously. 'Bumpy, you know. But the box was certainly, what you describe — a simple, open affair, hitched to the back of an estate-wagon. Gunton had a reliable man called Merry, who saw to getting Pantomime into the thing at about dusk one fine autumn evening. Gunton himself came out and saw that the creature was safely locked in; and then Merry and a stable-lad got into the wagon and drove off. Short of a road accident, Pantomime seemed as safe as houses. And until Salisbury, if Merry could be believed, he *was* safe. After that, it grew dark. And in the dark — again if Merry could be believed — some mysterious violation of the very laws of nature took place. In other words, when the box arrived at Newbury, Pantomime had disappeared.'

Mutter raised his eyebrows. 'Lock tampered with?'

'No. And they hadn't had to pull up during the whole journey.'

'Then Pantomime must have *jumped*.' Mrs Mutter was horrified.

Appleby shook his head. 'Quite impossible. Those boxes give a horse no room for tricks. There seemed only one conceivable explanation: that some Brobdingnagian bird had descended on poor little Pantomime and carried him off in his beak.

'I was working on a case in Oxford when I got the message

asking me to take over this queer affair. There wasn't much more information forthcoming than what I've given you, but of course there was a description of the horse; a chestnut with black spots on the hind quarters – like Eclipse and Pantaloon, I was told by a man at the Yard who specializes in the Stud-Book. With this I set out very early on the morning following the disappearance, intending to drive straight to Blandford, and from there retrace Pantomime's last journey if it should be necessary.

'I had got to Newbury, and was wondering whether Andover would be a good place to stop for breakfast, when I ran into fog. It seemed best to press on – and I must confess that probably I pressed on pretty fast. Still, policemen do well always to drive with a bit of extra care; and I was doing nothing that any normal contingency could render dangerous. Nevertheless, I had an accident. At one moment I had been staring into empty air – or fog. The next, there was a solid object plumb in front of my bonnet, and this was followed by a slight but ominous impact before I brought the car to a stop. For a second I wondered whether I'd fallen asleep at the wheel. For what I had *seen* in that moment decidedly suggested a dream. It had been a substantial chestnut mass, diversified with black spots.

'I climbed out and ran back. There, sure enough – and with all the appearance of having been hurled violently into a high hedge – I glimpsed the figure of a chestnut colt. But it was only for a moment; the wretched fog was getting worse, with drifting patches as thick as a horse-blanket. Pantomime was obscured for a couple of seconds – and when the place cleared again he had vanished.

'That was all to the good, since it meant he could scarcely have broken any bones. The road was empty, so I concluded he had forced his way through the hedge. I followed suit – it wasn't a comfortable dive – and there he was. But by *there* I mean a quarter of a mile off. He seemed to have done that in about twenty seconds.'

Mutter chuckled. 'A Derby horse, decidedly. Mahmoud's record for the twelve furlongs –'

'Quite so. Well, off I went in pursuit – and presently the dream

had turned to nightmare. It's an odd bit of country – open, un-
dulating, and covered with scattered patches of gorse which
seem to have been blown into all sorts of fantastic shapes by the
wind. What with the fog thrown in, it was easy to feel oneself
hunting the hapless Pantomime amid a sort of menagerie of
prehistoric monsters. And Pantomime was – well, illusive. For
one thing, he had more than flat-racing in him. At one moment
I even had a confused notion that he had cleared a hay-stack.
And this was the more surprising, since he did now appear to
have injured himself. I was getting no more than peeps at him,
but his gait was certainly queer. And if horses get concussion –
well, Pantomime was badly concussed.

The end came quickly. Somewhere near by there was a chap
out with a shot-gun after rabbits – a silly employment in those
conditions – and he was coming near enough to worry me. Suddenly I rounded a clump of gorse and came upon Pantomime
apparently cornered and at bay. I had just time to feel that there
was something pretty weirdly wrong when the creature rose in
the air like a tiger and came sailing down at me. At the same
instant I heard a patter of shot at my feet – it was the silly ass
with the gun blazing away at goodness knows what – and Pantomime just faded out. I found myself looking down, not at a
horse, but at the punctured and deflated remains of a highly
ingenious balloon.

'Not Pantomime but Pegasus.' Mrs Mutter offered this unexpected piece of classical learning with a brilliant smile.

'Quite so. The thieves' object, of course, had been to gain time.
They managed to substitute their extraordinary contrivance for
the real Pantomime just before Gunton came out in the dusk,
locked the horse-box, and told Merry to drive off. The thing was
tethered by no more than a nicely-calculated fraying cord, so
that eventually it freed itself and simply soared up into the
night. Probably it was designed that it should blow out to sea.
Poor Merry and his lad were going to look very like the guilty
parties – and while the trail was thus hopelessly confused at the
start, the real Pantomime could be smuggled abroad.'

'And it was!'

'Certainly. The colt was discovered some months later in France. I believe there may be a good deal of litigation.'

Mutter, who had for some minutes been engaged in applying the friction of a silk handkerchief to his top-hat, paused from this important labour. 'Haven't you told us rather a *tall* story?'

Appleby nodded. 'I'm assured the false Pantomime may have gone up to something like twenty thousand feet. So I suppose it *is* tall.'

'Perhaps you could say something about Pantomime's pedigree?'

This time it was Lady Appleby who spoke. 'By Airborne, without a doubt,' she said. 'And from Chimera.'

'Chimera? I don't believe there was ever any such –'

'No more do I.'

William the Conqueror

'Judith,' Appleby said, 'is fond of theatre people. She even continues to be fond of them when they take to films. That is how we came to be at the Bullions' house-party.'

'But of course!' Mrs Crisparkle glowed. 'Lady Appleby is so at home in the larger world of art.'

'Perhaps the Bullions' was that. Their concern at that time was certainly with art on the large scale. The film people, it seems, have gone back to enormities. Vast crowds and illimitable vistas are the things to plug on the screen if you want to keep television in its place. And the real trump card is a pitched battle, preferably with a great deal of cavalry, and chain-mail, and improbable-looking tents.'

'I know those tented fields.' Mrs Crisparkle nodded brightly. 'Like a counter covered with lamp-shades in an art-and-crafty shop.'

'Quite so. Well, the Bullions were to be starred in a tremendous film called *William the Conqueror*. And one of its highlights, needless to say, was the Battle of Hastings.'

'Ten-sixty-six.' The fine certainty of Mrs Crisparkle's expression gave way to misgiving. 'But were there cavalry at Hastings?'

'I've no idea. But there were no end of archers, and in the film their arrows were going to darken the heavens. That's why archery was all the go at the Bullions during that fatal week-end.'

Mrs Crisparkle was sympathetic. 'Those fatal week-ends! My dear Sir John, how well I know them.'

But Appleby shook his head. 'This,' he said gravely, 'was a *fatal* week-end. It led to murder.

'I doubt whether Mark Bullion or any of his guests was actually going to draw a long-bow in the film. Most of them must have been booked for nobler roles – dashing about on horseback, chiefly, and encouraging their vassals with heroic cries. Nevertheless, everybody was fooling about with bows and arrows at some improvised butts. And that went for the women too. Claire Bullion, as a matter of fact, was uncommonly good – the best even of the scattering of people with whom archery was a regular sport. She spent most of Saturday instructing a handsome chap called Giles Barcroft. You may recall his name. He had left the London stage for Hollywood about five years before, and now he was back in this country with a considerable reputation. He was even to play a big part – one of King Harold's principal nobles, torn between loyalty and his reawakened love for a great Norman lady.'

Mrs Crisparkle nodded intelligently. 'The Norman lady being played by Claire Bullion?'

'Precisely. And now I must tell you about the Sunday evening. The Bullions had rather a grand house, which I suppose they had rented – furniture, servants, and all – from some impoverished peer. Half-a-dozen of us were drinking cocktails on a terrace before the west front. Beneath us was a long, narrow sunken garden in what used to be called the Dutch taste, and immediately beyond that was the park – of which, however, we could see no more than a line of rising ground, parallel to our terrace and rather higher, with two magnificent oaks at either end of it. Beyond, there was simply the sunset sky.'

'It sounds rather impressive, Sir John. I get the suggestion of a natural theatre.'

'That describes it very well.' Appleby glanced at Mrs Crisparkle with approval. 'We might have been an audience looking across the orchestra-pit of that sunken garden and through the great proscenium-arch constituted by those tremendous oaks. What we were viewing was an empty stage, closed by the vast luminous backcloth of the evening sky.

'What was in fact concealed from us by the line of rising ground that formed our immediate horizon, was that part of the park in which the archery mostly went on. I could hear a couple of my fellow-guests rather maliciously discussing what *else* might be going on there at the moment. "They were fooling round together all yesterday." "True enough. But it's my guess they've had a glorious row." "So what, my dear fellow? Before Giles went to the Coast they were always having rows, but everybody knew that that was just by the way." "I can't make out what Mark thinks about it – can you? Have another of the poor old chap's drinks?"

'All this wasn't exactly obscure – and decidedly it wasn't edifying. The people concerned were talking the more freely because Bullion was securely out of hearing – down in the sunken garden in front of us, in fact, playing the lord of the manor and showing off his roses to some enraptured old woman.

'So much for the setting. In another moment, the thing happened.

'Barcroft's head and shoulders appeared silhouetted on that horizon – plumb centre, you might say, of that natural stage. He had the motions of a man scrambling up a bank – and indeed the ground did, as I knew, fall away sharply on the other side. Then he was on the ridge, and suddenly raising an arm. I believe we all supposed that he was going to wave to us. But he was raising both arms – flinging them above his head – and at the same moment his knees collapsed under him. With a horrible cry – I can hear it with an effort of terror yet, and I've heard some nasty noises in my time – with a single horrible cry, Giles Barcroft stumbled backwards and disappeared.

'We were all stunned – and the next sound was Bullion's voice calling out hoarsely in the garden. But it wasn't Barcroft's name that rang from him. It was his wife's.

'I believe I jumped pretty smartly from that terrace, and I wasn't much behind Bullion himself in scrambling up that incline and down on the other side. He was kneeling by Barcroft, who lay on his face, rolled over and over in dust. "Giles", he was calling out, "Giles – my God, what's happened?" And then he started back – as well he might. Barcroft was transfixed by an arrow, dead between the shoulder-blades. The feathered shaft had a glint of sunlight on it, and was quivering as if from some last pulsation of the body of the dying man.'

Mrs Crisparkle drew a long breath. 'That glint of sunlight. It's all terribly good theatre still.'

Appleby nodded soberly. 'Certainly a veritable *coup de théâtre* succeeded at once. Claire Bullion appeared in the background – horrified, scared, and carrying a bow. Her husband took one look, jumped to his feet, and in a high, cracked voice denounced her as a murderous fiend. But that wasn't all. In the silence that followed, Giles Barcroft spoke. It was no more than two whispered words, but they were perfectly clear. "I ... win," he enunciated. Within five seconds he was dead.'

'How very bewildering.' Mrs Crisparkle was round-eyed. 'Sir John – whatever did you do?'

Appleby smiled grimly. 'I grabbed Bullion.'

'It had indeed been a natural theatre, and we had been decidedly invited to watch a play. What Barcroft had won was, of course, a bet – a bet that, returning from his archery, he would put over that death-agony convincingly, and hold the illusion until the entire house-party was weeping round the supposed corpse – that sort of thing. And Bullion had carefully planted himself down there in the garden, thereby giving himself a start that would take him over that bank seconds before anyone else – a sufficient number of seconds to drive that waiting arrow straight to the heart of his play-acting friend. It was a pretty plan for disposing of his wife's lover – and his wife, as you will have seen, was to have come in for a spot of trouble too.'

'I see – I see!' Mrs Crisparkle's eyes were now saucers. 'But how did you *know*?'

'Barcroft had done his turn whole-heartedly – rolling, as I have told you, over and over in the dust. But the arrow that was supposed to have occasioned this, was sticking straight out of the body, with its very feathering unruffled. It was a bad slip on Mark Bullion's part. May I get you a drink?'

And Mrs Crisparkle nodded. 'Yes,' she said rather faintly. 'I think you may.'

Dead Man's Shoes

Catching the eight-five had meant an early start for Derry Fisher. A young man adept at combining pleasure with business, he had fallen in with some jolly people in the seaside town to which his occasions had briefly taken him, and on his last night he had been dancing into the small hours. As a result of this he was almost asleep now – and consequently at a slight disadvantage when the panting and wide-eyed girl tumbled into his compartment. This was a pity. It was something that had never happened to him before.

'Please ... I'm so sorry ... I only –' The girl, who seemed of about Derry's own age, was very pretty and very frightened. 'A man –' Again speech failed her, and she swayed hazardously on her feet. 'You see, I was alone, and –'

By this time Derry had collected himself and stood up. 'I'm afraid you've been upset,' he said. 'Sit down and take it easy. Nothing more can happen now.'

The girl sat down – but not without a glance around the compartment. Derry guessed that she badly felt the need of some person of her own sex. 'Thank you,' she said.

This time she had tried to smile as she spoke. But her eyes remained scared. It suddenly occurred to Derry that part of the nastiness of what had presumably happened must be in its anonymous quality. 'My name is Derry Fisher,' he said. 'I work for an estate agent in London, and I've been down to Sheercliff on a job. I caught this train so as to be back in the office after lunch.'

Whether or not the girl took in this prosaic information Derry was unable to tell. Certainly she did not, as he had hoped, do anything to supply her own biography. Instead, she produced a handkerchief and blew her nose. Then she asked a question in a voice still barely under control. 'I suppose I must look an utter fool?'

Derry resisted the temptation to say that, on the contrary, she looked quite beautiful. It mightn't, in the circumstances, be in terribly good taste. So he contented himself with shaking his head. 'Not a bit,' he said. 'And I wish I could help in any way. Did you have any luggage in the compartment you had to leave? If you did, may I fetch it for you?'

'Thank you very much.' The girl appeared steadied by this unexciting proposal. 'I have a green suit-case, and the compartment is the last one in this coach. But first I should tell you about ... about the man.'

Derry doubted it. He knew that, unless the man had been so tiresome he ought to be arrested, it would be wise that no more should be said. The girl could tell her mother or her best friend later in the day. She would only regret blurting things out to a strange young man. 'Look here,' he said, 'I wouldn't bother about the chap any more – not unless you feel it's only fair to other people to bring in the police at Waterloo. In that case, I'll see the guard. But at the moment, I'll fetch the suit-case. And you can think it over.'

'I don't think you understand.'

Derry paused, his hand already on the door to the corridor. 'I beg your pardon?'

'Please stop – please listen.' The girl gave a sharp laugh that came out unexpectedly and rather uncomfortably. 'I see I've been even more of a fool than I thought. You've got the ... the wrong impression. The man didn't –' Suddenly she buried her face in her hands and spoke savagely from behind them. 'It was nothing. I imagined it. I must be hysterical.'

Derry, who had sat down again, kept quiet. He knew that women do sometimes get round to imagining things. This girl didn't seem at all like that. But no doubt it was a trouble that sometimes took hold of quite unexpected people.

'I mean that I imagined its *importance*. I certainly didn't imagine the *thing*. Nobody could have a ... a hallucination of that sort.' As if nerving herself, the girl put her hands down and looked straight at Derry. '*Could* they?'

It was Derry who laughed this time – although he could scarcely have told why. 'Look here,' he said. 'I think I *have* misunderstood. What was it?'

'It was his shoes.' For a moment the girl's glance was almost helpless, as if she was aware of the absurd anti-climax that this odd statement must produce. 'It was something about his shoes.'

The engine shrieked, and the express plunged into a tunnel. In the wan electric light which had replaced the early summer sunshine, Derry stared at the girl blankly. 'You mean – this isn't about anything that . . . *happened*?'

'No – or yes and no.' For a moment the girl appeared to struggle for words. Then she squared herself where she sat. 'May I tell you the whole thing?'

'Please do – I'm awfully curious.' Derry spoke sincerely. The story, whatever it might be, was not going to be an awkward chronicle of attempted impropriety. 'You did say *shoes*?'

'Yes. A brown shoe and a black one.'

The train had returned to daylight. This did not prevent Derry Fisher from a sensation of considerable darkness. 'You mean that this man –'

'Yes. He was wearing one brown shoe and one black . . . how incredibly trivial it sounds.'

'I don't know. It's not a thing one ever sees.'

'Exactly!' The girl looked gratefully at Derry. 'And when you see it, it gives you a shock. But the real shock was when *he* saw that *I* saw it. You see?'

Derry smiled. 'Not really. Hadn't you better start at the beginning?'

'The beginning was at Sheercliff. I thought I'd only just catch the train myself, but this man cut it even finer than I did. He tumbled in just as we moved off. With any sort of baggage, he couldn't have managed it. But he has nothing but a brief-case.'

'Is he tidily dressed apart from this business of the shoes?'

The girl considered. 'He certainly isn't noticeably untidy. But what chiefly strikes me about his clothes is that they look tremendously expensive. He's in the sort of tweeds that you could tell a mile off, and that must be terribly good if they're not to be ghastly.'

'Is he a loud sort of person himself?'

'Not a bit. He's middle-aged and intellectual looking, and quite clearly one of nature's First Class passengers. I think he jumped into a Third in a hurry and hasn't bothered to change. He simply put his brief-case down beside him – there were only the two of us in the compartment – and disappeared behind *The Times*. I had a book, and I didn't do much more than take a glance at him. It wasn't perhaps for half an hour that I noticed the shoes. They gave me a jar, as I've said. And although I went on reading, the queerness of it stuck in my head. So presently I had another look, just to make sure I hadn't been mistaken. And as I looked, *he* looked. That is to say, he happened to glance over *The Times*, saw the direction of my eyes, and followed it. What he discovered was a terrific shock to him. His legs jerked as if he'd been stung, and his feet made a futile effort to disappear beneath the seat. I looked up in surprise, and just caught a glimpse of his face before he raised *The Times* again. He had gone a horrible grey, as if he was going to be sick. It made me feel a bit sick myself. And matters didn't improve when he turned chatty.'

'But not, surely, about the shoes?'

'Yes, about the shoes. He put down his paper and apologized for them – just as if the compartment was ... was my drawing-room and he felt that he had come into it too casually dressed.'

'He made a kind of joke about it?'

'That was what he seemed to intend. But he was very nervous. He was smoking those yellow cigarettes – aren't they called Russian? – and he kept stubbing out one and lighting another. He asked me if the shoes made him look like an absent-minded professor.'

'And what did you say to that?' Derry guessed that it was doing the girl good to talk about her queer encounter. And it sounded merely eccentric rather than sinister. Presently she ought to be able to see it as that.

'I said it didn't. I said it didn't, somehow, look a thing of which absent-mindedness would be the explanation. I said it *ought* to; that it was the sort of thing one might make an absent-minded person do in a story; but that when one actually *saw* it, that just didn't seem to fit.'

Derry Fisher smiled. 'You gave him quite good value for his money. It was what might be called a considered reply.'

'Perhaps. But he didn't like it.' To Derry's surprise the girl's agitation was growing again. 'I suppose I was tactless to do more than murmur vaguely. He stubbed out another cigarette, and I felt a queer tension suddenly established between us. It was a horrid sensation. And what he said next didn't at all ease it. He said I was quite right, and that he wasn't at all absent-minded. He was colour-blind.'

Derry was puzzled. 'That's certainly a bit odd. But I don't see –'

'I happened to know that it was almost certainly nonsense.'

This time the girl sounded slightly impatient; and Derry decided, quite without resentment, that she was cleverer than he was. 'I'm not absolutely certain that colour-blindness of that sort doesn't exist. But I know that anything other than the ordinary red-green kind is excessively rare. So this was a very tall story. And, of course, I had another reason for disbelieving him. Wouldn't you agree?'

Derry stared. 'I'm afraid I don't at all know.'

'If this man *is* unable to distinguish between black and brown, he couldn't possibly have received such a shock the moment his glance fell on his shoes. Don't you see?'

'Yes – of course.' Derry felt rather foolish. 'And what happened then?'

'This time I didn't say anything. I felt, for some reason, really frightened. And I was even more frightened when I detected him cautiously trying the handle of the door.'

'The door to the corridor?'

'No. The door on the other side.'

Derry Fisher, although not brilliant, had a quick instinct for the moment at which action was desirable. 'Look here,' he said, 'it's about time I had a look.' And with a reassuring glance at his companion, he rose and stepped into the corridor.

They were moving at speed, and had been doing so steadily since some time before the beginning of his encounter with the frightened girl. He walked up the train in the direction she had indicated, glancing into each compartment as he passed. In one there was a group of young airmen, mostly asleep; in another a solitary lady of severe appearance seemed to be correcting examination papers; in a third an elderly clergyman and his wife were placidly chatting. Derry came to the last compartment and saw at a glance that it was empty.

Conscious of being both disappointed and relieved, he stepped inside. The girl's green suit-case was on the rack. On the opposite seat lay an unfolded copy of *The Times*. There were two or three yellow cigarette-butts on the floor. The window was up.

Derry felt obscurely prompted to make as little physical impact upon the compartment as might be. He picked up the suit-case and went out, shutting the corridor door behind him. The girl was sitting where he had left her, and he set the suit-case down beside her. 'He's gone,' he said.

'Gone! You don't think –'

'It's very unlikely that anything nasty has happened.' Derry was reassuring. 'The window is closed, and he couldn't have chucked himself out without opening the door. In that case, it would be open still. Nobody clinging to the side of the train could get it shut again, even if he wanted to. Your tiresome friend has just made off to another carriage. It's the end of him – but quite harmlessly.'

'He could only have gone in the other direction, or we'd have seen him.'

'That's perfectly true. But he naturally would go off in the opposite direction to yourself. And the greater length of the train lies that way. It's more crowded, too, at that end. He realizes that he's made an ass of himself, and he's decided to submerge himself in the crush.'

The girl nodded. 'I suppose you're right. But I haven't really told you why I bolted.' She hesitated. 'It's too fantastic – too silly. I didn't think he had any notion of killing himself. I rather thought he was meaning to kill *me*.' The girl laughed – and it was her unsteady laugh again. 'Isn't it a disgusting piece of hysteria? It must mean that my unconscious mind just won't bear looking into.'

'Rubbish.' Derry felt it incumbent upon him to speak with some sternness. 'This chap is a thoroughly queer fish. It was perfectly reasonable to feel that he might be quite irresponsible. You say he actually began fiddling with the door-handle?'

'Yes. And I really thought that he was thinking out what you might call two . . . two co-ordinated movements. Getting the door open and pitching me through it. And when I did get up and leave, I felt that it was a terrific crisis for him. I sensed that he was all coiled up to hurl himself at me – and that he decided in the last fraction of a second that it wouldn't do.' The girl stood up. 'But this is all too idiotic. And at least I already see it as that – thank goodness.' She smiled rather wanly at Derry. 'I shall go along and try the effect of a cup of coffee.'

'May I come too?'

'I'd rather you didn't. But you've already been terribly kind. You've helped me to pull myself together. It's just that I feel I can finish the job better alone.'

Left in solitude, Derry Fisher reflected that he had learnt very little about the girl herself – nothing at all, indeed, except the disturbing episode in which she had found herself involved. Might he, when she returned, ask her for her name – or at least attempt a more general conversation? The probability was that he would never see her again; and this was a fact which he found himself facing with lively dissatisfaction. Her appearance in his compartment had been after a fashion to make the imagination expect some further succession of strange events, some romantic sequel.

But when the girl did return, her own manner was notably prosaic. Coffee and reflection seemed further to have persuaded her that she had already dramatized an insignificant circumstance too much. She remained grateful and talked politely. But Derry guessed that she felt awkward, and that at Waterloo she would be glad to say good-bye, both to him and to the whole incident. So he forebore to make any suggestion for the bettering of their acquaintance. Only when the train reached the terminus he insisted on accompanying her through the barrier and to the taxi-rank. The man who had scared her – the man with the black and brown shoes – must be somewhere in the crush; and if, as seemed likely, he was crazy, there was a possibility that he might bother her again. But they caught no sight of him.

The girl gave an address in Kensington and stepped into her cab. 'Thank you,' she said. 'Thank you so much.'

Derry took his dismissal with a smile – regretful, but with the feeling that he was doing the right thing. 'Good-bye,' he said. 'At least, you're safe and sound.'

Her eyes widened, and then laughed at him. 'Yes, indeed. He can't despatch me now.'

The cab moved off. Derry stepped forward to wave regardless of the traffic, was nearly bowled over by one of the next cabs out; inside it, he glimpsed a man's amused face as he skipped nimbly to safety. He had been in danger, he saw, of making an ass of himself over that girl. He hurried off to catch a bus.

Shortly after lunch Derry went in to see his uncle – at present his employer, and soon, he hoped, to be his partner. Derry sat on one corner of his uncle's desk – a privilege which made him feel slightly less juvenile and on the mat – and gave an account of himself. He described his few days at Sheercliff and his labours there on behalf of the firm.

His uncle listened with his customary mingling of scepticism and benevolent regard; and then proceeded to ask his customary series of mild but formidably searching questions. Eventually he moved to less austere ground. Had Derry got in any tennis? Had he found the usual agreeable persons to go dancing with? On these topics, too, Derry offered what were by now prescriptive replies, whereupon his uncle buried his nose in a file and gave a wave which Derry knew was to waft him from the room.

All this was traditional. But as he reached the door his uncle looked up again. 'By the way, my dear boy, I see you left Sheercliff just before the sensation there.'

'The sensation, Uncle?' Only vaguely interested, Derry saw his relative reach for a lunch-time newspaper.

'An unidentified body found on the rocks in mysterious circumstances – that sort of thing.'

'Oh.' Derry was not much impressed.

'And there was something rather unaccountable. Now, where did I see it?' Derry's uncle let his eye travel over the paper now spread out before him. 'Yes – here it is. The body was fully dressed. But it was wearing one black shoe and one brown ... My dear boy – are you ill? Too many late nights, if you ask me.'

2

At nine o'clock that morning – it was his usual hour – Superintendent Lort had come on duty at Sheercliff police station and found Captain Meritt waiting for him. The circumstance gave Lort very little pleasure. He was an elderly man, soon to retire; and he felt from the first that Meritt belonged to a world that had passed beyond him. Meritt was an ex-army officer, and so to be treated with decent respect. His job was that of bodyguard – there could be no other name for it – to a certain Sir Stephen Borlase, who had been staying for some weeks at the Metropole Hotel. It was not apparent to Lort why Borlase should require other protection than that provided by the regular police. Meritt, it appeared, was paid by the great industrial concern whose principal research chemist Borlase was. But it was an important Ministry that had yanked Meritt out of one of the regular Security Services and seconded him to the job. Borlase's research, it seemed, was very much a work of national importance. And so there was this irregular arrangement. This *most* irregular arrangement, Lort said to himself now – and greeted his visitor with a discouraging glare.

'Borlase has vanished.' Meritt blurted out the words and sat down uninvited. He looked like a man whose whole career is in the melting-pot. Probably it was.

'Vanished, sir? Since when?'

'Well, since last night – or rather early this morning. I saw him then. But now he's gone. His bed hasn't been slept in.'

'Do I understand, Captain Meritt, that it is part of your – um employment to visit Sir Stephen Borlase's bedroom before nine a.m., and at once to communicate with the police if he isn't found there?'

'Of course not, man. The point is that he hasn't *slept* there. And that needs inquiring into at once.'

'But surely, sir, such an inquiry is precisely what you are – er – paid for?'

'Certainly. But I naturally expect the help of the police.' Meritt was plainly angry. 'Borlase is a damned important man. He is working now on the devil knows what.'

'That probably describes it very well.' And Lort smiled grimly. 'But are we to raise an alarm because this gentleman fails to sleep in his hotel? I know nothing of his habits. But the fact that he has been provided with a somewhat peculiar – um – companion in yourself, suggests to me that he may not be without a few quiet eccentricities.'

'He's a brilliant and rather unstable man.'

'I see. But this is not information that has been given us here in our humdrum course of duty. Do I understand it to be thought possible that Sir Stephen may bolt?'

Meritt visibly hesitated. 'That's not for me to say. I am instructed merely to be on guard on his behalf. And *you*, Superintendent, if I am not mistaken, have been instructed to give me any help you can.'

'I have been instructed, sir, to recognize your function and to co-operate. Very well. What, in more detail, is the position. And what do you propose should be done?'

'Part of the position, Superintendent, I think you already know. Sir Stephen is here as a convalescent, but in point of fact he can't be kept from working all the time. Apparently his stuff is so theoretical and generally rarified that he can do it all in his head, so all he needs to have about him is a file or two and a few notebooks. He has been pottering about the beach and the cliffs during the day, as his doctors have no doubt told him to do. And then, as often as not, he has been working late into the night. It has made my job the deuce of a bore.'

'No doubt, sir.' Lort was unsympathetic. 'And last night?'

'He sat up until nearly one o'clock. I have a room from which I can see his windows; and it has become my habit not to go to bed myself until he seems safely tucked up. You can judge from that how this job has come to worry me. Well, out went his lights in the end, and I was just about to undress when I heard him open the outer door of his suite. He went downstairs. It seemed to me I'd better follow; and when I reached the hall, there he was giving a nod to the night porter and walking out of the hotel. He hadn't changed for dinner, and in his tweeds he might have been a visitor leaving the place for good. He was merely bent, however, on a nocturnal stroll.'

'It was a pleasant night, no doubt.' Lort offered this comment impassively.

'Quite so. Sir Stephen's proceeding was no more than mildly eccentric. But if I'd let him wander off like that in the small hours, and if anything *had* happened, it would have been just too bad for both of us. So I took that stroll too – some fifty yards in the rear. He went straight through the town and took the short cliff path out to Merlin Head. It's an extremely impressive spot in full moonlight, with the sheer drop to the sea looking particularly awe-inspiring, I imagine. Of course there was nobody about. And as there is only one narrow path to the Head, I didn't follow him to the end of it. He doesn't like being dogged around.'

'I'm not surprised.' Lort was emphatic. 'I don't know what things are coming to that such antics should be considered necessary in a quiet place like this. But go on.'

'You will remember that there's a little shelter on the verge of the Head, with a bench from which you can command the whole sweep of the bay. Borlase disappeared into that, but didn't sit for long. Within ten minutes he was making his way back towards me – and at that I slipped out of sight and followed him discreetly back to the hotel. Perhaps I should mention having a feeling that there was something on his mind. His walk out to the Head had been direct and decisive. But on the way back he hesitated several times, as if doing a bit of wool-gathering. So I kept well in the background, and he had gone to his bedroom by the time I re-entered the hotel. I waited, as usual, until his lights were out, and then I turned in.'

'And now, you say, he has vanished?'

'Yes. I've got into the way of taking him along his letters in the morning. That is how I've discovered that he never went to bed at all.'

Lort frowned. 'But you say all the lights went out in his suite? Could there have been one still burning when you went to bed yourself – one that wouldn't be visible to you?'

'I think not.'

'And the night porter? Was he aware of Borlase's leaving again?'

'No. But he potters around a little, although not supposed to quit the hall. I doubt if it was difficult for Borlase to let himself out unobserved.' Meritt paused. 'And that, Superintendent, is the position now. What do you make of it?'

'I'm far from feeling obliged to make anything of it at all.' Lort allowed himself some tartness in this reply. 'Here is a man, devoted to abstruse scientific thought, who takes a reflective stroll at one o'clock in the morning. Moonlight doesn't help with whatever problem he's chewing over, so for a time he sits in the dark and tries that. Presently he wanders out again, and very probably walks till morning. Eventually he emerges from his abstraction, discovers himself to be uncommonly hungry, breakfasts at the first inn he sees, returns to Sheercliff at his leisure, and finds that the conscientious Captain Meritt has persuaded the police to start a manhunt.' And Lort favoured his visitor with a bleak smile. 'The truth may not be precisely that. But my guess is that I'm well within the target area.'

'I see.' Meritt had produced his watch and glanced at it. Now he put it away and turned a cold eye on the elderly and sardonic man before him. 'And you think mine a very queer job?'

'I do, sir – decidedly.'

'And so it is, Superintendent. But then Borlase, as it happens, is a very queer man. Just how queer, I think I must now take the responsibility of telling you.'

'I am very willing, sir, to hear anything that makes sense of your anxieties.'

'Very well – here goes.' Meritt paused as if to collect himself. 'Perhaps I can best begin by repeating what I have just said – but with a difference. The Borlases are a very queer couple of men.'

Lort stared. 'You mean there is a brother – something like that?'

'I mean nothing of the sort. I mean that Sir Stephen Borlase – the man stopping at the Metropole Hotel – is much more easily understood as two people than as one.'

Lort sat back in his chair. 'Jekyll and Hyde?'

'Or Hyde and Jekyll. That is undoubtedly the popular expression of the thing, and perhaps the best for laymen like you and me, Superintendent, to hang on to. Or possibly we might think of him as a sort of Hamlet – the man who couldn't make up his mind.'

'Frankly, sir, I don't find this easy to believe. I suppose Dr Jekyll may have been a man of some scientific attainment, but I can't see Hamlet as an eminent research chemist.'

'Perhaps not.' Meritt took a moment to estimate the cogency of this pronouncement. 'But the fact is that Borlase combines immense drive and concentration as a scientist with a highly unstable personality. Commonly his ideological convictions are very much those of any other man of his sort in our society. For the greater part of his days, that is to say, he is completely reliable. But every now and then he is subject to a fit of emotional and intellectual confusion, and from this there emerges for a short time what is virtually a different personality. It's an awkward thing in the days of the cold war, as you can see. Let certain folk effectively contact Borlase when he has swung over to this other polarity – this other set of values – and goodness knows what they might not get out of him. And now I think you can understand why I was given my job – and why I think the present situation genuinely alarming.'

'I still feel, sir, that I've a good deal to learn.' Lort was clearly preparing to plod doggedly round the queer story with which he had been presented. 'Am I to understand that Sir Stephen Borlase is fully aware of his own condition?'

'In a general way – yes. But he plays it down. When normal, he declines to admit that these periods of disturbance go, so to speak, at all deep. He won't treat himself as potentially a cot case. Nothing in the way of regular visits by the appropriate sort of medical man would be tolerated by him. So he has been persuaded that he is in the first flight of V.I.P.s – as indeed he pretty well is – and provided with –'

'– The new style of guardian angel represented by yourself.' Lort, having given his cautious antagonism this further airing, reached for a scribbling-pad as if to indicate that the matter had entered a new phase. Have you been given to understand that there does now exist against Borlase a specific threat? Are there, in fact, supposed to be persons aware of his condition and actively planning to exploit it?'

'It is thought very likely that there are – particularly a fellow called Krauss.'

'I see. And you have been told what signs to look for in Borlase himself?'

'He is said to go moody, restless, distraught – that sort of thing.'

Lort nodded. 'What about the last few days? Has he appeared all right?'

'The devil of it is, Superintendent, that he has always appeared a bit of a queer fish to me. I can't claim to have noticed any change in the last few days.'

'Then, Captain Meritt, it remains my guess that this is a false alarm. When did you leave the Metropole – half an hour ago? Likely enough, Borlase has returned in the interval. I'll call the place up and find out.'

Two telephones stood on Lort's desk – and now, as he was in the act of reaching for one, the second emitted a low but urgent purr. The Superintendent picked it up. 'Yes . . . Yes . . . Dead, you say? . . . *Where?*' Lort's glance, as he listened, fleetingly sought Meritt's face. 'The *tide*? If that was so, you did perfectly right . . . Unidentified? I hope he remains so . . . I said, I hope he remains so . . . Never mind why . . . Yes, of course – within ten minutes . . . Thank you.'

When Lort had snapped down the receiver, there was a moment's silence. Meritt had gone pale, and when he spoke it was with an odd striving for a casual note. 'Not, I suppose, anything to do with –?'

'Probably not.' Lort was on his feet. 'Still, you might care to come along, sir – just in case.'

'In case –?'

'In case it *is* the body of Sir Stephen Borlase that has just been found below Merlin Head.'

'Accident?'

The Superintendent reached for his cap. 'That's what we're going to find out.'

The sky was almost cloudless, the air filled with a mild warmth, the sea sparkling within its far-flung semicircle of gleaming cliffs. On the front and in the broad, tree-lined streets, visitors – at this early season mainly recruited from the superior classes of society – made their way to and from the baths, the Winter Gardens, the circulating libraries, or exercised well-bred dogs with due regard to the cleanliness and decorum which is so marked a feature of the Sheercliff scene. As he drove the agitated Captain Meritt through this pleasing pageant, Superintendent Lort discernibly let his spirits rise. But the effect of this was only to give a more sardonic turn to his speech. An accident, he pointed out, whether in the sea or on the cliffs, was an undesirable thing. The City Council deprecated accidents. Accidents were dissuasive; potential visitors read about them and decided to go elsewhere. But a crime was another matter. Many pious and law-abiding Sheercliff citizens would ask for nothing better than a really sensational crime. The present season, it was true, was somewhat early. Even a murder extensively featured in the national Press would have little effect upon Metropole or Grand or Majestic folk. But the August crowds – the true annual bearers of prosperity to the town – were another matter. A course of events culminating in the Central Criminal Court in about the third week of July, Superintendent Lort opined, might take threepence off the rates.

Captain Meritt showed no appreciation of this unexpected vein of pleasantry in his professional colleague. He sat silent during the drive. He remained silent in the small police-station which they entered at the end of it. Here a melancholy sergeant led them out to a shed at the back for the purpose, as he expressed it, of viewing the remains. This, however, was for some minutes delayed. With a due sense of climax, the sergeant chose to pause in the intervening yard and favour his superior with a fuller account of the case.

An elderly clergyman, early abroad in the interest of bird-watching, had been the first to peer over Merlin Head and see the body. It lay sprawled on an isolated outcrop of rock at the base of the cliff, and only by an unlikely chance had it not fallen directly into the sea. Had this happened, it would probably have disappeared – at least as an identifiable individual – for good. For the currents played strange tricks on this coast, and it was only after some weeks that the sea commonly rendered up its dead. On this the sergeant was disposed to be expansive. 'Nibbled, sir – that's how they often are. Some quite small fish, it seems, are uncommonly gross feeders. But come along.'

On this macabre note, the three men entered the shed. The body lay on a long table, covered with a sheet. The sergeant stepped forward and drew this back, so that the face was revealed.

'It's your man, all right.' Lort's voice was decently subdued.

'It's my man.' Meritt, very pale, glanced at the sergeant. 'Any certainty how it happened?'

'The back of the head's stove in. He might have been hit, and then thrown over the cliff. Or he might just have jumped and the damage been done by the rocks. The surgeon thinks they'll be able to tell just which, once they've gone into the body more particular.'

'I see.' Meritt moved closer to the body, gave a startled exclamation, and drew the sheet down farther. 'It's Sir Stephen Borlase, all right. But those aren't his clothes. At least, I never saw him in them.'

Lort frowned. 'He wasn't dressed like this when you followed him last night?'

'He wasn't in anything like this dark stuff at all. He was in country kit – a light tweed with rather a bold pattern.'

'Odd.' Lort turned to the sergeant. 'Anything on those clothes – a tailor's label with the owner's name, for instance?'

'Nothing of the sort, sir. I'd say they were ordinary, good-class, off-the-peg garments. But there's something queer about the shoes.'

'They don't fit?' Lort pounced on this.

'It's not that. It's *this*.' The sergeant, his sense of drama reasserting itself, whipped away the sheet altogether. 'Did you ever see a corpse in one black shoe and one brown?'

'Suicide,' Lort had driven halfway back through Sheercliff before he spoke. 'Suicide planned so that it could never be proved. Borlase was simply going to disappear. When you followed him last night – or rather early this morning – he was spying out the land. Or it might be better to say the cliff and the sea.'

'Look before you leap?' Meritt was moodily stuffing a pipe.

'Just that. And perhaps he didn't like what he saw. You told me that he walked up there briskly enough, but that his return to the Metropole was a bit irresolute. But he went through with the thing. Knowing that he had to give you the slip this time, he changed into those anonymous clothes in the dark – which is how he managed to land himself with different-coloured shoes.'

'That may be true,' Meritt was suddenly interested. 'And the shoes were, in fact, to give him away! It might be one of those queer tricks of the mind – and particularly of a mind like Borlase's. Part of him didn't want anonymity and extinction. So he made this unconsciously motivated mistake and betrayal. An instance of what Freud calls the psychopathology of everyday life.'

'No doubt.' Superintendent Lort did not appear to feel that his picture of the case was much strengthened by this speculation. 'Well, Borlase slipped out again later, and simply pitched himself over Merlin Head. He reckoned to go straight into the sea, and to be drawn out by the current. Later, we might or might not have got back an unrecognizable body in unidentifiable clothes. Of course, further investigation may prove me wrong. But I'd say it's a fair working supposition. Do you agree?'

Without interrupting the business of lighting his pipe, Captain Meritt shook his head. 'I don't see it. Borlase was an odd chap, or I wouldn't have been given my job. He might, I suppose, feel driven to take his own life. And he might feel the act as disgraceful – something to disguise. But why not disguise it as an accident? He had plenty of brains to work out something convincing in that way. Why should he try to make his death look like an unaccountable disappearance?'

'Might it be because he disliked you, sir?'

'What's that?' Meritt was startled.

'I mean, of course, disliked the way you'd been set on him. He resented having a gaoler disguised as a bodyguard – and quite right too, if you ask me.' Lort delivered himself of this sentiment with vigour. 'So he resolved to leave you in as awkward a situation as he could. Had he seemed just to clean vanish, you'd have been left looking decidedly a fool.'

'I see.' Meritt digested this view of the matter in silence for some seconds. And when at length he pronounced upon it, it was with unexpected urbanity. 'Well, Borlase is dead, poor devil – and it's a bad mark to me either way. I'll be quite content myself if your interpretation is accepted by the coroner.'

'But you doubt whether it will be?'

'I do.' And Meritt puffed at his pipe with a sombre frown. 'My guess is that there's more to come out, Superintendent. And probably with more bad marks attached. The country has lost Stephen Borlase. I have a nasty feeling it may have lost something else as well.'

3

Derry Fisher felt rather like the Bellman. 'What I tell you three times is true.' It was just that number of times that he had now told his story: first to his uncle, then at the local police-station, and now – rather to his awe – to Sir John Appleby, high up in this quiet room in New Scotland Yard. Appleby himself, Derry saw, must be pretty high up. He was, in fact, an Assistant Commissioner. Derry was already guessing that the queer situation in which he found himself involved was important as well as conventionally sensational. Appleby was not at all portentous. His idea of police investigation appeared to be friendly and at times mildly whimsical conversation. But Derry sensed that he was feeling pretty serious underneath.

'And you say you saw this girl into a taxi? But of course you did. Pretty or not, it was the natural and proper thing. And then you took the next taxi yourself?'

'No, sir.' Derry shook his head, genuinely amused. 'I found my natural level on top of a bus.'

'Quite so. Taxi queues at these big stations are often longer than bus queues, anyway. I suppose there *was* a queue – streams of taxis going out?'

'Yes, sir. Parts of our train had been pretty crowded. I had to wait a moment while several more taxis shot past. One of them nearly bowled me over.'

'Did you find yourself staring at people's shoes?'

Derry burst out laughing. 'As a matter of fact, I did. I keep on doing it now.'

'You do indeed. You had a look at mine the instant you entered this room.' And Appleby smiled genially at his embarrassed visitor. 'You'd make a detective, Mr Fisher, I don't doubt. And you tell your story very clearly.'

'To tell you the truth, sir, I'm very relieved to find it credited. It seems so uncommonly queer.'

'We get plenty of queer yarns in this place.' Appleby companionably held out a box of cigarettes. 'But of yours, as a matter of fact, we have a scrap of confirmation already.'

Derry Fisher sat up eagerly. 'You've heard from the girl.'

'Not yet – although we ought to today, if she ever looks at a newspaper or listens to the wireless. Unless, of course –' Appleby checked himself. 'What we've had is news of an angry traveller at Waterloo, complaining of theft from his suit-case while he was absent from his compartment.'

'Isn't that sort of thing fairly common.'

'Common enough. But this was on your train from Sheercliff this morning. And what was stolen was a pair of shoes – nothing else. I've no doubt that you see the likely significance of that. By the time you had got to Waterloo, there was certainly nobody on your train in the embarrassing position of wearing a discernibly odd pair of shoes. Only the dead body in Sheercliff was still doing this . . . By the way, have you any ideas about this?'

Derry, although startled, answered boldly. 'Yes, sir. At least, I see one way that it might have come about. The two men – this Sir Stephen Borlase who is dead and the man who was on the train – for some reason changed clothes rather hastily in the dark. And they muddled the shoes.'

Appleby nodded approvingly. 'That's very good. Borlase, as a matter of fact, has been found in clothes which, it seems, can't be positively identified as his. Correspondingly, the clothes which your girl described as worn by the fellow on the train sound uncommonly like those being worn by Borlase when he was last seen alive. He may, of course, have been dead when the exchange took place. Indeed, that would seem to be the likely way of it. I wonder, now, what it would be like, changing clothes with a dead man – say with a murdered man – in the dark.'

'I'm sure I'd muddle a good deal more than the shoes.' Derry Fisher's conviction was unfeigned. 'One would have to possess nerves of steel to do so ghastly a thing.'

'Either that or be in an uncommonly tight corner. You'd be surprised at the things that timid or even craven folk will brace themselves to when really up against it.' Appleby paused. 'But aren't we supposing a darkness that can't really have been there? Unless, of course, we can place the thing in a cave or cellar or shuttered room.'

'The moonlight.'

'Precisely. I asked about that during my last phone-call to Sheercliff half an hour ago. There can be no doubt that there was a full moon in an unclouded sky. I dare say you were aware of it yourself.'

'Yes, sir. As a matter of fact, I was dancing in it.'

'Then, there you are.' Appleby appeared much pleased. 'Are you fond of Rubens as a landscape painter.'

'Rubens?' Derry felt incapable of this abrupt transition to a polite cultural topic. 'I'm afraid I don't know much about him.'

'He has one or two great things done in full moonlight. Everything marvellously clear, you know, but at the same time largely drained of colour.' Appleby chuckled. 'If you knocked me out by the light of the moon, Mr Fisher, you could exchange clothes with me without the slightest difficulty. But you might very well go wrong over brown and black shoes. My guess is that they wouldn't be indistinguishable to a careful scrutiny, but that they would be the next thing to it ... And now I must really go across to Waterloo. I should be greatly obliged if you'd come along.'

'While you inquire – investigate?'

'Just that. You might be a great help to us.'

'I'll certainly come.' Derry stood up – and suddenly a new view of this invitation came to him. 'You don't mean to lose sight of me?'

'That is so.' For the first time, Appleby spoke with real gravity.

'You may as well know, Mr Fisher, that this affair may be very serious indeed. Nobody connected with it will be lost sight of until it is cleared up.'

'You make me wish I hadn't lost sight of the girl.'

'I wish you had not. We must face the fact that she is the only person who could identify the man on the train – the living man in the odd shoes.'

Slowly it dawned on Derry. 'And I –'

'You are the only person who could identify the girl. Supposing – well, that she was no longer in a position to speak up for herself.'

'You think she may be in danger.'

'I'd like to know who was in the next taxi or two after hers.'

It chanced that the morning's train for Sheercliff had been neither broken up nor cleaned through, and a clerk led them to it over what, to Derry, seemed miles and miles of sidings. It stood, forlorn, dusty, and dead, in the rather bleak late-afternoon sunshine. Once aboard, Derry had less difficulty than he had expected in identifying the compartment in which his adventure had begun. It looked very impersonal and uninteresting now. He felt suddenly depressed, and watched with growing scepticism the minutely careful search that Sir John Appleby made.

Whether after any success or not, Appleby eventually gave over. 'This fellow who complained of losing shoes,' he said. 'Where was he?'

The clerk consulted some papers. 'We have a note of that, sir. It was three carriages down, next to the restaurant-car. The passenger had gone to get himself an early lunch, leaving his suit-case on the seat of the empty compartment. When he got back, he found it open, with the contents tumbled about, and a pair of shoes missing. Of course he has no claim.'

'Except on our interest.' Appleby turned to Derry. 'Now, I wonder why our elusive friend didn't substitute his own troublesome footwear and close the case? That *would* have given the other fellow a bit of a shock in time. But perhaps it was no occasion for a display of humour.' Appleby spoke absently. His glance was still darting about the uncommunicative compartment, as if reluctant to give it best. Then he stepped into the corridor and moved up the train. 'A group of airmen,' he said, 'mostly asleep. A solitary lady. A clergyman and his wife. Is that right?'

Derry nodded. 'Quite right.'

'And then the compartment where your girl made her awkward observation. If you don't mind, I'll go into this one alone.' He did so, and moved about as if the whole place was made of egg-shell. Derry watched fascinated. His scepticism was entirely gone. To his own eye the compartment looked blank and meaningless. Yet it suddenly seemed impossible that to so intent and concentrated scrutiny it should not at once yield some clamant and decisive fact.

'You can still smell what she called the Russian cigarettes.' Appleby spoke over his shoulder. 'And here in the ash-tray are two or three of the yellow stubs you saw yourself. I at once produce pill-boxes and forceps. Also a pocket lens.' Derry glimpsed the railway clerk watching wide-eyed as Appleby actually performed these legendary operations. 'I sniff. This tobacco – my dear Watson – is manufactured only in Omsk. Or is it Tomsk? At any rate, I distinctly begin to see Red. Only Commissars are ever issued with this particular brand. The plot thickens. The vanished man has a slight cast in his left eye. A joint – one of the lower ones – is missing from his right fore-finger . . .' On this surprising rubbish Appleby's voice died away. Regardless of the two men waiting in the corridor, he painfully explored the confined space around him for a further fifteen minutes. When he emerged, he was wholly serious. And Derry Fisher thought that he saw something like far-reaching speculation in his eye.

'Those young airmen, Mr Fisher – you say they were asleep?'

'Not all of them.'

'And the clergyman and his wife?'

'Chatting and admiring the view.'

'On the far side?'

'No, the corridor side.'

'And the solitary lady?'

'She struck me as a headmistress, or something of that sort. She was working at papers.'

'Absorbed in them?'

'Well – not entirely. I think I remember her giving me rather a formidable glance as I went by. You think these people may have seen something important, sir?'

'They are a factor, undoubtedly.' Appleby was glancing at his watch. 'I must get back. The mystery of the rifled suit-case is something that we needn't pursue. What we want is your girl. And there ought to be word of her by now. What would be your guess about her when she saw all this in the papers? Is she the sort who might lose her head or panic and lie low?'

Derry shook his head. 'I'm sure she's not. She would see it was her duty to come forward, and she'd do so.'

'Kensington, you said – and you absolutely didn't hear any more?' Appleby had dropped to the line, and they were now tramping through a wilderness of deserted rolling-stock. 'And you gleaned absolutely nothing about her connections – profession, reason for having been in Sheercliff, and so on?'

'I'm afraid I didn't.' Derry hesitated. 'It wasn't because I didn't want to. But she'd had this shock, and it would have seemed impertinent –'

'Quite so.' Appleby was curtly approving. 'But I wish we had just the beginning of a line on her, all the same.'

Derry Fisher for some reason felt his heart sink. 'You really do think, sir, that she may be in danger?'

'Certainly she is in danger. We must find her just as soon as we can.'

Back in his room half an hour later, and with Derry still in tow, Appleby was making a trunk-call.

'Stephen Borlase?' The cultivated voice from Cambridge wasted no time. 'Yes, certainly. I have no doubt that I count as one of his oldest friends. The news has saddened me very much. A wonderful brain, and on the verge of great things ... Mentally unbalanced? My dear sir, we all are – except conceivably at Scotland Yard. I know they were worried about Stephen, but if I were you I'd take it with a pinch of salt. He was not nearly so mad as Mark is, if you ask me?'

'Mark?'

'Mark Borlase – Stephen's cousin. Haven't you contacted him?' The voice from Camridge seemed surprised. 'Mark is certainly next of kin ... Address? I know only that he lives in a windmill. From time to time I should imagine that he goes out and tilts at it ... Precisely – an eccentric. He goes in for un-worldliness and absence of mind ... The same interests as Stephen? Dear me, no. Mark is literary – wrote a little book on Pushkin, and is a bit of an authority on Russian literature in general. An interesting but ineffective type.'

'Thank you very much.' Appleby was scribbling on a desk-pad. 'Just one more thing. I wonder if you can tell me anything sig-nificant about Sir Stephen's methods of work?'

'Yes.' The voice from Cambridge took on extra precision. 'It happened in his head, and went straight into a small notebook which he kept in an inner pocket. That – and perhaps a few loose papers lying rather too carelessly about – was nowadays pretty well his whole stock-in-trade. I hope that notebook's safe.'

'So do I. Sir Stephen had a bodyguard who ought to have kept an eye on all that. I expect to contact him at any time. You'd say that the notebook may be very important indeed?'

'My God!' And the telephone in Cambridge went down with a click.

As Appleby dropped his own receiver into place, a secretary entered the room. 'A caller, sir – somebody I think you'll want to see about this Sheercliff affair.'

Derry Fisher was conscious of sitting up with a jerk as Appleby swung round to ask crisply, 'Not the girl?'

'I'm afraid not, sir. A cousin of the dead man. He gives his name as Mark Borlase.'

'Bring him in.' Appleby turned back to Derry. 'Lives in a windmill, and pops up as if he were answering a cue. He may interest you, Mr Fisher, even though he's not your girl. So stay where you are.'

Derry did as he was told. Mark Borlase was a middle-aged, cultivated, untidy man. He had a charming smile and restless, tobacco-stained hands. His manner was decidedly vague, and one felt at once that his natural occupation was wool-gathering. Only good breeding and a sense of social duty, Derry guessed, kept him from relapsing into complete abstraction straightway.

'Sir John Appleby? My name is Borlase. They got hold of me from Sheercliff, and asked me to come along and see you here. This about Stephen is very sad. I liked him, and hope he liked me. We had nothing to say to each other, I'm afraid – nothing at all. But he was a good sort of person in his dry way. I'm very sorry that his end should be a matter of policemen and inquests and so forth. I wonder what I can do?' As he spoke, Mark Borlase produced a pair of glasses from a breast-pocket and clipped them on his nose. 'Perhaps I could identify the body – something like that?' And Mark Borlase looked slowly round the room, as if confidently expecting a corpse in a corner. Not finding this, he let his glance rest mildly on Derry Fisher instead. 'This your boy?'

'Your cousin's body is naturally at Sheercliff, Mr Borlase. It has been adequately identified. And this gentleman is not my son' – Appleby smiled faintly – 'but Mr Derry Fisher, who happened to travel up from Sheercliff this morning in circumstances which give him an interest in your cousin's death.'

'From Sheercliff this morning? How do you do.' And Mark Borlase gave Derry a smile which, for some reason, sent a prickling sensation down the young man's spine. 'You were a friend of poor Stephen's?'

'No – nothing of that sort. I never knew him. It's just that on the train I ran across a – another passenger who'd had a queer experience – one that seems to connect up with Sir Stephen's death. That's why the police are interested in me.'

'Indeed.' Mark Borlase did not appear to find this ingenuous explanation sufficiently significant to hold his attention. He turned his mild gaze again to Appleby. 'They say, you know, that there were times when Stephen wasn't quite himself.'

'But you have no personal experience of that?'

'I didn't see him very often. Of course, we corresponded occasionally.'

'About what?'

Mark Borlase seemed momentarily at a loss. 'Well – don't you know – this and that.'

'You said a moment ago that you and Sir Stephen had nothing at all to say to each other. Can you be a little more specific about the this and that which occupied your letters?'

'As a matter of fact' – and Mark Borlase hesitated – 'Stephen got me to look at things for him from time to time.'

'Things, Mr Borlase?'

'Articles in Russian. It's my subject.'

'I see.' And Appleby nodded. 'Articles, that would be, in learned and scientific journals? Sir Stephen's own stuff?'

'Dear me, no.' Mark Borlase evinced a sort of absent-minded amusement. 'I'm a literary person, and would be no good on anything technical. Stephen had his own experts to do all that sort of thing, as a matter of course.'

'Philosophy, then – and sociology and so forth? He used you to acquaint himself with untranslated writings of – well, an ideological cast?'

Mark Borlase's hand moved uneasily. 'Is this what they call a security check? But it *was* matter of that sort. Stephen had an intermittent – but occasionally intense – interest in Communist theory and the like. I'm bound to confess that it irritated me very much. Not the doctrine – I don't give twopence for one political doctrine or another – but the style. I like my Russian good.'

'You would have viewed with indifference your cousin's entering upon treasonable courses, but would have deprecated his continued concern with inelegant Russian prose?'

Rather surprisingly, Mark Borlase was on his feet and flushing darkly. 'Damn it all, man, you understand the conversation of gentlemen better than that. I don't give a tinker's curse, I say, for one or another sort of hot air. But of course I wouldn't have a kinsman make a fool of himself and disgrace the family if I could help it. I used to translate or explain whatever rubbish Stephen in these occasional fits sent along – and do my best to laugh at him for his pains.'

'And you were never seriously uneasy.'

Mark Borlase's hesitation was just perceptible. 'Never. I realize there has been a certain amount of sinister talk. Stephen himself told me that some fool of a Cabinet Minister had decided he was a dangerously split personality, and that he had been plagued with a lot of nonsense as a result. For all I know of the present facts, such idiocy may have driven Stephen to suicide.'

'I sincerely hope not.' Appleby's tone was sober. 'And I am sorry, Mr Borlase, to have had to sound you on some rather unpleasant ground. It was good of you to come along so quickly. One of my assistants may want a little routine information at your convenience in a day or two. At the moment, I have only one further question. When did you see your cousin last?'

This time Mark Borlase answered promptly. 'Six weeks ago. And he was perfectly well. I'm at the Junior Wessex, by the way, should you want me.'

'Thank you very much.'

For some moments after the door closed on Mark Borlase, there was silence. Appleby sat quite still, lost in thought. Then he turned to Derry. 'Well?'

'I've seen him before.'

'*What!*'

'I've seen him before. It came to me when he smiled. I've seen him quite recently.'

'Be careful, man.' Appleby had sat up at his desk, square and severe. 'This sort of thing is new to you – and sometimes it sets people fancying things. We don't want a false scent. So think.'

Derry's mouth was dry and he guessed that he looked queer. For a full minute he, too, sat quite still. 'I *know* I've seen him recently – and it connects with Sheercliff.'

'Mark may be like Stephen in personal appearance. And you may have caught a glimpse of Stephen down there in the streets.'

'No – I've seen *him*.' Derry felt his heart pounding. 'In a taxi . . . smiling . . . driving out of Waterloo today.'

4

Sir John Appleby appeared quite unsurprised. 'That is capital. It looks as if we are on the track of something at last. Let us suppose that you are not mistaken. The overwhelming probable inference is that Mark Borlase has himself been down to Sheercliff, and indeed travelled back by the same train as yourself.'

'Then he lied, didn't he? He said he hadn't seen his cousin for six weeks.'

'It certainly sounded like a lie. But he may have gone down intending to see Stephen, and then for some reason changed his mind. You didn't manage to see how he was dressed?'

Derry shook his head. 'I'm afraid not. He *may* have been in those tweeds of Stephen's. All I saw was his face – leaning forward, and rather amused that I had to skip out of the way of his cab. But look here, sir' – Derry was suddenly urgent – 'it was the cab immediately behind the girl's. *Could* he have followed it, and tracked her down? Can one really tell a taxi-driver to do that? It's always happening in stories.'

Appleby smiled. 'Certainly you can. Men occasionally want to follow girls without necessarily having it in mind to commit murder. You can imagine cases in which the motive might even be laudable. And most taxi-drivers wouldn't mind a bit of a chase. Try it, some time.'

Derry, although accustomed by now to the intermittent levity of the Assistant Commissioner, was rather shocked. 'But, sir, oughtn't we ... I mean, if there's a chance he knows where to find her –'

'Quite so. One or two arrangements must certainly be made.' Appleby was scribbling as he spoke, and now he touched a bell. 'Here they are.' He held up a sheet of paper and then handed it to his secretary. 'See that this is acted on at once, Hunt, please. And are there any developments?'

'Captain Meritt just arrived, sir.'

'Excellent. Show him in.' Appleby turned to Derry. 'The man who knows all about the Sheercliff end. It will be a bad business if we don't get somewhere now.' He frowned. 'And also, perhaps, if we do.'

Captain Meritt was military, brisk, and (Derry suspected) inwardly somewhat shattered. He listened to what Appleby had to say, nodded an introduction to the young man, and plunged straight into his own narrative.

'I waited in Sheercliff for the doctors to make up their minds. It seems there can be no doubt about what happened, and that the local man's notion of suicide is all wrong. Borlase was killed by a terrific blow on the head, and then within a few minutes was pitched over the cliff. I've tried to get medical help on the clothes. You know how scalp wounds, even when only superficial, bleed in a profuse and alarming way? I wondered if the clothes he was actually wearing when killed would by any chance remain wearable and presentable.'

Appleby nodded. 'A good point.'

'But the leeches won't be positive one way or the other. It isn't certain there would have been any great mess. It's my bet now that the murderer stripped the dead man of his clothes and got him into the ones he was found in.'

'I agree.' Appleby was incisive. 'But why? What was the situation?'

'*I* was the situation, if you ask me.' And Meritt laughed, but without much effect of mirth. 'As I see it now, the murder happened not on a second trip of Sir Stephen's to Merlin Head, but on the first and only trip. I saw Sir Stephen go up there. I thought I saw him come down. But all I really saw was his clothes. In fact, I came a first-class crash.'

'It's certainly a possibility.' Appleby spoke with a hint of professional commiseration. 'And can you name the man who fooled you?'

'Krauss.'

Appleby nodded. 'I gather he may be involved. The Minister made a great point of it when he contacted me this morning.'

'You see, Krauss –' Meritt hesitated. 'Is Mr Fisher here interested in Krauss?'

Appleby smiled. 'I don't think it will much endanger the country, Mr Fisher, to tell you about Krauss. He is a foreign agent whom we suspect of specializing in approaching scientists with the object of extracting secret information from them. Krauss's is the ideological and not the venal approach. We don't know that he has ever made much success. But it is believed that he keeps on trying. And Captain Meritt is perfectly correct in saying that Krauss is supposed to have been on the track of Sir Stephen Borlase. So Krauss is a likely suspect enough.' Appleby turned his back to his colleague. 'Fisher and I, as it happens, have another one. But carry on.'

'Another suspect?' Meritt was startled.

'Not a bad one. But first come, first served. So continue.'

Meritt laughed. 'Very well. Here is the crime as I see it. Stephen Borlase was an unstable fellow, with fits in which he didn't very well know his own mind on certain vital matters. As a result, Krauss got a long way with him – got, in fact, as far as Merlin Head in the small hours of this morning. He persuaded Borlase to an appointment there – to a moonlight confabulation, you may say, in the little shelter by the cliff edge. The meeting, however, was a failure. Borlase was not disposed, after all, to see treason as a piece of higher duty. Conceivably he never was. These, after all, are jumpy times. If they were not, some of us would be out of a job.'

'Quite so.'

'Krauss, then, was stuck. And, being stuck, he struck.' Meritt paused, as if mildly surprised at his own command of the resources of English. 'Primarily he was out to suborn Borlase. But there was this other possibility. Borlase carried on his person notes that were the vital growing-point of his researches. These would be enormously worth stealing – and particularly if the brain capable of producing them could simultaneously be destroyed for ever. That is why Krauss killed Borlase.'

'If he did.'

'I'm only putting a case.' Meritt was patient. 'Now, what would be the first thing one would do after committing murder and robbery? I think one would scout around. Krauss took a peer out from that cliff shelter – and just glimpsed me at the far end of the path leading to it. He would realize the situation in a flash, and see that it was pretty grim.'

'Grim enough to take the fantastic risk of donning Borlase's clothes and hoping to evade you that way?'

'Yes. And it wasn't really so fantastic. He would know I was being as unobtrusive as possible, and that I would keep well back. So he chanced it.'

'It's a first-class hypothesis.' Appleby drummed absently on the deck before him. 'But one point worries me. Borlase was found in *entirely* strange clothes? And why a *complete* exchange? And why bother to re-dress the corpse at all?'

'Krauss suddenly tumbled to the significance of the cliff, the sea, and the currents. With luck, he could get rid of the body for days or weeks. That would be valuable in itself. Moreover, if it was then recovered entirely unidentifiable, either in its own person or by any of its clothes, the eminent Sir Stephen Borlase would simply have disappeared without explanation. There was a neat little propaganda trick to take in that.'

'Very well. Krauss – or another – effects this change of clothes, and then pitches the body into the sea. Or rather, *not* into the sea. It lands on a small outcrop of rock. And so the murderer's plan – as you see it, that is – partly fails. Now, there is a point that occurs to me there. Suppose that the murderer, for some reason, was – so to speak – *aiming* not at the sea but at that rock. Would it have been a practical target? Could he have reckoned on keeping the body *from* the sea?'

Meritt frowned. 'I'm not clear about the bearing of your question.'

'Conceivably it has none. But one ought, I think, to consider the question *Accident or design?* on every occasion that one possibly can.'

'I entirely agree.' Meritt thought for a moment. 'Yes, I think the rock would prove, if one experimented, a reasonably easy target.'

'Well, then – let's go on. The disguised Krauss, with Borlase's notebook happily in his pocket, does succeed in getting past you.'

'I'm afraid so. But he is by no means out of the wood. There I am, discreetly behind him. If he wants to avoid suspicion, there is only one natural thing for him to do at the end of this nocturnal stroll. He must return to Borlase's hotel. He must accept the risk of being confronted, face on, by a night porter. Moreover, he probably has not more than Borlase's key as a clue to what room he must make for. And he must find it before I, in my turn, regain the Metropole.'

'In fact, it was all pretty sticky – all the time and without knowing it – he had made that ghastly slip-up over the shoes, and was now wearing one of Borlase's and one of his own.'

'Exactly. But he did get to Borlase's suite quite safely. Later he crept out again, and took the first train to Town. He can't, I think, have had any base in Sheercliff, or he would have made for it first and got into other clothes.'

Derry Fisher had listened fascinated to this hypothetical re-construction of events in which he himself had been obscurely involved. Now he broke in. 'This man Krauss, sir – have you ever seen him?'

Meritt nodded. 'Certainly. I was given an unobtrusive view of a good many of his kidney when I took on my present job.'

'Could he be described as middle-aged and intellectual looking; and does he smoke Russian cigarettes?'

'I don't know about his smoking, although there are people who will. But the description certainly fits.'

'It certainly fits.' Appleby nodded thoughtfully. 'But then – it would fit Mark Borlase as well.'

'*Mark* Borlase?' Meritt was puzzled.

'Stephen's cousin. They don't seem to have briefed you in the family, Meritt, quite as they should. Mark Borlase appears to have travelled up from Sheercliff today, although he has kept quiet about it. Fisher here saw him at Waterloo – and believes that he may even have followed the taxi of the girl who spotted the shoes. When I hear of anybody claiming actually to have seen your friend Krauss there, I shall begin to take rather more interest in him. Meanwhile, I keep my eye on Cousin Mark. You don't happen to be a member of the Junior Wessex? A pity. He told us he's putting up there for the night. You could have gone and taken a peep at him for yourself.'

'I'm going to do my best to take a peep at Krauss.' Captain Meritt rose. 'I haven't much hope for that notebook – but one never knows. These fellows have queer ways. He may hold on to it till he gets his price.'

'There's some comfort in that. Or Mark Borlase may.'

Meritt moved to the door. 'I think your Mark Borlase is a rank outsider.'

'Fisher and I have our money on him, all the same.'

When Meritt had departed, Appleby looked at his watch. 'I wonder,' he asked, 'if you would care for a cup of tea? We make astonishing tea at the Yard. And capital anchovy toast.'

'Thank you very much.' Derry Fisher was disconcerted. 'But oughtn't we – ?'

Appleby smiled. 'To be organizing the siege of the Junior Wessex – or otherwise pushing effectively about? Well, I think we have the inside of an hour to relax in.'

Derry stared. 'Before – before something *happens*?'

'Before – my dear young man – we take a long shot at finally clearing up this odd business of a dead man's shoes.'

5

'A black shoe and a brown one – how very curious!'

'What did you say?' Jane Grove set down her tea-cup with a surprising clatter.

'And – dear me! – at Sheercliff.' Jane's aunt, enjoyably interested, reached for a slice of cake. 'You might have run into it. Which just shows, does it not? I mean, that in the midst of life we are in death. I've got a whole cherry.'

'I don't know what you're talking about.' Jane's voice trembled slightly.

'Something in the paper, dear.' Jane's aunt propped the folded page against the milk-jug. 'A poor man found dead beneath the cliffs quite early this morning.'

'Early this morning!'

'And something about *another* man. Will you have a third cup?'

'No. Go on.'

'I intend to, dear. I *always* take three cups.'

'I mean about the other man.'

'The other man? Oh, yes. He seems to have travelled on a train, and to have worn mixed-up shoes too. There are people at Scotland Yard who want any information about him.'

'May I see?' Jane took the evening paper and read without speaking.

'It couldn't be a new fashion?'

'A new fashion, aunt?'

'Wearing different-coloured shoes. *Two* men, you see. But one – of course – now dead.'

Jane laughed a little wildly. 'No – not a new fashion.' She got abruptly to her feet. 'I think I must –'

'Yes, dear?'

Jane hesitated. 'I must water the pot. You might like a *fourth* cup.' She performed this commonplace action with a steady hand, and when she spoke again her tone was entirely casual. 'I'm afraid I have to go out.'

'To go out again, Jane – after your long day?'

'I – I've got to do something I forgot. It's rather important.' Jane fetched her handbag and gloves. 'I don't suppose I shall be very long.'

'Very well, dear. But don't forget – you can't be too careful.'

Jane Grove jumped. 'Careful?'

'Of the traffic, dear. So dangerous nowadays.'

Jane, standing by the window, smiled wryly. The quiet Kensington road was deserted. She lingered for some minutes. Then, as if reproaching herself for some lack of resolution, she grabbed her bag and hurried out.

Sir John Appleby's tea and anchovy toast, although it had all the appearance of being a leisurely and carefree affair, had a steady accompaniment of messages despatched and received. Finally, Appleby's secretary came in and spoke with a trace of excitement.

'Fifteen Babcock Gardens, sir. And at five-forty-five.'

'Good.' Appleby rose briskly. 'He did as he was told, and said he'd walk?'

'Yes. He's making for the Green Park now.'

'That gives us all very good time. You've got three cars ready.'

'They should be pretty well posted by now. We've studied the maps and had a report from the section.'

Appleby nodded and signed to Derry Fisher to follow him. 'And what sort of a problem does this house in Babcock Gardens look like presenting?'

'Tricky, sir – but it might be worse. At a corner, but very quiet. All the houses there have basements with areas. There's a deserted cabmen's shelter over the way. The secretary hesitated. 'Are you taking a bit of a risk, sir?'

'That's as it will appear.' Appleby's tone suggested that he found this question not wholly in order. 'And now we'll be off.'

'Your car's outside, sir – with the short-wave tested and correct.'

Below, a discreetly powerful limousine was waiting, and into this Derry Fisher found himself bundled. It had a table with street-plans, and it was filled with low-pitched precise speech. Appleby had no sooner sat down than he joined in. The effect, as of an invisible conference, was very queer and very exciting. Derry had been involved in this sort of thing before – but only in the cinema. He rather expected the car to go hurtling through London with screaming sirens. The pace, however, proved to be nothing out of the ordinary. Turning into the Mall, they moved as sedately as if in a procession. Carlton House Terrace seemed to go on forever, and the Royal Standard fluttering above Buckingham Palace drew only very slowly nearer. When they rounded Queen Victoria on her elaborate pedestal and swung round for Constitution Hill, it was at a speed that seemed more appropriate to sightseers than to emissaries of the law.

But if the car dawdled, Derry's mind moved fast – much faster than it was accustomed to do in the interest of his uncle's business. He had never heard of Babcock Gardens, but he guessed that it was an address in Kensington – and the address, too, which he had failed to hear the girl giving at Waterloo that morning. And somebody was walking to it – walking to it through the Green Park. And Appleby had acknowledged that the girl was in danger, and Appleby's secretary had let slip misgivings over the riskiness of what was now going on. What *was* now going on? Quite clearly, the setting of a trap. *Appleby was setting a trap, with the girl as bait.*

'I ought to tell you that there may be a little shooting before we're through with this.'

Derry jumped. Appleby apparently unconscious of any strain, had murmured the words in his ear. 'Shooting, sir – you mean at the girl?'

'But all this is itself a very long shot.' Appleby had ominously ignored the question. 'It mayn't come off at all. But it's going to be uncommonly labour-saving if it does ... I think we turn out of Knightsbridge at the next corner.'

Derry was silent. He felt helpless and afraid. The crawl continued. Appleby was again absorbed in listening to reports and giving orders. But he had time for one brief aside. 'Complicated, you know. Lurking for lurkers. Requires the policeman's most cat-like tread. Not like marching up and arresting a fellow in the name of the law.'

Again Derry said nothing; he didn't feel at all like mild fun. Suddenly the pace increased. Appleby's dispositions – whatever they were – appeared to be completed. The car ran through broad, quiet streets between rows of solidly prosperous-looking houses. Presently it turned left into a narrower road, and then left again into what seemed a deserted mews. And there it drew to a halt.

Appleby jumped out. 'The unobtrusive approach to our grandstand seat.'

Derry followed. 'A grandstand seat?'

'We are at the back of Babcock Gardens. A surprised but obliging citizen is giving us the run of the dining-room. Number fifteen is just opposite.'

It seemed to Derry Fisher afterwards that what followed was all over in a flash. The dining-room of the obliging citizen was sombre and Victorian, and this gave the sunlit street outside, viewed through a large bay-window, something of the appearance of a theatrical scene – an empty stage awaiting the entrance of actors and the beginning of an action.

Suddenly it was peopled – and the action had taken place. The house opposite stood at a corner. Round this came the figure of a man, glancing upwards, as if in search of a street number. Derry had time only to realize that he was familiar when the door of number fifteen opened and a girl came down the steps. It was the girl of Derry's encounter on the train that morning. She had almost reached the footpath when she staggered and fell – and in the same instant there came the crack of a revolver shot. The man was standing still, apparently staring at her intently. Derry could see only his back. But he now knew that it was the back of Mark Borlase.

Borlase took a step forward. Simultaneously, another figure leapt across the road – it must have been from the corresponding corner – and made a dash for Borlase. It was Meritt. What he intended seemed to be a flying Rugger tackle. But before he could bring this off, yet another figure dramatically appeared. A uniformed policeman, hurling himself up the area-steps of number fifteen, took the charging Meritt in the flank and brought him crashing to the ground. In an instant there were policemen all over the place.

'Come along.' Appleby touched the horrified Derry Fisher on the arm. They hurried out. Mark Borlase had not moved. Shocked and bewildered, he was looking from one side to the other. On his left, Meritt had been hauled to his feet, and stood collared by two powerful constables. On his right, still sprawled on the steps of number fifteen, lay the girl – a pool of blood forming beneath one arm.

Derry ran towards her, his heart pounding. As he did so, she raised herself, and with a groping movement found her handbag. For a moment, and with a queerly expressionless face, she gazed at Meritt and at the men who held him. Then with her uninjured arm she opened her bag, drew out a small glittering object, and thrust it in her mouth.

'Stop her!'

Appleby's cry was too late. Another revolver shot broke the quiet of Babcock Gardens. Incredibly – incredibly and horribly – Derry Fisher's beautiful girl had blown her brains out.

6

Later that evening Appleby explained.

'There was never much doubt, Mr Borlase, that your cousin had been murdered. And clearly the crime was not one of passion or impulse. The background of the case was international espionage. Sir Stephen was killed in order to obtain an important scientific secret and to eliminate the only brain capable of reproducing it. There may have been an attempt – conceivably by the man Krauss – to get at Sir Stephen by the ideological route. But that had certainly come to nothing. You agree?'

Mark Borlase nodded. 'Stephen – as I insisted to you – was really perfectly sound. He worried me at times, it is true – and it was only yesterday that I felt I ought to go down and have a word with him. Actually, we didn't meet. I got him on the telephone, and knew at once that there was no question of any trouble at the moment. So I concealed the fact that I was actually in Sheercliff, put up at the Grand for the night, and came back this morning. I ought to have been franker when you challenged me, no doubt.'

'It has all come straight in the wash, Mr Borlase. And now let me go on. Here was a professional crime. This made me at once suspicious of the genuineness of any *muddle* over those shoes. *But they might be a trick designed to mislead.* And, if that was so, I was up against a mind given to doing things *ingeniously*. I made a note that it might be possible to exploit that later.

'Now the train. I came away from my inspection of it convinced that the girl's story was a fabrication from start to finish. The fact stared me in the face.'

Derry Fisher sat up straight. 'But how *could* it? I've chewed over it again and again –'

'My dear young man, these things are not your profession. This girl, representing herself as badly frightened, ignored three compartments – in two of which she would have found feminine support and comfort – and chose to burst in upon a solitary and suitably impressionable young man of her own age. Again, while the mysterious man with the different-coloured shoes would certainly have retreated *up* the train, the rifled suit-case was *down* the train – the direction in which the girl herself went off unaccompanied, for her cup of coffee. Again, the Russian cigarettes had discernibly been smoked in a holder. On one of them, nevertheless, there was a tiny smear of lipstick.' Appleby turned to Derry. 'I think I mentioned it to you at the time.'

'Mentioned it?' Derry was bewildered – and then light came to him. 'When you made that silly – that joke about seeing red?'

'I'm afraid so. Well now, the case was beginning to come clear. Sir Stephen's body had been dropped on that rock, and not into the sea, deliberately; we were meant to find it in the strange clothes and the unaccountable shoes – otherwise the whole elaborate false trail laid by the girl on her railway journey would be meaningless. But *why* this elaboration? There seemed only one answer. To serve as an alibi, conclusive from the start, for somebody anxious to avoid any intensive investigation. My thoughts turned to Meritt as soon as he produced that streamlined picture of the man Krauss as the criminal.'

Mark Borlase nodded. 'And so you set a trap for him?'

'Precisely. But first, let me give you briefly what my guess about Meritt was. He had been offered money – big and tempting money – to do *both* things: get the notebook and liquidate Sir Stephen. He saw his chance in Sir Stephen's habit of taking that nocturnal stroll. Last night he simply followed him up to the Head, killed and robbed him, and dressed the body in clothes he had already concealed for the purpose, including the odd shoes. Then he dropped the body over the cliff so that it would fall just where it did, returned to the Metropole, and telephoned his confederate to begin playing her part on the eight-five this morning. The girl – her name was Jane Grove – was devoted to him. And she played up very well – to the end, I'd say.'

For a moment there was silence in Appleby's room. Then Derry asked a question. 'And your trap?'

'It depended on what is pretty well an axiom in detective investigation. A criminal who has – successfully, as he thinks – brought off an ingenious trick will try to bring off another, twice as ingenious, if you give him a chance. Still guessing – for I really had no evidence against Meritt at all – I gave him such a chance just as irresistibly as I could.

'The girl, you see, must come forward, and repeat the yarn she had told on the train. That was essential to the convincingness of the whole story. It was, of course, a yarn about encountering a man who doesn't exist. For this *nobody* I determined to persuade Meritt to substitute a *somebody*: yourself, Mr Borlase. You had been on that train and concealed the fact. I let Meritt have this information. I gave him the impression that I strongly suspected you. I let slip the information that you could be contacted at your club, the Junior Wessex. And as soon as Meritt had left I got a message to you there myself, explaining what I wanted and asking you to co-operate. You did so, most admirably, and I am very grateful to you.'

Mark Borlase inclined his head. 'A blood-hunt isn't much in

my line, I'm bound to say. But it seemed proper that Stephen's murderer should be brought to book.'

Derry Fisher looked perplexed. 'I don't see how Meritt —'

'It was simple enough.' Appleby broke off to take a telephone call, and then resumed his explanation. 'Meritt represented himself to Mr Borlase on the telephone as my secretary, and asked him to come to my private address – which he gave as fifteen Babcock Gardens – at five-forty-five. He then got in touch with the girl and arranged *his* trap.' Appleby smiled grimly. 'He didn't know it was *our* trap too.'

'He was going to incriminate Mr Borlase?'

'Just that. Remember, you would have been able to swear that you saw Mr Borlase leaving Waterloo in a taxi just behind the girl. From this would follow the inference that Mr Borlase had tracked her to her home; and that after his interview here he had decided that he must silence her.'

'But Meritt didn't himself mean to – to kill the girl?'

'He meant to stage an attempted murder by Mr Borlase; and to that he must have nerved her on the telephone. It all had to be very nicely timed.'

Mark Borlase suddenly shivered. 'He was going to arrest me, after he had himself winged the girl? He would have said the revolver was mine – that sort of thing?'

'Yes. He may even have meant to kill you, and maintain that it had happened in the course of a struggle. Then the girl would have identified you as the man with the odd shoes. And that would have been that.'

'How could he have explained being on the scene – there in Babcock Gardens, I mean – at all?'

'By declaring that I had prompted him to go and have a look at your club; that he had spotted you coming out and had decided to shadow you. It would have been some such story as that. He had lost his head a bit, I'd say, in pursuit of this final ingenuity. It was criminal artistry, of a sort. But it was thoroughly crazy as well.'

'And Stephen's notebook?'

'That telephone-call was to say it has been found with Meritt's things. Meritt thought himself absolutely safe, and he was determined to hold out for a good price.' Appleby rose. 'Well – that's the whole thing. And we shall none of us be sorry to go to bed.'

As they said good-bye, Derry Fisher hesitated. 'May I ask one more question?'

'Certainly.'

'The shooting in Babcock Gardens was an afterthought of Meritt's – and I think it was the afterthought of a fiend. But why – after you had examined the train and guessed nearly the whole truth – did you tell me that the girl was in danger?'

'She was in danger of the gallows, Mr Fisher. But at least she escaped *that*.'

The Lion and the Unicorn

Lady Appleby glanced reproachfully at her husband as he slipped into his place on the stand in Pall Mall. 'We thought you wouldn't get here at all. The streets have been closed for ages.'

The Assistant Commissioner laughed. 'My dear, it's one of those occasions on which I find it useful to be known to the police.' He looked at his watch. 'And we still have a good deal of time on hand. Was the breakfast up to scratch?'

'Sir John – that breakfast was out of this world!' It was Mrs Harbot who replied – dropping, in order to do so, the binoculars with which she had been studying whatever of British institutions came within their field. 'I think your London clubs are wonderful. But what I don't figure out, Sir John, is why you're here with us in these seats. I'd guess that a man high up with the police would be down there on a horse, with a uniform and a sword. Like the one going past now. Isn't he beautiful? Would he be an Inspector?'

Appleby looked – and paused civilly, as if the question required some little skill to answer. 'He's a major, as a matter of fact, in the Brigade of Guards. The police, you know, require a bit of a helping hand on occasions of this sort.'

Mrs Harbot again surveyed the scene. 'Wouldn't it be wonderful, Sir John, if something marvellously unexpected happened?'

This clearly, was a largeness of expectation with which Appleby found it hard to sympathize. 'I'll be quite content with what's on the programme. I've had my share of the unexpected, as a matter of fact, during the small hours of this morning.'

Lady Appleby looked up quickly. 'Is that why you didn't come home?'

'Yes. A little encounter with the Lion and the Unicorn.'

Mrs Harbot's eyes rounded. 'The Lion and the Unicorn? Were they heralds or pursuivants – something like that?'

'Dear me, no. They were just a Lion and a Unicorn.'

'But doing something unexpected?'

Appleby looked doubtful. 'That's rather hard to answer. In a sense, their behaviour was quite conventional. They were fighting for the Crown.'

Mrs Harbot was horrified. 'Not the crown that –'

'Dear me, no. The traditional crown of the ancient kingdom of Ruritania.'

Lady Appleby eyed her husband with frank scepticism. 'Ruritania, John?'

'I'm calling it that.' And Appleby turned gravely to Mrs Harbot. 'Even so, you must treat this as a most confidential communication. It is true that Ruritania – the country I am calling Ruritania – disappeared as an independent monarchy round about 1918. That is how its crown jewels came to be alienated. But if the facts that I am about to tell you became generally known, I assure you that the Chancelleries of Europe would be rocked to their foundations.'

Mrs Harbot smiled brilliantly. 'If this isn't just like Sherlock Holmes!'

'I hope you will continue to think so. But let me proceed.

'The offices and showrooms of the Jeweller's Company,' Appleby began, 'are just round the corner. You can see them from the card-room of this club. It was from there, indeed, that Colonel Busteed – one of our oldest members – saw the thing being installed late yesterday evening. It seemed a belated effort in the way of decoration, but it was all done with great speed and efficiency. A lorry with a tall extension-ladder drove up just after office hours, and within fifteen minutes an elaborate affair had been erected at the level of the mansard roof: an enormous coat of arms, flanked by two handsome beasts, pretty well as large as life and done very much in the round. Busteed concluded that the Jewellers had felt something more than the general scheme of decoration in the street was required, and that they had arranged for this imposing display pretty well at the eleventh hour. He thought no more about it – or no more about it just then. But he did happen to mention it to me as I was leaving the club. It was pretty well dusk by that time, but I caught a glimpse of the contraption myself as I turned the corner.

'As it happened, I had to pay a call at the Home Office, and coming out I ran into Lord Anchor. He is a distinguished elderly man, and among other things a former Master of the Jewellers' Company. By way of making conversation, I said something about this last-moment embellishing of their building. To my surprise, he said he had never heard of it. Indeed, the old boy took quite a high line.'

'A high line?' Mrs Harbot was puzzled.

'He said that the greatest propriety had to be observed in using the royal coat of arms, or anything like it; and that if he had been consulted he would have vetoed the proposal at once. Well, I concluded that the other Jewellers had by-passed old Anchor in the matter, and that I had properly put my foot in it. So I endeavoured to escape. I didn't get away, however, until I had heard a good deal more in the way of criticism of the Jewellers' recent policies. For instance, there was this business of the Ruritanian regalia.'

Mrs Harbot sighed delightedly. 'The crown jewels?'

'Precisely. The Jewellers were displaying them in a window, behind a steel grill, and Lord Anchor believed that this was likely to cause some resentment in *émigré* Ruritanian circles in this country. There was no doubt about the Company's legal right to the jewels – the intrinsic value of which, indeed, was not very considerable. They had been handed over with the authority of the former royal family and its minister as part-security for a loan that went west in the abortive counter-revolution of 1925. But there had been some sore feelings – even litigation – and Anchor felt that to make the ancient crown and so forth part of a topical display had been an error in tact. He pointed out that the beautiful young Grand Duchess Paulina, the claimant to the Ruritanian throne, was in London at this moment.'

'Isn't that just too romantic?' Mrs Harbot was enthralled.

Appleby shook his head. 'I assure you that I haven't come to the romantic part yet. Anchor held forth for some time in this vein, and my impression was that the old chap was talking sense. I left him in a state of considerable indignation. But it was nothing to the state in which I found Colonel Busteed when, later in the evening, I came back to the club. It appeared that the Lion and the Unicorn were automata.'

'Automata?' It was Lady Appleby who was startled this time. 'You mean they moved – were worked by machinery?'

'So Busteed had convinced himself. There are such things round about London at the moment, you know – and quite amusing some of them are. But the application of the principle to these particular heraldic symbols had apparently struck Busteed as grossly unsuitable. I wasn't myself all that shocked; it seemed to me that the Lion and the Unicorn could bob or beck at each other harmlessly enough. I was surprised, however, when Busteed told me what the Lion did. It scratched.'

Mrs Harbot stared. 'Scratched the Unicorn?'

'Not even that. The Lion scratched *itself*. Busteed had only glimpsed the phenomenon in the dusk on his way to dinner, but he was quite sure of it. I confess that I was a good deal puzzled. Busteed, although our great authority here on both port and Madeira, is a most abstemious man, and I found it hard to imagine that he had been other than quite sober.

'As it happened, I hadn't much leisure to consider the matter, for I was simply eating a hasty late meal before going back for some hours' work at the Yard. It was after midnight before the problem came into my head again – but when it did come, it came to stick. Lord Anchor's ignorance and Colonel Busteed's impression were both mildly surprising; taken together, they constituted something really odd. I ended by setting the telephone going and eventually tracked down the Jewellers' secretary in his bed. My story was news to him. He had never heard of a proposal to put up any decoration of the sort I described. He suggested contacting his night-watchman at once.

'I had already tried ringing the Jewellers' premises, and there had been no reply. It seemed clear that there was trouble, so I called out a car and came round with a couple of constables straight away. The street-lighting illuminated the lower part of the building clearly enough, but above the cornice it faded into darkness, so that there was no more than a vague blob to suggest what we were looking for. The car, however, had a powerful spotlight, and we had this focused in a matter of seconds. The coat of arms was there. But both the Lion and the Unicorn had gone.'

'Gone?' Mrs Harbot was perplexed. 'I don't see how automata could *go*.'

Appleby chuckled. 'Augustly employed automata don't scratch themselves either. But humans may be tempted to do so – particularly if constrained to maintain uncomfortable postures in unusual habiliments. I had no doubt that we were in the presence of an ingenious plot to gain access to the Jewellers' building by the one vulnerable route – the windows in the mansard roof.

'There was an awkward pause while we waited for keys. When the secretary arrived with them he brought Lord Anchor as well – in high feather, it seemed to me, that the Company had run into a spot of trouble. He hadn't the slightest doubt that it was the Ruritanian regalia that was the occasion for it. We hadn't got far in our search of the building when we knew that he was right.

'From somewhere in the bowels of the place there came a muffled thumping and hollering. I needn't say that this was from the night-watchman, who had met the invasion of his territory with singularly little efficiency and had been ignominiously locked up. But another sound was more commanding – and for some seconds thoroughly perplexing as well. I had a queer impression that it was something I had heard often enough – and yet never, so to speak, in the workaday world. The truth appeared when we burst into the main showroom of the place. A wide space had been cleared in the middle, the Ruritanian crown stood isolated on a table at the side, and before it the Lion and the Unicorn were at a ding-dong duel with sabres. It was first-class cinema stuff.'

'Of the Walt Disney sort?' Lady Appleby was again sceptical. 'Animals fighting duels –'

'The Lion I recognized at once. Even with the headpiece of this bizarre disguise laid aside he was leonine – none other, in fact, than the venerable Count *X*, formerly Lord Chamberlain at the court of Ruritania. And the Unicorn, as it happened, I also knew. He was the dashing young Baron *Y*, youngest son of that almost legendary Ruritanian –'

'And they had fallen out?' Mrs Harbot was distressed. 'Now, if that wasn't just too bad! When they could have got clean away, too, with that wonderful old crown.'

Appleby shook his head. 'It wasn't precisely falling out. Each of these noblemen had discovered that the other was pledged to recover the crown for the beautiful Grand Duchess. They had agreed therefore to join forces until the prize was actually in their grasp – and then to fight for the privilege of laying it at the feet of their adored mistress.'

'Sir John – if that wasn't a chivalrous thing!'

'Indeed, yes. Well, it was the younger man who reacted the more quickly to the new situation. Dropping his sabre – the Jewellers, you know, have a mass of such things dating from the early history of their Company – the young Baron *Y* seized his country's historic crown, evaded us, and dashed from the building. Still retaining his own weapon, the venerable Count *X* pursued him. We followed.'

Lady Appleby looked at her husband in what might have been either admiration or profound distrust. 'The Lion, in fact, beat the Unicorn all round about the town?'

'Precisely, Judith – you express it very well. And the pursuit, as you will immediately realize, was much complicated by the state the streets had by this time assumed. Time being short, I will not describe it in detail. Suffice it that both noblemen eventually took refuge in their own Embassy. It is much to the credit of the present republican régime in Ruritania that they were admitted without hesitation. . . . Do I hear a band?'

Mrs Harbot drew a deep breath. 'And the crown? That is now in the hands of the Republic too?'

'By no means. The young Baron *Y*, with all his famous father's happiness in such ticklish situations, secreted it as he fled. Look around you, my dear Mrs Harbot. Very tolerably colourable crowns of all sizes hang as thick as blackberries in the streets of this loyal city today. The young Baron has simply added to the display by climbing to the top of some lamp-post and depositing a real one. As soon as his escapade is composed with the authorities – which I can promise you will be in a few hours' time – he will recover it, and thus claim the victory over his venerable countryman and rival.'

For a moment Mrs Harbot was almost awed. 'But the Jewellers?'

'Lord Anchor has declared that he will put his foot down. The incident is to be declared closed, and no restitution of the crown will be demanded. The Grand Duchess, I don't doubt, will be permitted to carry it off in triumph to her beautiful Californian home.'

Mrs Harbot was much affected. Lady Appleby regarded her with some compunction. 'I must really explain that my husband is given to rather tall –'

But Appleby suddenly leant forward.

'They're coming!' he said.

More about Penguins and Pelicans

Penguinews, which appears every month, contains details of all the new books issued by Penguins as they are published. From time to time it is supplemented by *Penguins in Print*, which is a complete list of all available books published by Penguins. (There are well over four thousand of these.)

A specimen copy of *Penguinews* will be sent to you free on request. For a year's issues (including the complete lists) please send 30p if you live in the United Kingdom, or 60p if you live elsewhere. Just write to Dept EP, Penguin Books Ltd, Harmondsworth, Middlesex, enclosing a cheque or postal order, and your name will be added to the mailing list.

Note: *Penguinews* and *Penguins in Print* are not available in the U.S.A. or Canada

The New Sonia Wayward

Michael Innes

'Colonel Petticate stared at his wife in stupefaction. He could scarcely believe the evidence of his eyes – or of the fingers which he had just lifted from her pulse. But it was true. The poor old girl was dead.'

From its first splendid paragraph to its comically shocking end, *The New Sonia Wayward* is a blissful tangle of humour, irony and real suspense, in which Michael Innes surpasses himself with the subtlety and wit of his characterization.

'A gem. How rare an item this is. A polished, urbane, and funny thriller. Wonderfully written. On no account to be missed' – *Evening Standard*

Not for sale in the U.S.A.

Appleby's End

Michael Innes

Appleby's End was the name of the station where Detective-Inspector John Appleby got off the train from Scotland Yard.

That could have been a coincidence. But, from then on, coincidences came too often, too fast and too many to be genuine.

Everything that happened related back to stories by Ranulph Raven, Victorian novelist. Animals were replaced by marble effigies. Someone received a tombstone that told him when he would die. A servant was found buried up to his neck in snow – dead. Even Appleby's End, it turned out, was a story by Ranulph Raven. And why did Ranulph Raven's mysterious descendants make a point of inviting Appleby to spend the night at their house?

Maybe Appleby's End was in sight.

Not for sale in the U.S.A.

Appleby at Allington

Michael at Allington

Although Sir John Appleby had retired, his detective's instincts and experience hadn't.

When the first body was discovered at Allington Park, he was quite content to believe that it was an accident. But the second body starts him thinking. Two deaths, one after another, is tragic coincidence and Sir John doesn't believe in coincidence.

So he digs around. How did Owain Allington buy back the family estate? Why was he so attached to his rather dissolute nephew, Martin Allington?

In a recent 'Son et Lumière', there had been mention of treasure at Allington Park. But everyone who could gain from it had shrugged it off as pure fiction.

Only some of them had shrugged it off a lot more intensely than others.

Not for sale in the U.S.A.